the Space between

the Space between

Kali VanBaale

RIVER CITY PUBLISHING
MONTGOMERY, ALABAMA

Published in the United States by River City Publishing
1719 Mulberry St.
Montgomery, AL 36106

Designed by Lissa Monroe

First Edition—2006
Printed in the United States of America
　　　1 3 5 7 9 10 8 6 4 2

This is a work of fiction. Names, characters, places, and incidents either are
the product of the author's imagination or are used fictitiously, and any
resemblance to actual persons living or dead, events, or locales is entirely
coincidental.

ISBN-10: 1-57966-058-4
ISBN-13: 978-1-57966-058-1

Library of Congress Cataloging-in-Publication Data

VanBaale, Kali, 1975-
The space between / by Kali VanBaale. — 1st ed.
p. cm.
Summary: "Judith's son has shot two students, a teacher, and himself at
school. An ordinary wife and mother must suddenly grapple with
extraordinary grief and horror, struggling to be the center of her remaining
family but plagued by doubts and questions that may disrupt her life more
completely than the shooting"—Provided by publisher.

1. High school students—Crimes against—Fiction. 2. Teachers—Crimes
against—Fiction. 3. School shootings—Fiction. 4. Housewives—Fiction. 5.
Loss (Psychology)—Fiction. 6. Psychological fiction. I. Title.
PS3622.A5859S63 2006
813'.6—dc22
2006008794

for Troy
for giving me Tuesdays

"No one ever told me that grief felt so like fear."
—C. S. Lewis

"It isn't for the moment you are struck that you need courage,
but for the long uphill climb back to sanity and faith
and security."
—Anne Morrow Lindbergh

Contents

St. Valentine's Day

THE LAST MORNING JUDITH ELLIOTT saw her son alive, he asked for blueberry pancakes drowned in maple syrup, with a side of cinnamon toast and orange juice. She obliged, hauled out her mixer and hot griddle, happy to see him forego his usual breakfast of cold cereal and soda. She cracked eggs and measured out milk while Lucas allowed his kid sister to chat him up with breathless twelve-year-old enthusiasm about her upcoming symphony concert.

Lindsey had probably been stunned by any amount of attention he was willing to toss in her direction. Normally, she seemed to be like an annoying insect he just swatted away with a roll of his eyes, a heavy sigh, or the occasional shove into a door or table. But something had changed in his face overnight, softened it and taken away the hard edge to his voice. He was attentive as his sister spoke, listening with genuine smiles and nods to her story about a recent prank played during orchestra practice, her blond ponytail swishing back and forth in time with her hand gestures.

Peter joined them at the table in a crisp blue suit and starched gray shirt the same color of his eyes, the morning edition of the *Wall Street Journal* under his arm, whistling some advertising jingle between his teeth. As Judith set a stack of hot pancakes in front of him, he tucked a napkin over his collar to protect his silk tie and double-checked the gold watch on his wrist. It was, Judith knew, set exactly seven minutes fast.

She watched her son's hands, his long gentle fingers, as he passed the butter and leaned into his plate of hot food with a fork and knife balanced between his ink-stained fingertips. How seldom she had experienced that kind of pleasant family moment in the last few years, father talking to son, brother talking to sister. No empty silences with only the occasional clatter or scrape of utensils.

After breakfast, Lucas voluntarily helped his mother clear the table and load dirty dishes into the washer. They stood, shoulders touching, at the same diminutive height with matching shades of red hair and fair, freckled skin. He wore a plaid button-up shirt and slacks she had bought him for Christmas, never worn until that day. He was almost unrecognizable without his paint-smudged T-shirt and baggy jeans with holes in the knees and frayed edges around the ankles.

"Why doesn't anyone call you Judy instead of Judith?" Lucas asked once they were alone.

Judith rinsed a glass in the sink and thought for a moment. "I don't know. I never really thought about it."

"Or call Dad Pete instead of Peter. It sounds so formal."

"I guess we never liked nicknames," she finally said.

"Is that why no one ever called me Luke?"

"Well, if we wanted to call you Luke, we would've named you Luke, not Lucas." She handed him a crusty spatula. "Why do you ask?"

"No reason," he shrugged. "Just curious."

Judith watched him wipe toast crumbs from the counter with a wet rag, and a brief thought nagged her, a memory of his recent visit to the police station, those horrible minutes in the garage between her husband and son once they'd gotten home. Lucas switched off the faucet and smiled at her. All the unhappy business of the past months must be smoothing over, she told herself. Just look at him, finally feeling better, maybe putting it all behind him for good.

"Doesn't Lucas look nice today?" she commented to Peter as he reentered the room in search of his briefcase.

"He needs to tuck in his shirt," Peter said and brushed a kiss across his wife's cheek. His dry lips barely grazed her skin as he straightened the knot in his tie at the base of his throat. "Don't forget about dinner. Seven o'clock reservations."

"I know," Judith said and settled into a chair at the table while Lucas adjusted the buckle on his belt to tidy his shirt.

"Bye, Dad," Lucas said.

"And my dry cleaning," Peter added.

"I know." Judith snapped the morning paper open.

"Hey, Dad, I wanted to—" Lucas called. But Peter was already in the garage starting the rental car. Lucas picked at the teeth of the comb in his hand for a moment before checking his appearance in the mirror one last time.

He retrieved his ski jacket from the hall closet, offering Lindsey a ride in his battered Toyota as he slung a blue canvas backpack over his shoulder. He hadn't carried a bag to school in years but Judith thought little about it, then.

Lindsey bent to give Judith a kiss on her way out the door and knocked the back of her mother's head with her violin case in her rushed excitement, no doubt thrilled to arrive at Hyatt Middle School in a car driven by a sixteen-year-old chauffeur instead of in a big yellow bus.

Lucas propped the door to the garage open with his elbow. "Happy Valentine's Day, Mom."

She twisted around in her chair to look at him. "Oh, Happy Valentine's Day, Lucas."

He hesitated then, paused as if he wanted say something else, as if it were something important or difficult that stuck to the roof of his mouth. But he only gave her an awkward little wave, a flap of his hand, with his usually slouched shoulders squared and straight. And she waved back. Did not stop him. Did not ask him to sit down with her for a few more minutes, to talk about anything that might be on his mind. Lucas turned to leave, and the last thing Judith saw was the blue backpack heading out the door.

Transit

AS HER FAMILY CLATTERED out of the house with banging doors and grinding car motors, Judith lingered over another cup of coffee with her daily planner. She jotted down a list of errands for the day—dry cleaning, hair appointment, birthday present for her mother. She pulled a cardigan over her shoulders and shivered under her silk pajama top as a draft swept through the kitchen. She flexed her fingers and toes, her extremities always cold, and surveyed the heavy sheets of plastic drooping over the gaping hole in the kitchen wall. The original deck and sliding glass doors were being replaced by an enclosed sun porch to accommodate Judith's large collection of houseplants. The family had been in suburban Fairlawn only a few months, and the new house at 817 Culver Lane had yet to really feel like home. It was a sprawling brick two-story with oversized windows and a massive oak front door showcasing an ornate stained-glass inlay. Judith had liked the floor plan when they built the house, but now the spacious rooms echoed and felt hollow in spite of the furniture and accessories the decorator had helped her select. Her thought, when they'd moved in July of the previous year, had been that by adding a sun porch, her own personal touch, the house might finally feel theirs. But all the project had done so far was increase the frequency of her daily headaches. She glanced at the clock. The construction crew was thirty minutes late. Again.

Judith dialed her younger sister's cellular number, but Penny's voicemail recording said she was out of the office showing a house.

"Hey, it's me," Judith said. "We need to talk about going in on a birthday present for Virginia. Call me back if you get this before eleven; otherwise I'll be home between three and five. But try to get me before lunch, because I want to get my shopping done today before Peter and I go out."

She felt a building annoyance for another day that would be consumed by the porch construction and her mother, both of which seemed to demand most of her time on a regular basis. Virginia's birthday was still weeks away, but she was already laying the groundwork for requests, veiled by long sighs and breathy comments like, "Oh, you'll never guess what Paula Frey's husband bought her for their anniversary. He's so *thoughtful*." Judith thought it really would be easier on everyone if Virginia just submitted her gift list in writing. Like an office memo to distribute between her only two employees, her daughters.

Peter was scheduled to fly out to Dallas in the morning, another five-day stretch of meetings that was becoming routine, so it would be a quick dinner at her favorite downtown restaurant in keeping with their Valentine's Day tradition. Judith considered what she and Peter should wear for the evening, as dressing with coordination for his approval had become essential since his marketing promotion last spring. He had been more preoccupied with things like image and reputation since earning a senior title at Goodyear Tires, stressing his aspirations to certify a position for them among the elite in Fairlawn. She knew they made an attractive couple, with her long red hair and tiny stature next to his tall physique and sharp jaw line. And she understood that people noticed when they entered a restaurant or party together, wearing handsome clothes or fine jewelry, so they should treat their appearances like an extension of his profession. But she often thought about their public perception, the image they were cultivating in this new circle of people, and sometimes, something inside her turned away from the mendacious-feeling picture they created. She and her husband portrayed what others expected to see, but it was never clear to her if she really wanted to be what they portrayed.

It had been difficult to leave their old house by the airport in Akron, and, regardless of their making a move to the suburbs within blocks of her sister's townhouse, the new area felt like a different planet at times. Peter worked longer hours than before and was away from home more days of the month than a marriage should tolerate. Judith struggled with the added expectations and constant competition she felt they were involuntarily swept up in. The move had been particularly hard for Lucas, who, even though he hadn't left behind many friends, still had trouble adjusting to a new high school. And Judith herself had never taken much interest in socializing or making close friends, with the exception of her sister, who still had not called her back.

Judith collected an armful of damp towels the kids had left on the bathroom floor and nudged Lucas's bedroom door open to gather his dirty laundry. A pile of slacks and shirts and empty hangers covered the bed, as if he had tried on a number of different outfits that morning, putting some real consideration into what he would wear for the day. Again, the thought of his unusual demeanor at breakfast nagged her, smiling and talking, so pleasant, so different.

Judith showered and dressed, remembering as she blow-dried her hair that she needed to pick up new strings for Lindsey's violin at the music store. Another item to add to her list. As she brought down a basket of laundry, Wanda, the weekly cleaning lady, let herself in the back door, carrying her plastic caddy of rubber gloves, bottles, and assorted floral aprons. Wanda was a nice enough woman, widowed with five grown children she had raised on her own. She worked at a slow but steady pace, breathing hard and perspiring as she moved from room to room with a slight limp after a knee replacement years ago. But Judith suspected that Wanda secretly disapproved of her, seeing her as a pampered wife and mother paying a stranger to keep her house clean, paying someone to pick up after her two spoiled children who left potato chip crumbs on the floor in front of the television and never put their shoes away. Judith made a point to run errands or work in the basement when Wanda was around, hoping to avoid the woman's sideways glances of subtle criticism, the clicking tongue, the *tsk tsk* when she made the children's rumpled beds or capped the open tube of toothpaste left on the bathroom vanity. It had never occurred to Judith to fire Wanda and find someone else who would happily scrub a toilet without passing judgment, because the woman had been hired at Peter's insistence in the first place, and Judith learned long ago not to fight his punctilious nature.

"Wanda," Judith said before she went downstairs to work. "Don't worry about the bedrooms this morning. I think it'll take a while to dust down here." She gestured to the film of construction grime coating everything that wasn't protected by old bed sheets.

"That's fine," Wanda answered, rinsing out her rag in the kitchen sink. "How about the bathrooms?"

"No, don't worry about those either. And before I forget, you won't need to come the first week in April. We'll be gone the second through the tenth."

"Vacation?" Wanda asked, raising her brows.

"Yes," Judith nodded. "We're taking a cruise to Mexico with some people from Peter's company."

"How nice," Wanda smiled nicely, but her tone indicated otherwise.

After leaving a check for Wanda on the table, Judith escaped into the basement and shut the door to her corner room, relieved to be alone. She slipped her hands into a pair of canvas gardening gloves and buttoned one of Peter's discarded flannel shirts over her clothes for protection while she worked. Her long-time hobby of raising African violets had slowly turned into a full-time job. Three years ago, she'd joined the Ohio chapter of the African Violet Society, attending their annual conventions and shows, and last spring, she had taken home a twenty-five dollar prize for best miniature. She'd never thought of herself as a competitive person, but here she was, working on a Victorian Flirt hybrid with frilled pink stars and wide white stripes, eyeing another award in a new category.

The sunroom was her pet project, more space for her expanding collection of plants. She liked to think of herself as an amateur horticulturist, widely known amongst friends and family for her skills in growing lush indoor plants and blooming flowers all year round. There was a gracious sun window over the kitchen sink and another off the formal living room, but they were already overcrowded with asparagus ferns, Christmas cacti, and philodendrons, and every east and west window of the house was filled with some kind of greenery. The master bathroom had turned into a jungle of sorts, with a towering bamboo palm she'd tended since Lindsey was born and a four-year-old ficus that had taken over an entire corner of the room. And the luxurious jet tub was lined with both English and Swedish ivy, creeping and spiraling around her bottles of bath salts and scented oils. Peter complained that he needed a machete just to get to the john. She ignored his gripes, knowing her plants to be her trademark, her passion. They suited her solitary nature. But with her serious hobby overwhelming the house, she had been forced to devise a plan for the sunroom. More space, additional shelving, better lighting. And she was ready to get her most precious plants, her violets, out of the basement.

Judith checked a temperature gauge attached to the wall and turned on the fluorescent grow lights suspended above her racks of violets. She checked the soil of each plant with her fingers, adding water from a small can to a few saucers under the pots that felt dry. Today she was repotting three violets, as she rotated each plant every six months. In a plastic bucket, she mixed her own soil: one-third peat moss, one-third vermiculite, and one-third perlite. She lined up three new ceramic pots and carefully scooped out the mixture with a spoon.

"I'm leaving now, Mrs. Elliott," Wanda called down the stairs.

Judith opened the door to her workroom. "Thank you, Wanda. See you next week," she hollered back. She was back at her worktable when the telephone rang upstairs. It was probably her sister finally returning her call —two hours late. Her hands were dirty, so she would let the machine get it. But the ringing stopped for only a few seconds before it started right back up again.

Judith decided she should see who it was and dashed upstairs with a pot of dirt in one hand and an uprooted violet in the other. She dropped everything on the kitchen counter, discarding her gloves in a messy pile.

"Hello?" she said, breathless, barely catching the call before the machine picked up again.

Peter's voice sliced through the line. "Judith, finally. Are you watching TV? Something's happened at the high school, at Roosevelt. I heard it on the radio. A shooting in one of the classrooms."

"A what?" She scrambled over a chair to reach for the television remote.

"It's all over the news. Has Lucas called home yet?"

"No. No one's called." She flipped through the channels, finding nothing on the local stations yet. "Oh, God. Was anyone hurt?"

"I don't know. They're busing kids over to Dell Elementary."

"Oh, my God. Okay. Should I go over there? I'll drive over," she said, grabbing her purse and a set of keys. The phone jostled between her head and shoulder as she wrangled with her coat, nearly dropping the handset.

"Take the cell phone," Peter said. She could hear him opening and slamming drawers. "And get Lindsey, too. It'll be an hour before I can get home."

"Okay." She turned in confused circles. "Should I call the school first or the police—no. Okay. I'm just going over there. I'm leaving right now."

"Call me as soon as you find him and—" But she hung up before Peter could finish.

THE TAILORED NEIGHBORHOODS of Fairlawn stretched and curved for what felt like infinite miles as Judith stabbed at the buttons on the car radio, at last finding a local news report when a DJ cut into the morning talk show.

"We've just received a report of a shooting in an Akron area high school. Roosevelt High School in the suburb of Fairlawn. We're already getting reports of two dead, one possibly a teacher, and at least three injuries taken to the hospital, but we do not have a report on their conditions." There was a moment of muffled discussion away from the microphone before the DJ returned. "Okay, this was just handed to me. We have two already confirmed dead, one student and one teacher. Local authorities are asking parents, please, *do not* go to the high school. They are busing students from Roosevelt over to nearby Dell Elementary on Gibson Avenue. Parents are advised to go to Dell Elementary."

The cell phone slid from one end of the dash to the other as Judith careened around the corners. She pulled out in front of another car, and the man behind the wheel honked and shook his fist at her. Her hands were sweating, leaving dark prints on the leather steering wheel. Still unfamiliar with many areas of town, she couldn't think of how to get to Dell. Around the park or straight down Jefferson? The streets became busier as she neared the school, with people wandering down the sidewalks or standing at the end of their driveways, staring in the direction of Gibson Avenue. The sudden heavy traffic, she realized, was other parents racing to get to the elementary school.

A school shooting. At Roosevelt. Two dead. Two dead. She slammed on the brakes to avoid rear-ending the car in front of her. She took a deep breath and tried to calm herself. Maybe it had just been a prank, she reasoned. Kids playing a joke with blanks or firecrackers, thinking they were being funny. But then a picture flickered through her mind. Lucas at the breakfast table that morning, so different. She felt the tiniest pinprick at the back of her neck, a split-second feeling of something darker, like a minute drop of spilled ink slowly spreading across a white tablecloth.

The blue backpack.

The Blindest Eye

AFTER THE SLIDING GLASS doors had been removed weeks before, Judith found the strangest thing. Inside the wall was a square of soft wood, probably a scrap from the framing or deck, with a message carved on it in crude letters, maybe with a screwdriver or pocketknife. She had discovered it late one night while trying to secure the plastic cover after a winter storm had blown it free, leaving it slapping and cracking against itself and creating such a racket that she couldn't sleep. As Judith pulled the sheeting snug against the naked studs and reached for a tack, she glanced inside the wall and saw the block, neatly wedged between the sheetrock and studs, obviously placed there with some special care and purpose. She pried it out with a butter knife and blew the dust off, seeing the words gouged deeply into the grain.

Save me, O God

For the waters have come up to my neck.

She read the words, frowning, and ran her fingers across the rough, splintery wood as the block weighed heavy against her hands. Intrigued, she went to the computer in Peter's office and logged on to the Internet. She searched first a poetry and then a classical literature website before finally finding a match on a Biblical website. Psalm 69. She hunted through Peter's dense bookshelves until she located the only Bible she knew to be in the house, a yellowed King James version he had been given at his parents' funeral when he was twelve. She flipped to Psalm 69 and read the entire passage. *Save me, O God . . .*

She closed the Bible and stared once again at the piece of wood on the desk. So odd. Such a deep sentiment left behind in such an unusual place, hidden in her house, unbeknownst, for all those months. Put there by someone, most likely one of the men on the construction crew, who was in some sort of emotional pain. She thought about who the person could be—one of the young men always smoking in the driveway during break, the overweight general contractor with a tracheotomy scar at the base of his throat, or the Hispanic man who always ate lunch alone, sitting atop an overturned bucket on the porch. She wondered what could be going on in their lives to compel one of them to think about such words, to feel driven to carve them out and then hide them in a stranger's home. Judith kept the block of wood, putting it on the top shelf of her closet underneath a pile of sweaters. And for weeks after she had found it, she got an unsettled feeling in the pit of her stomach every time she went to her closet to select a cable knit or crew neck.

She wondered what else existed in her house without her knowledge.

THE PARKING LOT AT DELL Elementary overflowed with traffic—cars, trucks, and minivans bumper to bumper, horns honking and drivers yelling at each other. Some vehicles had been left in private driveways or just abandoned on the side of the road. Sirens screamed from every direction, and lights flashed around both entrances. Police barricades blocked all but two access streets as officers tried to funnel the congested traffic away from a steady stream of buses threading their way to the playground area. Groups of kids from the senior high were deposited at the doors of the gymnasium in the east wing of the school, where teachers attempted to take names down on clipboards and clump the students together alphabetically.

Judith found a tight parking spot near the ball diamonds and joined the throngs of frantic adults trying to make their way to where police officers were giving information at the drop-off point. She followed a path of trampled snow and brown grass, stumbling as her feet tangled in a dropped scarf. People around her were crying, talking loudly to each other or into cell phones. News vans were already set up next to the schoolyard, and a female reporter approached each person who attempted to pass.

"Ma'am! Ma'am! Do you have a child at the high school?"

"Sir! Have you had any contact from your child since the shooting occurred?"

A man next to Judith snatched the microphone out of the reporter's hand and threw it into the bushes. "Get out of my way!" he yelled.

The school was deteriorating into chaos, the outnumbered authorities unable to control the masses of people fighting their way to the emptying buses. Judith pushed and elbowed her way to the playground until she stood in the crowd and watched the buses as they arrived, her unbuttoned coat flapping in the breeze. All about her, students flung themselves into the arms of terrified, relieved parents. She recognized a few faces, red and tear-streaked, and scanned each one, watching for Lucas's mop of light red hair. It was a deafening scene, impossible for her to call out his name over the wails of emotional students. More reporters thrust themselves into the mix, pushing cameras into the faces of any teenager within reach.

"I'm Kevin Bradshaw from Channel Five news. Can you tell me where you were when the shooting occurred?"

An overweight boy stumbled off a bus and stopped next to Judith, gasping for breath as he spoke, wiping at his eyes with the cuff of his sweatshirt. "Um, I was in biology, and we heard these pops, like fireworks going off—"

"Where was your classroom located in proximity to the room where the shooting took place?" the reporter yelled over the noise.

"I was on the second floor—"

"I'm sorry, please speak up!"

"The second floor," he yelled back. "You know, a-above the gym and I think, I mean, I don't know, but I think it happened on the first floor—"

The reporter turned his back on the boy, looking for someone else to interview. "Move over there, get to that group of kids!" he snapped at his cameraman. He squashed Judith's foot as he shoved her out of his way.

The crowd swarmed each bus as it arrived, and she was swept forward, like being caught in the crush of crazed fans at a rock concert. She searched the bus windows for her son's face, checking off each kid who filed out. None of the students wore coats, and they shivered violently from fear and cold as they descended the steps. Judith suddenly could not remember what color Lucas's shirt was. Long-sleeved, but her brain was spinning too fast to conjure up a picture.

"Back up! Back up! Give them some room to get off the bus!" someone screamed.

"I can't find my parents! Where do I go?" a girl cried as a uniformed man muscled through to help her.

Judith spotted a woman she recognized from the club. She was crying, smothering her son to her chest. Judith couldn't think of their names. But maybe the boy had seen Lucas. Maybe they would help her search for him.

"Allison!" Judith yelled, attempting a name that felt vaguely familiar. "Ellen!" But the woman couldn't hear her over the hundreds of petrified cries. The crowd surged toward another bus, and the pair was swallowed up in the abyss of faces.

Judith's eyes started to water, and she fought to hold it together, checking the phone in her frozen hand since she would never be able to hear it ring. A gust of wind raked through the crowd and whipped her hair into her eyes and mouth as a roaring news helicopter swooped overhead. There was no organization, no one to ask for help. A few parents tried to circulate the area, to write down names on scraps of paper as they encountered students, but they were soon mobbed by parent after parent crying out names. The sleepy community of Fairlawn had in no way been prepared for this.

"Kelsey Daniels? Kelsey Daniels? She's a junior," a man yelled out to no one listening.

"My son! Jason Geary? Light brown hair, he was wearing a football jersey. He's a freshman."

"Please! I can't find my daughters! Jenna and Josie Fitzpatrick. They're identical twins. Are they here yet?"

A woman fainted, and her husband propped her up so she wouldn't be trampled, fanning his hand in front of her face. Her purse slipped off her shoulder and fell open—lipstick, pens, and photos scattered across the ground, crushed under the stampede of feet. Judith bent down to help retrieve the woman's things, then quickly stood up, thinking she heard someone say Lucas's name to her left. Then again from another direction a few moments later, like an echo bouncing around off the bodies. She spun helplessly, trying to locate the voices. She was crying openly now, continuously wiping at her cold, wet cheeks.

"Lucas!" she called in desperation, not knowing what else to do. She cupped her hands around her mouth and dropped the phone. It smashed against the pavement.

"Lucas Elliott!"

A few people around her started to move away, creating a small clearing where she stood alone. Her hands fell to her sides, and she felt eyes staring while a few fingers pointed in her direction.

A girl she recognized from Lucas's grade was talking to a reporter and television cameraman. The girl was clinging to a friend, and both of them appeared to be near tears.

"And what class were you in?" one reporter asked.

"Um, I, it was second-period English with—"

"Where is that classroom located?"

"Uh, on the first floor," the girl sniffed.

"And you were in the room when the shootings occurred? Describe to me what you saw."

"This boy, from my grade, he's, um, he's new this year. He, like, walked in and just started shooting." She broke down into sobs and buried her face into her girlfriend's shoulder.

"Who did you see him shoot?" the reporter asked when she recovered a bit.

She wiped her hands across her nose. "Mr. Kranovich, our teacher, and this girl, her name is Hannah Myers, and she's like a freshman or something, but I didn't know her—"

"Was anyone else shot?"

"Yeah, Matt Michaels. He's a football player, and he sat in front of me. He got shot in the head, and there was like, blood just everywhere." She gulped for another breath. "It was horrible, and I didn't know what to do. This blood and, and like, stuff flew all over, and I, and I—"

"And what did you do then?" The reporter knitted her brows together as she listened, glancing over her shoulder to make sure she was still in the camera shot.

"I screamed and got under my desk. I thought I was going to die. I was so totally scared. Everybody just started screaming, and he kept firing. It was really loud like firecrackers, and some of the kids thought it was a joke at first, until they saw the people falling and the blood, and then everyone just flipped out."

Judith could not look away from the girl's moving lips and flushed cheeks. She felt a numbness seeping through her hands and feet, a faintness fanning out behind her eyes.

No. Don't say it.

"And you saw the shooter?"

No.

"Yeah," the girl broke down again, her face twisting up in tears. "He just came in and pulled out this gun and fired a bunch of times, and I was so scared—"

"Do you know his name? Where is he now?"

No.

"Um-hmm. He's new this year, and he walked in and just started firing and then I, like, um, I saw him shoot himself in the head, and it went, tons of blood and stuff, hit the chalkboard. It was Lucas Elliott, this boy from my grade."

All sound fell away, deafened by the pulsating blood in Judith's eardrums as she shook her head. Cold hands slid up her chest and wrapped around her throat. Her own hands, she did not realize, foreign and removed. She could not blink, could not breathe.

The staring eyes were now everywhere.

No. Her mind refused. *No. No. No.* But the eyes were still there.

Watershed

THE GARAGE WAS OPEN. Doors unlocked. Coffeemaker still on, the last bit of liquid scorched to the bottom of the pot. Soil lay spilled out of the ceramic pot turned on its side, gardening gloves flat and empty on the counter. The answering machine showed no messages. The television blared from the kitchen counter with what Judith had already seen and heard at the school: police sirens, traffic jams, frightened parents waiting, waiting. A police officer spoke with a reporter and made a plea for family members to please wait at home for information. A phone number for families to call for a list of students arriving at the elementary school flashed across the bottom of the screen. Judith squeezed her eyes shut, pressing her hands hard over her ears until the only sound she heard was her own blood pumping around and around her body like some nutty carnival ride at the fair. She swayed on her feet, dizzy, light-headed, and when she opened her eyes, the interview with the young girl was airing. Judith lunged at the television, yanking the cable wire from the wall and the back of the set.

Upstairs, she fell onto the bed still wearing her winter coat, her purse still slung over her shoulder, and drew the blankets over her like a protective shroud. The air inside her self-made tent was thick with her own sweat and breath and the earthy dampness of her boots as they left wet muddy circles on the sheets. She did not move. She did not think. She did not cry.

Just closed her eyes and curled into the tightest ball her body would form. Under the blankets, she retreated from the rest of the world, from all the families and good people in Fairlawn who would soon know the Elliott name as well as their own. She cowered from the parents she knew were still standing at the elementary school, waiting, hoping for a child to be on a bus that would never come.

No. No. No. The only word in her mind.

Brakes squealed in the driveway, and the front door banged open. "Judith?" Peter's voice called breathlessly from downstairs. His heavy shoes shuffled across the kitchen floor and up the carpeted stairwell to the bedroom.

"Judith?" Peter squinted into the darkness. "Judith, what are you doing in here? Why didn't you call me back? Did you find Lucas?"

She said nothing.

"Judith? Get up! What in the hell's the matter with you?"

She peeled the blankets away from her face.

He didn't know.

He hadn't heard the news reports. Hadn't heard the interview with the girl being played over and over on the television. But then a thought occurred to her and she bolted upright. *Maybe.* Just maybe she hadn't heard the girl correctly. Misunderstood what she'd said to the reporter in front of the buses. Maybe that girl had been wrong, misidentified the boy she'd seen in the classroom. After all, Lucas had been enrolled at Roosevelt for only one semester, and it was a big school. The kids couldn't know each and every student there.

A small bubble of hope filled Judith's chest and helped to pull her out of bed. *Peter hadn't heard anything*. If Peter didn't know, if it hadn't been uttered from his lips, then it couldn't be true. Lucas could be anywhere. At someone else's house. Riding around with that boy, Travis, his friend from art class, talking about what happened. It would be just like Lucas not to call home, not to think about how worried his parents might be and that they needed to hear from him. A new, frightening thought gripped her. What if he was still in the school? Trapped or stuck hiding somewhere, too terrified to come out? Yes, there were all kinds of scenarios now. That girl was mistaken.

"I picked Lindsey up," Peter said. "She went home with Amy when you didn't go get her. She's scared to death."

He turned on the bedside lamp and removed his suit jacket. "Any messages on the machine?"

"No," she shook her head.

"Well, we'll figure out where he is. It just might take a little time with all the confusion."

Judith nodded hopefully and followed him downstairs where Lindsey was waiting to bombard them with questions. She continuously cleared her throat and made small, guttural noises, an old nervous tic. Peter ignored her, rifling through the loose papers and notes piled near the telephone. "Where is the Boyds' number?"

"Why do you want their number?" Judith asked.

"To ask if they've seen Lucas."

"Lucas never runs around with Jacob Boyd."

"Well, I'm just thinking. I'm trying to come up with some ideas, Judith. Could you be a little more helpful? I swear you are absolutely worthless in a crisis."

Lindsey followed her father around the kitchen, close at his heels. "Dad? Dad? Why isn't Lucas home yet? Where is he? Maybe you should call Travis?"

Someone pounded on the door in the garage and rattled the knob.

"Hey! Judith? It's Penny. Let me in."

Lindsey unlocked the dead bolt and threw herself against her aunt's chest.

"Peter called me," Penny said, hugging Judith with her free arm. "Any word yet?"

"No. We're still looking." Peter flipped through the phone book.

"This is madness," she said and offered a slip of paper to Peter. "I jotted a number down from the radio. You know, for parents . . ." Penny's smooth cheeks were flushed from the cold. She had not put a coat on over her suit, and her name tag was still clipped to her lapel. She pulled her dark hair down from the neat ponytail at the back of her head and toyed with the elastic band between her fingers.

"Thanks." Peter took the paper and dialed the number but shook his head. "Busy signal." He frowned at the static on the television screen and picked up the remote, trying to change the channel. "Judith, what's wrong with the TV?"

Judith thought she heard a vehicle pull into the drive and rushed to the front window of the living room to see if it was Lucas's car, but there was nothing. She broke out into a sweat again, and her damp wool coat felt heavy, smelled like a wet animal. *Where was he?* She craned her neck to look further down the street, praying for just a glimpse of his silver Toyota.

Culver Lane was flooding with cars and, as she studied the busy traffic, two cruisers from the sheriff's department stopped at the curb in front of their house. She shuddered, the brief moment of hope wrenched from her feeble grasp like a thief twisting her wrist to steal her purse. She willed the deputies away, begged them to continue driving down to one of the other houses on the block. The Huffmans' or the Petersons', whose eighteen-year-old son had stolen a car for a joyride last year. He was a known troublemaker, and Judith wanted him to be the reason the officers were conducting business in their neighborhood.

No. No. No.

Three uniformed men exited the cars and marched up the sidewalk to the house, silver handcuffs dangling off their belts. She thought again about that morning. How Lucas had eaten every last bite of his large breakfast, the nice clothes he'd worn, and the unusual expression on his face. What was it she had thought sitting at the table? That he and Kristin had gotten back together? Maybe met another girl? *Maybe he's finally feeling better.*

She jumped when the chimes sounded over her head. She opened the door, and the men filled the entryway with their wide shoulders and polished badges as she let them in single file, each officer wiping his wet boots on the welcome mat.

"Mrs. Elliott?" one of the men asked.

"Yes," she whispered, wishing she could lie, tell them they had the wrong house. *No, we're the Smith family . . . .*

"I'm Sheriff Klass with the Summit County Sheriff's Department. We need to speak with you and your husband." His eyes were black and serious, and an overgrown mustache obscured his top lip.

One by one, she took their hats and coats, her movements stiff, the muscles in her face wooden. When she opened the closet to hang up their things, there on the floor, tucked perfectly in the corner, were Lucas's schoolbooks. She thought again of the blue backpack and reached for her chest, squeezed a handful of skin over the place where her heart used to be. She ran her fingers over the smooth spines, *Geometry, Biology, American History.* On top of the stack was a Spanish take-home quiz, blank.

The men assembled around the kitchen table.

"Lindsey, please go upstairs to your room and close the door so we can talk with these gentlemen," Peter said.

"I want to stay, Dad," she whined, and moved into the circle of Penny's arms.

"Lindsey, just do what I ask," he ordered.

She started to protest once more, but Penny took the cue and ushered her down to the family room in the basement.

"I'm Peter Elliott. This is my wife, Judith, and that was my sister-in-law, Penny Campbell," Peter said, and sat down at the table. Amazingly calm and formal. Judith dropped into a chair next to him with her coat still on, perspiration now dripping down her face.

Klass gestured to the men standing behind him. "This is Deputy Sheriff Dorian and Deputy Cedillo." Dorian sat down next to Klass and removed a notebook and pen. His uniform seemed too small, stretched tightly across his round chest until the gold buttons strained. The other man, Cedillo, young and nervous-looking, hovered against a wall, shifting from one foot to the other.

"We're here in the matter of the shooting at Roosevelt High this morning," Klass said.

Penny returned from the basement, slid onto a stool at the breakfast counter, and smiled reassuringly at her sister. A slow ache had begun to creep up Judith's back and neck, and she felt as if she couldn't hold her eyes open. Still clinging to her purse, she pressed it tighter under her arm, like a life preserver.

"I'm very sorry to have to tell you this," Klass continued, "but your son, Lucas Elliott, has been identified as the gunman. He also took his own life before the incident was over."

"Oh, my God!" Penny gasped. "Oh, no. Lucas, Lucas . . ."

Peter crossed his arms over his chest and shook his head vehemently. "You have to be mistaken. You can't mean our son."

"I'm very sorry, Mr. Elliott, but we've—"

"No, no. It's not Lucas. It can't be. That's the most ridiculous thing I've ever heard. We know our son. He would never, ever do something like this." He motioned to Judith. "Tell them. It can't be Lucas. Tell them. Tell them they're wrong."

Judith clasped her hands tightly in her lap, still sweating inside her coat. Her fingers and toes had gone numb. She didn't answer. She didn't move. Not even to blink her dry, burning eyes. Judith imagined a boulder rolling down the side of a mountain, crushing her. Being flattened out by a train roaring across metal tracks. Thrown through a windshield in a head-on car collision. Any other horrible experience. Anything but this.

"Well," Peter continued in his quest for rationalization. "We're worried right now because he hasn't turned up. But, but I'm sure he just rode home with a friend," he paused, his breath fast. "Or something. And in all the confusion hasn't called us yet."

"Mr. Elliott, we've identified him."

Klass handed over a small clear bag containing a brown leather wallet. Peter opened the sack and removed the wallet. Inside, under a plastic cover, was Lucas's driver's license.

"Again, I'm so sorry to have to break this to you," Klass said quietly.

"But you have to be wrong," Peter said, his voice trembling. He clutched the bag to his chest and dropped the wallet onto the table where it tumbled open, Lucas's picture staring up from the center of the table. "I mean, you could be wrong. Someone could have stolen his wallet or, or . . ."

"Sir," Klass said in a low voice, "It's him."

Peter slumped onto the table as his sobs shook him and rattled the cups in their saucers, spilling coffee over the edges. Penny jumped off the stool and wrapped her arms around his neck, patting his back and whispering useless words of comfort. Judith remained with her hands clenched in her lap and stared at the open wallet. *Organ donor . . . Y.*

Dorian spoke for the first time. "The incident at Roosevelt High this morning is still in the early stages of investigation. Over the next few days we'll need to do extensive interviews with each member of your family. We'll also conduct blood and urinalysis tests on your son in the next—"

"What for?" Penny interrupted, her voice cracked and husky.

Dorian appeared tired under the hard lights of their kitchen, maybe even sad as he watched Judith do nothing next to her husband, who was trying so hard to compose himself. "We'll need to run a drug screen," he replied.

Judith sat on her deadened hands to quell the urge to dig through her own flesh.

"A drug screen? Lucas has never done drugs!" Peter cried.

"It's standard procedure, Mr. Elliott," Klass said, exhaling deeply. He fingered the long whiskers in his moustache. "Does your son have access to a personal computer? One in his bedroom?"

Peter's response was slow, his expression bewildered. "There's one in Lindsey's room. And a laptop in my office, but it's my work computer. He never touches it."

"We'll need to take any and all hardware tonight that he may have used." Klass signaled for Dorian to go upstairs. "We can speak more in depth tomorrow. Give you the evening for you and your family. You might consider staying in a motel for the night."

Peter glanced at Judith but she shook her head.

"Then I'll post Deputy Cedillo here to keep crowd control and do a visual sweep of the bedroom for now, and ask that you not enter the room until we can conduct a more thorough search first thing in the morning. We'll obtain a warrant in the meantime."

Klass paused. "There is also the matter of identifying the body. Perhaps Ms. Campbell—"

Judith shoved her chair away from the table, scooted it backwards with a grinding scrape until it bumped into the wall behind her. "No, I can't. I don't want . . . I can't . . . "

Peter straightened in his chair and wiped his eyes. "I want to see him. Tonight. I won't believe it until I see him for myself."

"We usually recommend an extended family member to do this. It can be an unbearably painful thing for a parent," he said.

"I'll go with Peter," Penny offered.

"We can escort you and Mr. Elliott to the medical examiner's office." Klass stood and pushed his chair under the table.

"Fine," Penny nodded and coughed back a sob. "We'll need to call our mother. Someone should tell her before she hears it on the news."

"Do we need a lawyer?" Judith asked in a tiny voice.

"Well, Mrs. Elliott, I'll be totally honest with you," Klass answered. "Our department has never dealt with anything of this sort before. I'm probably not the best person to answer that question, but if I were you, I would want legal advice."

"We'll leave you our cards." Dorian slid two paper rectangles across the table. "And we don't advise leaving town until further notice."

"I just can't believe it," Peter said, his eyes and movements bewildered as he tucked the cards into his shirt pocket.

The officers gathered their coats and shook hands, everything so civil and polite. They were met outside on the porch with an explosion of blinding lights, people swarming over the curb and sidewalk. News trucks circled the block, filming the house and the cars in the driveway, reporting live on the front lawn. Peter and Penny fought their way through the gauntlet to the first squad car, shielding their faces with gloved hands.

JUDITH DRAGGED HERSELF TO the staircase, where she found Lindsey seated on the top step, knees pulled up to her chest, weeping noiselessly into the crook of her arms. Judith squeezed into the carpeted spot next to her daughter, still wearing her winter coat and handbag slung over her shoulder. She pulled Lindsey's shaking body against her own and rocked back and forth, back and forth, until the child fell asleep, and Judith curled up on the steps next to her, too exhausted to move.

Waiting for the After

A STEADY *BEEP BEEP BEEP* went off somewhere in the house. Judith blinked, disoriented, and groped for a pillow to cover her face. The morning sun had already heated the bedroom through the open window blinds. She stretched her aching legs and ran a foot over Peter's empty side of the bed. She peeked from under the pillow at the clock on the nightstand. 7:02.

She sat up, pushed the blankets off, and looked down at her clothes from the day before, damp and rumpled from sweat. Her gait was unsteady as she tracked the source of the beeping out of her bedroom and into the hall. The door was closed, and she entered thoughtlessly, greeted by a lucent glow from the sun reflecting off the snow outside. Once the clock was silenced, she rubbed her bleary eyes and realized where she was, what day it was, and the pieces fell into place. It was the day after. Lucas was gone. Not asleep under the covers in his bed, pushing the snooze button on his alarm three or four times, making himself late for school. She held her breath, squeezed her eyes shut, and ground a fist into her chest.

The contents of his bedroom were unchanged, as if nothing of importance had occurred in the last twenty-four hours. The dresser was piled with neat stacks of laundry folded by Wanda the morning before, waiting to be put away. The unmade bed was a tangle of sheets and blankets, his pillow tossed on the floor. A collection of paintings leaned against the closet door, more sketches taped to the wall around the window. A completed order form for an art supply catalog dated two months ago was tacked to the bulletin board.

Judith stumbled out of his bedroom into the bathroom, moving painfully, as though she'd been in a terrible car accident and nursed serious injuries. She splashed icy water from the faucet over her face and neck, bending to let it run over her head until her wet hair dripped down her shoulders and back. She removed her stale shirt and clutched it to her bare breasts, staring at herself in the full-length mirror behind the door. The same eyes, the same nose and mouth she had examined every morning for thirty-nine years. To her disbelief, her reflection was unchanged. A tremendous swell of panic barreled through her stomach and up her chest. The room tipped and swayed and she reached for the counter.

It was Lucas Elliott, this boy from my grade.

Her breathing quickened, as if her lungs were fighting against every necessary breath. She kicked the lid of the stool up and doubled over, her empty stomach churning until she retched and gagged.

He's new this year, and he walked in and just started firing.

Still on her hands and knees, she yanked open the overflowing cabinet and rifled through bandages, vitamins, ointments of every kind. At the back, she found a bottle of sleeping pills prescribed for her last fall after the move. She stood up, popped the top off the half-full container, and carefully extracted each perfect little capsule, one at a time, lining them up along the sink like twenty-seven soldiers marching into battle. Trying to steady her hand, she pinched the last one between her fingers and stared at the blue gelatin covering. She thought about the other families, somewhere in Fairlawn, also waking up to empty bedrooms and alarm clocks going off for children who weren't asleep in their beds. How much those families must hate the Elliott name. She was not strong enough for this. She pressed the pill to her lips.

"What are you doing?" Lindsey asked as she pushed the bathroom door wide open.

Startled, Judith dropped the pill down the sink. She hastily whisked the remaining pills into the palm of her hand and threw them into the trash. "Nothing. Just looking for something to take for my headache."

"My head hurts, too," Lindsey said, wrapping her thin arms around herself and shivering.

"Here." Judith opened a bottle of aspirin and handed her a tablet. "Where's your dad?" She grabbed a clean bra. Her throat felt raw.

"Downstairs." Lindsey swallowed the tablet dry.

"Lindsey," Judith started to say, and reached out for her, but the girl pushed past and slipped into her bedroom, locking the door behind her.

AFTER CHANGING INTO A pair of sweatpants, Judith trudged downstairs and found Peter in the kitchen, hunched over a cup of coffee, the morning paper spread out in front of him. He rubbed at his receding hairline over and over with the tip of his index finger. His clothes were wrinkled, as if he'd slept folded up and stuffed into a suitcase.

"It's everywhere," he croaked, and waved his hand as though an imaginary bug were pestering him. "On TV, the radio, in the papers." There were patches of dark gray stubble on his chin and upper lip, his hair greasy and uncombed. The front of his shirt was spotted with jelly, maybe a drop of coffee. The phone rang, and they both jumped.

"Don't answer it," he snapped.

A woman's voice sounded on the answering machine. "This is Rita Sherman again with the *Beacon*, and I was—"

Judith pulled the plug out of the wall, wrapped the cord around the machine and the phone together, and stuck them both in the microwave. Peter stared out the window, his eyes watery and bloodshot. "I don't know what to do next. Where do we—I mean, who should I call next? I don't know any funeral homes out here, or . . . or should I look in the yellow pages? I don't know what to do next." The white skin along his forehead was turning a painful red color under the pressure of his finger. "I called Howard Pierce because I didn't know who else to call, and he's agreed to meet with us tomorrow morning."

"We're talking to lawyers already?" Judith asked quietly.

"We're going to need all the help we can get," he said, and raked the back of his neck with his fingernails. A few angry red hives had broken out around his collar line. "I just didn't know who else to call."

"Oh, Peter."

"The sheriff will be here in about ten minutes, and we have to be ready," he said, stuffing the paper into the trash. "More questions, more questions." He got up from the table, went into the hall bathroom, and shut the door. She heard the faucet run, not quite drowning out the sound of his weeping.

Judith pressed her head against the closed door and told herself to go in. Sit down on the floor next to her husband where he was sobbing like a small, frightened boy, pull him into her arms, or burrow herself into his for warm comfort. But even with her hand on the knob, turning, turning until it nearly clicked, she let go and did nothing more. If she went into the bathroom and faced her husband, she would see the death of their son in his eyes.

She dug the main section of the *Akron Beacon-Journal* back out of the garbage and spread it across the dining room table, took a breath, and looked at the front page. Lucas's junior-year school picture dominated the center, the grainy photo making his eyes seem like tiny black beads glued onto his face. He had not smiled for the camera and wore the same morose expression he had offered the rest of the world in the last few months of his life. Judith had never liked that photo. His picture towered over the smaller photos of the victims: Ed Kranovich, the eleventh-grade English teacher, and two students, Matt Michaels and Hannah Myers. Matt Michaels, a name she had certainly heard before.

Mr. Kranovich had an open, friendly face. Round-frame glasses an English teacher who favored Walt Whitman might wear. Matt Michaels looked every bit the All-American football player. Good teeth, hair slicked back with too much gel. And Hannah Myers, a girl Judith vaguely remembered from a spring concert last year, so small and pretty, wearing a long, dark braid and a shy, closed-mouth smile. She had played a piano solo. Mozart.

The articles were long and repetitive: "Very little information or details about the shootings available at this point." There was a picture of their home on Culver Lane. The Elliott name was on every page—where they lived, Peter's job at Goodyear, how old they were. Like a resumé submitted to a potential employer. She flipped back to the front page and stared once more at Lucas's picture—the black, lifeless beads. She closed the paper, unable to bear the other photos, three other sets of eyes staring back at her, sad and accusing. She wanted to cry, thought she might finally, gratefully, break down as a hard lump pressed at the base of her throat, but nothing came. Stalled, wedged somewhere in her esophagus. The doorbell rang, and she checked the window to see the same parade of news vehicles planted along the street as the day before. A young man in a delivery uniform was waiting on the porch. He held a long narrow box across his arms and bounced up and down to keep warm. Judith let him in, barely opening the door enough for him to slide through.

"Hi. Floral delivery from Sam's." He handed her the box.

"Floral delivery?"

"Sorry about the delay. It was supposed to come yesterday, but we were just swamped." He glanced over his shoulder out the window. "You all famous or something?"

She opened the envelope and slid the small card out. *See you at seven. Love, Peter.*

"You all famous or what?" he repeated.

Her breaths were too quick and shallow for a response. She lifted the lid of the box. Underneath the thin green tissue paper were twelve perfect yellow roses. Her favorite.

She jammed a handful of cash from her wallet into his cold palm, and Sheriff Klass and Deputies Dorian and Cedillo passed the delivery boy on the congested sidewalk. Peter rushed from the bathroom at the sound of their voices, drying his hands and face on a towel.

"Mr. and Mrs. Elliott," Klass said, removing his overcoat. He paused for a moment, staring at the roses in her arms. "I'm sure you've had an unbearably long night, and I apologize for the early hour, but it's important for our investigation to move quickly."

"It's fine," Judith said. She set the box of flowers on the table and joined Peter where he sat fidgeting, crossing and uncrossing his slender legs.

"Again, we're very sorry for your loss," Dorian said.

"Thank you," Peter said.

"All right," Klass said, exchanging a quick glance with Dorian. "Since our last conversation, we've been able to compile some preliminary information on the shootings, and I'm just going to briefly run down what we know at this point." Klass flipped through a small spiral notebook. "And please, stop me at any point if you need a break." He exhaled loudly and began reading. "As we said last night, the three victims have been identified and their families contacted. A seventeen-year-old male, Matthew Michaels; Edward Kranovich, age thirty-one, the English teacher; and a fifteen-year-old female, Hannah Myers."

"They were shot in that order," Dorian said. "The morning paper had them listed wrong."

"Okay, so far what we know is that—" Klass stopped mid-sentence. "Um, Mrs. Elliott, this is extremely sensitive information, so if you would like to excuse yourself—"

"Just read it," Judith said, her voice as emotionless as her face.

"Okay. As I was saying, Lucas entered the building around eight AM, according to the surveillance videos from the school. At approximately nine-forty, he requested a bathroom pass from Mr. Kranovich. We have witnesses that place him at his locker and in the second floor boys' bathroom between nine-forty and nine-fifty, presumably to retrieve the gun, which had been wrapped in gym shorts, from his backpack. At about nine-fifty-one, he reentered Kranovich's classroom, removed the handgun, a forty-caliber Glock, from the back of his jeans, and fired the first shot at Matt Michaels."

Matt Michaels. Judith turned the name over in her mind. *He's Kristin's new boyfriend,* Lucas had said with an ice pack pressed to his bloody nose.

Peter leapt from his chair and paced in front of the unfinished porch. He kicked at a sliver of wood, mumbling to himself.

"Would you like me to stop, Mr. Elliott?" Klass asked.

"No, no. I'm . . . I just need a minute." He raked his fingers through the hair at his temples and took a deep breath before sitting back down. "I'm sorry. This is just—" He shook his head. "So difficult to hear. Still so hard to believe."

"I understand." The cell phone hooked to Klass's belt rang, and he went into the hallway to answer it. After a few seconds, he motioned for Dorian to join him while Cedillo remained at the table.

"Were you there when they told the other families?" Judith asked, watching him toy uncomfortably with the Styrofoam coffee cup in his hand, the rim dotted with bite marks.

He cleared his throat. "Yes, ma'am, I was."

She pressed her cold fingers to her forehead. "Was it terrible?"

"Yes, ma'am. It was." His hand shook as he spoke.

"How long have you been in the department?"

"Two and a half weeks," he answered. His body seemed too large for the narrow chair, and the change in his pocket jingled as he bounced his leg up and down under the table.

"I suppose this is your first case?"

"Yes," he nodded.

"Sorry about the interruption," Klass apologized as he and Dorian returned to their seats. "Okay." He ran down his notes with his index finger. "The other students in the room reported that Mr. Kranovich was the second person shot."

"Attempting to save the other students," Dorian interjected.

Judith closed her eyes and pictured Ed Kranovich, his salt-and-pepper hair and coffee-stained teeth. His kind eyes on the other side of his desk during parent-teacher conferences the previous fall. *I think he's got so much more potential than he's using. He's shy in class, he holds back, but I can tell he's got a lot to offer. And his current grade doesn't reflect at all what he's capable of.* Mr. Kranovich had liked Lucas.

"Then he fired one bullet at Hannah Myers, which grazed the ear of the student sitting one seat in front of her." Klass flipped around his notebook. "What's that student's name?" he asked, looking over Dorian's shoulder at the other pages of notes.

"Kristin Danforth," Dorian finished.

"Right. And then he turned the gun on himself. The whole incident lasted less than a minute."

"Kristin," Judith echoed. Peter choked back a sob and dropped his head.

"We haven't had a chance to talk at length with her yet. She's still at Akron General. But we understand she used to date your son?"

"Yes," Peter answered. "They broke up around the Christmas holiday. She started dating that boy, Matt Michaels, shortly after." He paused, his eyes welling with tears. "Did he say anything or leave a note for anyone?"

"No." Klass shook his head, seeming regretful. "He never spoke during the incident, and no written communications have been recovered at the school, in his personal effects, or in his vehicle. We still have to search your home, though."

"We've obtained a warrant." Dorian slid the paper across the table.

Peter took the document and removed his reading glasses from his front pocket, wiping his eyes with a handkerchief.

"And your twelve-year-old daughter is the only other child in the house?"

"Yes," he nodded. "She's still upstairs."

The front door opened after a soft knock, and Judith's mother entered the house amid an outbreak of camera flashes and reporters yelling questions from the street behind her. Virginia removed her cashmere coat and laid it across the bench in the foyer, gliding into the kitchen with her unbreakable posture. She wore her public face—fresh make-up and an elegant navy sweater set and pearls.

Peter stood to greet her, and they embraced. He bent his tall frame down to muffle his cries against her delicate shoulders. She patted his back with her white fingers, like a bird flapping its wings in alarm. Once Peter composed himself, she reached a cool hand out to Judith's arm and squeezed it gently for a moment.

"How are you holding up?" she asked her daughter, her eyelids fluttering back the teardrops that threatened to ruin her perfectly applied mascara. Judith didn't answer.

"I'm Virginia Campbell," she said to the officers, extending a hand to Sheriff Klass. "I'm Judith's mother."

"Nice to meet you, ma'am," Klass said. "I'll say again how sorry we are for your family's terrible loss."

"Thank you," she said, and cast her eyes down at the floor as she settled into a chair. "We're so shocked over what has happened."

"We understand, ma'am. And the sheriff's department is here only to help piece this tragedy together for answers."

"Of course," Virginia agreed. "It's just so incomprehensible. I keep asking myself why God couldn't have taken me? I've lived my life."

"God didn't take him, Virginia. He killed himself," Judith said. Everyone around the table shifted in their seats in an awkward silence.

Virginia leaned close and wrapped her arm around Judith's shoulder. "You're going to say and do some inappropriate and even shocking things in your grief," she whispered into Judith's ear. "But let's remember our dignity."

Klass and Dorian cleared their throats.

"Did Lucas ever show any signs of violent tendencies?" Dorian asked. "Has your son ever had problems with drugs? Troubles at school or home?"

Judith glanced at Peter as he shifted a bit in his chair. She heard her own pleading words from that awful night in the garage. *Peter! Let him go!* And Lindsey's terrified screams. *Mom! Make them stop!*

"No, we never had any troubles with drugs or alcohol," Peter finally said. "And he . . . he wasn't a violent boy."

"We pulled a report from the Fairlawn Police Department that says he smashed a windshield with a baseball bat—"

Peter interrupted. "Yes, well, there was the one incident recently, but we cooperated with the police and dealt with him accordingly at home."

"A vehicle belonging to Matt Michaels?"

"We dealt with it," Peter said, and averted his eyes away from both Judith and Sheriff Klass.

"So, there were problems with other kids at school? Bullying?" Klass asked.

"Yes," Peter nodded. "We had some trouble at his old school and again at Roosevelt."

"When?"

"It started after the holiday break. A group of football players started harassing him. Friends of Matt Michaels's."

"What kind of harassment?"

Peter spread his fingers out on the table and sighed. "They threw beer cans in our yard, egged his car, made prank phone calls at all hours of the night. He came home from school one day with a bloody nose after a fight with two of them."

"And when was this?"

"Two, three weeks ago, maybe. He served an in-school suspension."

"Did you report any of these harassment incidents to the authorities when he was taken into custody? Or to the school?" Dorian held a notebook and pen but did not write anything down.

"No," Peter answered softly. "I—I mean, we felt that it would only make things worse. Aggravate the boys further. We thought that the situation just needed time to cool off."

"I agree," Virginia chimed in. "I've always said boys will be boys. How are they supposed to grow up to be men in today's society? Everyone telling them to *cry* and *feel* and get in touch with their emotions. It's very confusing."

Klass stared at her blankly for a moment, then moved on without comment. "Who did Lucas hang out with at school? Who were his friends?"

"He hadn't been a student at Roosevelt very long," Peter said. "But he did make one friend named Travis. They were in some art classes together and used to ride around on Friday nights sometimes."

"And what is Travis's last name?"

Peter looked at Judith and shrugged. "We don't—I guess we never asked what his last name was. Judith was the only one who met him." He pulled at the fine blond hairs on his arms, twisting them between two fingers, then smoothing them back down. The hives had spread down to his wrists.

"We'll locate an address or phone number for this boy. We need to talk to him." Klass flipped a page in his notebook and continued to write.

"So, back to Kristin Danforth," Dorian said. "How long did they date?"

"Only a few months," Peter answered. "From maybe October to Christmas. She was Lucas's first girlfriend." Judith felt the room grow stuffy at the mention of Kristin's name. One of the men's uniforms smelled of stale cigarette smoke, and her mother's rose-scented perfume was suffocating.

"Were they serious or exclusive?"

"Oh, I don't think so," Peter said. "They were just kids."

"Were they sexually active?"

"I don't think they—"

"Yes," Judith interrupted. "They were."

Peter closed his mouth and clenched his jaw into a hard line. His angry, accusing stare caused a heat to rise in her cheeks. The obvious breakdown in their family's communication had been shamefully exposed.

"Did he ever express any feelings or verbalize any intentions to you that he wanted to harm himself or Kristin or anyone else?" Klass asked pointedly.

Judith put her hands against her throat and thought about what Lucas had said the day he came home with the bloody nose. *I wish I was dead. I don't want anyone else but her. Ever.*

The officers stared at her, waiting for an answer.

"No," she finally whispered.

"Well, we've concluded that he was probably aiming for Kristin Danforth and missed, hitting Hannah Myers," Klass said. "In the short statement we got from Kristin at the hospital, she felt positive he intended the shot for her."

"And you don't keep any firearms in the house?" Dorian asked.

"None." Peter peeled off his glasses and rubbed his eyes. "I already told you. We have never owned a gun or kept one in the house."

"Do you have any ideas about where Lucas could have obtained the gun?"

Judith and Peter shook their heads in unison.

"We're running the serial number for registration," Dorian said. "It's likely that the gun was stolen."

At that point, Lindsey floated into the kitchen and opened the refrigerator door to retrieve a can of soda. Her tangled hair hung over her pale, swollen face. The waistband of her cartoon pajama shorts was bunched and rolled up at the base of her spine. She appeared unaware of the group of adults watching her, even when her grandmother rose and tried to offer her an embrace. All conversation ceased until she slipped back out of the room like an apparition.

"We'll also need to speak with your daughter at some point," Klass said in a low voice.

"Please, can't we leave her out of this?" Peter asked. "I don't want her exposed to any more of this than she has to be."

"We understand your concerns, Mr. Elliott, but everyone in your family will need to be interviewed."

"We will help in any way we can," Virginia offered. "We're normally a very nice, decent family. Nothing like this has ever happened before. The shock of it . . ."

Virginia's smooth voice faded into a distant buzzing sound as a thick migraine rooted itself deep inside Judith's head, splintering down her neck and across her shoulders. It had been twenty-four hours since she had eaten anything. She felt removed from everything that was happening, hollow, as if she were sitting in for the Real Judith so the Real Judith could come completely apart in another room of the house. It was disturbing to be so disconnected and shut down.

Cry! Beat the walls! Kick the doors! Do something! Get this out! Your son is dead! Do you understand? He's dead!

But she only felt her throbbing head and heard the buzzing as she picked up the box of yellow roses and crushed it between her arms, then stuffed it into a garbage bag.

THE OFFICERS SPLIT UP and searched separate areas of Lucas's room, picking through his belongings with rubber gloves, tweezers, and flashlights. Klass started in the closet; Dorian went through the desk; and Cedillo sorted each drawer of the dresser. They deposited various items into clear plastic bags labeled by a black Sharpie marker. Judith watched from the doorway while notebooks, scraps of paper, and books were ferried away and added to the cardboard boxes by her feet. A teenage boy's innocent paraphernalia categorized as evidence to a terrible crime.

With the questioning over for the morning, Virginia took Lindsey back to her house, while Peter excused himself to meet Penny at the funeral home. He had left the house before the deputies entered the bedroom for their search. He took with him a nylon garment bag filled with clothes for Lucas to be buried in. Judith did not know what had been selected, had not offered to help or go with him, and could not bring herself to look inside the bag, to see the suit or sports coat her son would wear in his coffin. *His coffin.* The words in her head nearly brought Judith to her knees.

She knew Peter also carried an envelope in his coat pocket. A slim, white envelope containing a single sheet of paper that he would give to Penny at the funeral home for her to deliver to a local news station. A statement. An apology to the victims and their loved ones. *On behalf of the Elliott family* . . . He had written it after everyone left the kitchen, just three or so lines from what she had seen, scratched out on his yellow legal paper. She had watched unseen from the doorway as he wept, holding in his hand the gold fountain pen his grandfather had given him for his high school graduation. Watched as he pressed so hard against the paper that the tip snapped and exploded ink over the tablet and his hands. She had turned away while he cleaned up the mess and started all over.

She had led the deputies to Lucas's bedroom, opened the door, and politely switched on the light for them. She should have left at that point, waited in her own bedroom or the kitchen until they were finished, but she had to watch. Couldn't turn away from the little plastic bags. She felt her insides twist as his things were moved around and disturbed, no longer as he had left them, his fingers no longer the last to touch the knobs, the wood surfaces, the doors. It was her son's bedroom, his private space within their home. A place where she and Peter had never bothered him, never intruded or snooped. The same private area that they had prided themselves on giving him would now paint them as negligent and blind to all things critical that had gone on under their own roof with their own child.

Klass removed a small shoebox from the top shelf of the closet, lifted the lid, and fingered the contents, put it up to his nose.

"Cannabis," he said to Dorian and bagged it. He eyed Judith as she hovered in the doorway, perhaps checking for a reaction. But she had none. She had no idea what they might find in his room, and nothing would surprise her. Her son had become a complete stranger many hours ago.

"Did he do all these?" Dorian held up a stack of pencil sketches on large, cream-colored paper.

Judith stepped forward to look through them. Some were graphic, gruesome depictions of limp bodies at hangings, others of faceless people writhing in tall flames with their hair singed off and fingers clawing at the sky. She had never seen that kind of artwork from him before.

"Um, I guess so." Judith lingered over a soft drawing at the bottom of the stack of two naked bodies entwined on a bed, a rumpled sheet binding them close. And then another one of an elderly woman's face bent over a vase of flowers, peonies maybe, her softly wrinkled eyes closed as if she were savoring the sweet scent.

"Disturbing," Dorian said.

"Are you taking all of them?" she asked.

"Yes, ma'am." He pried the stack from her hands as she tried to hold back the couple on the bed and the old woman.

Cedillo glanced over Dorian's shoulder and studied the two drawings Judith had attempted to save from the inventory. She thought for a second he might speak up and make a move to get them back for her, but Dorian had already dropped them into the box.

"Cedillo," Klass said. "Help me with these." He held out a stack of CDs pulled from Lucas's bookcase. She read the titles quickly as Cedillo assigned them labels and retrieved another box. She understood. Hard rock and rap. Violent lyrics and parental warning stickers. Some she had heard when he played them in his room. Some she actually didn't mind and had purchased for him at Christmas to stuff his stocking.

She wanted to tell Klass to look harder. Read the titles of the other CDs on the shelf more carefully. Lucas hadn't listened to only one kind of music. He loved Billie Holiday. Bought every album Credence Clearwater Revival ever made. He had recently been on a seventies kick and bought a *Best of Disco* CD just last Thursday at the mall when she took him shopping for a new pair of jeans. *Just last Thursday*. They were painting an image of him, and Judith saw that it was to fit what he had done, not who he really was. But then, as of yesterday morning, she had no idea who he really was.

Once the deputies were finished, when the last box was loaded into their squad cars and driven away, she went back to his bedroom and saw the mess left behind. Items tossed about the floor after examination and determined useless. Concert ticket stubs, magazines, tattered paperback books, and a stuffed dog missing a leg. The dresser drawers gaped open, and the closet door stood ajar with the light on. It was no longer as Lucas had left it the day he died. *Just yesterday morning.* It was changed and spoiled.

He would never study for a test in there again. Or read comic books until three o'clock in the morning. Or sketch in his artist's notebook with colored pencils or charcoal as his stereo blared in the background. She would never have to nag him to turn the stereo down again. The realization of all that was happening to her family, of all that had changed since 9:51 yesterday morning, was so staggering, so incomprehensible, that she laughed. A tight, manic, frightening laugh that made her eyes water as she slammed the door shut and left the lights on.

Procession

THE CITY OF FAIRLAWN shut down. As a strong wind blew for two days, stores, banks, and businesses locked their doors. The schools remained closed. Neighborhoods were silent. Then, on Tuesday, vehicles crowded the streets from the First Methodist Church on Witmer Drive all the way to Norwood Avenue for Matt Michaels's funeral. Standing room only on the sidewalks an hour before the service. On Wednesday, the Beautiful Savior Lutheran Church on Ninth Street held services for Hannah Myers and Ed Kranovich. Hers in the morning; his, late afternoon. Two days of mourners' fighting the unusual wind, holding down dresses and skirts and hats. Local florists' trying to shield the deliveries of flower baskets and potted plants. Twenty-seven different church bells tolled for five minutes both days at noon, reportedly heard over a mile outside the city limits.

Friday morning, outside Judith's bedroom window, the brutal northeast wind carried an empty trash barrel down Culver Lane, rolling and banging it from curb to curb. The naked branches of a young birch next to the house clattered against each other, and an icy draft pushed through the cracks in the sill, grazing her face in puffs.

A lone reporter camped out in front of the house, braving the unfriendly weather in a thin leather jacket and knit stocking cap. He sat a notebook and camera on the roof of his car and wrapped his bare hands, probably frozen stiff, around a travel mug that emitted a withered plume of steam into the air. Another gust caught the notebook and camera, and both flew off the roof, papers scattering into nearby trees and bushes, while the camera cracked against the pavement and broke into two black pieces. The loose trashcan tumbled towards him and crashed into the rear bumper of his car. As if taking a cue from the container, he picked up the remains of his camera, dumped out the liquid in the cup, and drove away.

Judith, wearing only her brassiere, panties, and black control-top nylons, stared down at Culver Lane. A pile of blouses, slacks, and dresses buried the reading chair in the corner of the room. A navy blue jacket and skirt hung on the knob of the closet door. She had started to get dressed, but the energy it took to hook her bra and squeeze into pantyhose was too draining, and she had given up. She was groggy after taking too many sleeping pills on an empty stomach the night before. She just wanted to stay in bed, hidden under the blankets in the dark.

The drone of voices from downstairs swelled, permeating the quiet of her bedroom, where she sat coiled around a pillow in the bay window. Platters of finger food continued to crowd the kitchen table and counters, and the refrigerator was already overflowing with casserole dishes. Strange fruit salads and frosted cakes in metal pans with names written on labels taped across the lids. There were baskets of muffins and cold gelatin deserts, one with rotten-looking bananas suspended in it. Italian entrées seemed to be popular, with three lasagnas, two baked spaghettis, and a manicotti heavy on the spinach from Mrs. Clarkson next door, who made a point not to deliver it personally, instead sending over her unemployed forty-something son who mowed yards when he needed the cash.

Judith knew there were only about a dozen or so people downstairs planning to attend the graveside service. Her mother, serving coffee and crumb cake; Penny, handling the small number of cards and plants and flowers that trickled in; Mr. Morris, the funeral director; Peter's college roommate Tim and his wife, Brenda; and coworkers from Goodyear, including the CEO. Two women from Judith's chapter of the African Violet Society had stopped by the day before to give her pots from their personal collections, one Everdina and one Precious Pink. The women had stayed less than ten minutes.

Judith had been to many funerals in her lifetime—her father's as a teenager, two stepfathers since she'd been married, four sets of grandparents, aunts, uncles, and Peter's only cousin, who had been killed in a boating accident shortly before their move. But never had she been to a funeral for a child. Or a suicide. She wondered if *she* would've stayed less than ten minutes, uncomfortable, at a loss for words and anxious to just hand over her plant and leave. And she wondered what kind of plant she would've chosen to bring. A peace lily, maybe, or miniature rose bush that could be planted outside to keep blooming every summer. She wouldn't give an African violet. Too many people didn't know how to care for violets.

"Mom?" Lindsey called softly from the doorway.

"Hi. Come in." Judith patted the seat next to her. "Did you find a pair of tights that still fits?"

Lindsey tugged at the waistline of her simple A-line dress. "Yeah, but they're so itchy."

"You won't have to wear them very long."

Lindsey kicked off her leather pumps and curled up on the seat cushion to look out the window. The black dress made her skin appear even more pale and washed out, the line of her thin neck looking as white and breakable as an eggshell. She flipped her hair off her shoulders and laid her head down on her mother's legs.

"Have you eaten anything yet today?" Judith asked.

"I can't," she sighed. "Is Mr. Morris a preacher?" she asked.

"No. He's a funeral director from the funeral home."

"Why didn't you get a preacher?" Lindsey pulled at a snag in Judith's hose.

"We're not members of a church."

"Why isn't there a funeral for him?"

Judith leaned her head against the wall and reached down to stroke Lindsey's cheek with the back of her fingers. She felt the brush of Lindsey's eyelashes across the top of her thigh each time the girl blinked. "We didn't think anyone would come," Judith said honestly.

"Is that why he's getting buried so far away?"

"Yes."

"Is anyone else in our family buried there?"

"Yes. Your Grandma and Grandpa Elliott. They died when Dad was a young boy."

"Oh." Lindsey paused and relaxed her shoulders. "I didn't want him to be alone."

"Judith?" Penny tapped on the door as Lindsey moved away from her mother, straightening the hem of her dress. "Judith? Are you ready?" Penny's charcoal gray dress fit her athletic body perfectly, and the small black-rimmed glasses perched on the bridge of her nose helped to conceal the puffiness around her dark eyes.

"I had trouble finding my blue suit," Judith said and turned back to the long view of the window, the linen curtain still pulled aside in her hand.

"Oh. Well, get dressed, honey. It's almost, you know, time." Penny licked her thumb and smoothed down a stray hair atop Lindsey's head. "Linds, I think you'll need some warmer shoes. It's really cold and windy out there. Go find your black boots. The ones with the little heel that I bought for your birthday last year."

Judith heard her sister gather the pile of garments, probably to sort and return them to their place at the back of the closet where only her dressy clothes hung in nylon garment bags. A tangled mess of metal hangers jingled together as Penny worked to separate them. Would be a shame to let the clothes lie on the floor and wrinkle.

Virginia poked her head through the half-opened door. "Judith, why aren't you dressed?" Her black stiletto heels sank into the thick oatmeal-colored carpet.

"She couldn't find her blue suit," Penny said.

"Her blue suit? No, no, Judith. You need to wear a dress. In black. Where's that lovely black wool dress that you wore to cousin Andrew's baby's christening last year? With the buttons down the front? Little Peter Pan collar?" She flicked through a few garments on the rack and shook her head. "Black, definitely black. Much more appropriate."

"Whatever." Judith left the window and rooted around the back of her closet for black wool. Penny and Virginia busied themselves making the bed and fluffing pillows while she dressed.

"Judith, you should keep the house picked up. People will probably want to stop by this afternoon," Virginia commented.

"No one else is coming over, Mother," Judith said, buttoning the black dress.

"Oh." She turned away from Judith and adjusted the wide belt of her dress in the full-length mirror, tugging at the stretched fabric around her slender hips. "Still, it's always a good idea to keep—oh, Judith. Please don't wear your hair up. It's too windy out today to wear your hair up and ponytails are too casual for this type of occasion."

"Mother, stop bugging her," Penny said.

"I'm not bugging. I'm trying to help," Virginia said, her hands toying nervously with her clip-on earrings.

"Well, she probably doesn't give a shit what people think about her appearance at this point."

"Penny, please don't swear. I really hate it when you swear, especially—"

"It's fine," Judith said and yanked the rubber band from the back of her head, releasing the tumble of her long hair. "I'll wear it down."

Penny rolled her eyes and handed Judith a brush.

As she jerked the bristles though the new tangles, Judith remembered the morning of her father's funeral, how she and Penny had sat on the edge of their old pink tub to watch Virginia prepare herself.

∾∾

IT HAD BEEN MUCH LIKE this morning—people downstairs talking in hushed voices over coffee and bagels. Their aunts and uncles had brought plates of food, emptied trashcans and cleaned out the refrigerator, busy, always keeping themselves busy. Judith was fourteen and Penny barely eleven, small and huddled in the bathroom listening to their mother talk more to herself in the mirror than to her daughters waiting needfully at her knees.

"Thank the stars for waterproof mascara," she said, her array of cosmetics spread about the vanity. "Your father always told me I could have been a stage actress or opera star when I was done up. He liked me to look pretty on his arm. You girls should marry men who appreciate a wife who takes the time to present herself." She patted powder across her nose and chin. "Best face forward, I always say."

Judith squirmed as the hard porcelain pressed through her pleated skirt and slip. Penny sniffed a few times, swiped at her nose with an index finger.

"Use a tissue, dear," Virginia said. "Now, listen to me, girls. No sniveling. Your father would hate any big dramas. He had no patience for silly, weepy women."

She rubbed another layer of scarlet rouge into the flesh across her cheekbones and secured her teased hairstyle with a good helping of aerosol hairspray. The ventless bathroom was choked with a sticky alcohol cloud. Judith held her breath, inhaling only short gulps at a time when she had to. Penny tugged at the loose waistband of her skirt, one of her older sister's hand-me-downs, then was forced to cough and sputter to cover the small gasping sobs that continually worked their way past her lips.

"I think we're ready." Virginia draped a black-fringed shawl over her shoulders. "Now, now. Let's gather ourselves. No one looks attractive when they're all bunched up with tears." She leaned against the sink vanity and clasped her hands at her bosom.

"We need to talk about something important, girls. I think that you should both start calling me by my first name, Virginia, instead of Mother." She leaned in close to their faces, her breath sweet, like strawberries or watermelon. "This is a delicate thing to say, but I think you're old enough to understand the difficult position I'm now in. You should be prepared, that with children to provide for, I've got to think about getting married again someday. And I would hate to chase away any prospective suitors by throwing two young ones at him from the start." She smiled as she spoke but her eyes were glossy with tears. "Best to let things reveal themselves slowly, over time. Let someone get to know me first before introducing children into the picture."

Then she straightened up and lifted a red, lacquered finger. "I tell you what. I'm going to allow you girls a special treat."

She removed a tall, fragile perfume bottle from the shelf above the sink and dabbed her fingertip behind each of their ears.

"There, now. You'll feel like real women today."

Virginia stood back to admire them, her make-up like a finely painted china doll's. A queer smile was frozen below her nose, but her chin quivered and a small vein protruded down the center of her forehead as if she fought to hold the pleasant expression. Judith was terrified of her that morning. Not of the smile or startling make-up, but of what she was determined to conceal behind them.

AND HERE THEY WERE again. Preparing for a funeral in the same Campbell women's tradition—with enough blush and the right dress, all things bad could be made better.

Peter tapped on the door, and Judith gave up fiddling with her hair. There was nothing left for her to do to waste time.

"Are we ready?" he asked.

"Somebody needs to find Lindsey," Judith said. "She's changing her shoes."

"She's downstairs," he answered.

"Her hair isn't up, is it?" Virginia asked.

"Jesus Christ and all that is holy, Mother. Just get your coat and let's go!" Penny shoved her out the door as Virginia protested with every step.

"Are you ready?" Peter asked.

"Um-hmm." Judith nodded and swallowed down a sick lump in her throat.

"We'll ride with Mr. Morris, and Penny can drive your mother."

"Fine." She slipped on a pair of black leather knee boots and realized from the sticky discomfort under her arms that she'd forgotten to put on deodorant.

"Any flowers come yet?" she asked softly.

Peter shook his head. "And the flower shop isn't setting any up at the cemetery. It's too windy."

She pushed a strand of hair behind her ear. "So, there won't be anything at the grave today?"

Peter ignored the question and held out a pair of delicate diamond cuff links. "Help me?" The cubes sparkled in his milky palm.

Judith lifted his wrist and poked a link through one starchy sleeve, then the other. Her fingers worked the white cotton and hard gold, never making contact with his skin. She felt an urge to trace the thin blue vein that ran the length of his arm, to travel the raised line that led to a soft place between his shoulder and chest, where she could maybe rest her head. Close her eyes and listen to his heartbeat while he pressed her into someplace safe. *Save me*, she wanted to beg him. *Don't let me be that little girl with no tears on the side of the tub again. Please, make this all go away.*

But when she reached out for him, he pulled away and slipped a pale blue service folder into his coat pocket.

"Time to go," he said, and left the room.

Thereafter

THE PHONE NEXT TO THE bed rang, a pain to Judith's ears. She buried her head under a pillow until the answering machine mercifully clicked on. But within seconds, the phone rang again. This time she rolled over to answer it, groping through the darkness around the clutter on the nightstand, knocking over an empty pill bottle, the reading lamp, and a glass of water, liquid running over the sides of the table and soaking into the carpet. She squinted at the red numbers of the clock in front of her. 8:32. AM or PM? She did not know. It was Penny calling from work, firing off questions as soon as Judith put the receiver to her ear—questions that she was far too tired to answer, her neck muscles far too weak to hold her head up any longer.

"Mmm-hmm," she murmured. "Okay." Her voice turned sleepy as she let herself drift, floating back down to the pillow even though she was trying to understand her sister. All she heard were the muffled cotton sounds of sleep begging her back into medicated unconsciousness.

Some time later, Judith's bedroom door flew open, and she cowered under her pillow from the overhead light. Penny appeared and took the receiver out of Judith's limp hand, setting it back on the cradle. Judith blinked and tried to hold her eyes open.

"How many of these have you taken?" Penny demanded, picking up the empty container of sleeping pills.

"Wha-what?" Judith mumbled.

"How many?" Penny yanked the blankets off the bed. She placed a flat palm against Judith's flushed, clammy forehead. "You're running a low fever. Have you been taking your Lupron?"

Judith tugged her flannel nightdress over her exposed rear and curled into a tight ball against the chill of the room. She had been taking the anti-inflammatory for the past three years to treat serious fibroid tumors in her uterus, but since February she hadn't bothered, hadn't cared. "I can't find the bottle," she lied.

"Okay, then," Penny clapped her hands together. "Time to get up. Take a shower. I brought coffee and bagels, and then we're going to the pharmacy. In fact, we'll just go to the grocery store. Lindsey called me last night and said you've been out of toilet paper for three days."

"I can't go anywhere," Judith said.

Penny sat next to her on the bed. "Look," she said, softening her tone of voice. "I'll take you to a store away from, you know . . . here. Now, come on, get up."

Judith moaned and tried to wave her sister away, but Penny hoisted her to her feet and dumped her into a hot shower. She laid a clean outfit in a neat pile on top of the toilet lid, then leaned against the sink and supervised Judith like a mother with a misbehaving child.

Once dressed and with the last effects of the pills wearing off, Judith sat at the kitchen table and choked down half an apple-cinnamon bagel and a cup of coffee as though she were nursing a hangover. For the first time, she was aware of the state of their house, the mess and clutter, the filth of unwashed clothes and dishes and toilets. Her neglected herbs on the shelf over the sink had withered up and dried out, disintegrating to powder at her touch. Her houseplants were wilted, the yellowed leaves and vines drooping over the edges of their pots until they brushed the floor. She didn't even want to think about her violets in the basement—neglected now for nearly three months.

"Do you have any other errands you need to run?" Penny asked.

"I'm out of sleeping pills."

"Uh, negative on the tranquilizers. Where's your prescription for the Lupron?"

"I think it's on the bulletin board. Where's Peter?" Judith asked.

"On the computer." Penny loaded dirty dishes from the sink into the washer.

Judith pushed open the double doors of Peter's office and watched him from the threshold for a moment. He did not notice her as he sat at his desk with his back to the computer, staring at the blind-covered windows. She had often found him like this since Valentine's Day, on the rare occasions she left the bedroom to search for him, standing in his office or at the bathroom sink, just staring at nothing on the wall or floor, the task before him forgotten with an empty stapler in his hand or a slotted spoon poised over a boiling pot of water. She would ask him what he was making to eat, and he would not be able to answer, dumping the water down the sink and leaving the room.

Judith opened her mouth to say something but stopped when she noticed that his shirt was inside out, the rough seams zigzagging around his neck and shoulders like a hand-stitched doll. She cleared her throat. "Peter?"

He whirled around in his executive chair to face the computer screen. He shuffled a stack of papers and tried to scribble something on a notepad, but the cap was still on his pen.

"What are you doing?" Judith asked quietly.

"Bills. Paperwork." He coughed into his cupped hand.

"What kind of paperwork?"

Peter laid his forearms on the desk, covering the papers in front of him. "I'm closing his accounts at the bank and settling his insurance policies."

"Oh," Judith replied with a small nod. She didn't want to know any more about what he was covering under his arms. "Do you want to eat some lunch?"

"I already grabbed a sandwich."

"Okay. Has Lindsey eaten yet?"

Peter shrugged. "I don't know. I didn't ask her."

"WHEN DOES YOUR CLEANING lady come back?" Penny had an armful of dirty sheets to throw in the washing machine before they left.

Judith upended her purse and dumped out the contents in search of a bank deposit slip. "She quit."

"Quit? Why?"

"All the news people in our yard made her nervous."

"Do you want help finding someone else?"

"No one wants to work here," Judith answered, tossing the emptied bag onto the kitchen table. She wore a Cleveland Indians baseball cap with her hair braided in a messy line down her back. She shivered under her black windbreaker as the plastic sheets over the hole in the wall rustled and cracked against the spring wind, filling the kitchen with cool drafts. It was plenty warm outside, but only chilly air invaded the house. The builders had not returned to the house since *before,* and the naked studs still marked the shell of the porch. Judith paused at her daily planner abandoned on the counter next to the phone, frozen in the month of February. Each perfect square was filled with her handwriting: doctor's appointments, AVS meetings, Lindsey's winter symphony concert that had been canceled the weekend after Valentine's Day. She had been last year's Akron Youth Symphony Concerto Competition winner. Now, she barely left her bedroom.

Judith gave up on finding the bank slip and went upstairs to Lindsey's bedroom. She knocked once on the door and entered. "Are you awake?"

Lindsey lay curled on her side in bed, watching a game show on her small television set. With the lights off and the shades drawn, the normally bright, pink and purple daisy-print room was shrouded in gloom. Her violin stand was shoved in the closet and her case pushed under the bed. The large bulletin board above her desk, usually crowded with posters, clippings, and photos of her girlfriends, was stripped bare but for a single photograph.

"What happened to all your pictures?" Judith asked, stepping closer to look at the lone photo tacked to the center of the board. A moment, Judith recognized, snapped many autumns ago of Lindsey proudly smiling into the camera, dressed in an old fur stole of Judith's and one of Penny's rhinestone homecoming queen tiaras perched on her head. And Lucas standing next to her with his arm around her shoulders, wearing some sort of monster or goblin mask, holding a plastic pumpkin full of suckers, bubble gum, and jaw breakers. They were posed on the front step of the little brick house, their costumes lumpy-looking from the many layers of thermal underwear Judith always forced them to wear underneath. The last Halloween they went trick-or-treating. *Smile and say 'Smell my feet!'* Judith had yelled as the shutter clicked and Lindsey and Lucas laughed at her. *Smell my feet! Smell my feet!*

"Where are all the other pictures?" Judith repeated.

"I threw them away," Lindsey answered without moving her stare from the screen.

"Why?"

"Because I hated them," she snapped. "They were stupid."

Judith started to retrieve some of the crumpled papers from the trashcan. "You threw away the pictures of Amy—"

"I don't care," she interrupted. "She's not my friend anymore, anyway."

"Why not?"

Lindsey finally looked up at her mother. "Why do you think?"

Judith dropped the ruined memorabilia back into the trash. She didn't want to be in the dark room any longer. "I'm going to the store with Aunt Penny to get some groceries. Do you want to come with us?"

"No." Lindsey returned her vacant stare to the television program. A woman spoke intently into a microphone as a clock ticked away minutes at the bottom of the screen. Judith noticed the shrunken outline of Lindsey's body under the sheet, the plates of uneaten sandwiches and rotten apples with only a few bites out of them cluttering her desk next to full glasses of curdling milk and cans of stale soda.

"Is there anything special you'd like me to buy for you to eat?" Judith asked.

"No. I don't want to eat anything."

FRESH, DAMP GRASS SQUISHED under their feet as they cut across the yard to Penny's sports car. Judith shielded her eyes, even though the sky was a leaden overcast, and dug a pair of sunglasses out of her purse. She had not been outdoors in so long, and suddenly everything beyond the safety of her four bedroom walls felt overwhelmingly large and vacuous.

Penny's cell phone rang before she could start the engine. "Penny Campbell. Oh, hi. Yes, that's fine. I'll be in after lunch.

Thanks, Marjorie." She shut the phone off and dropped it into her purse. "Sorry. I'm showing a house at two."

"I thought your secretary's name was Janet?"

"New girl. Janet moved to Phoenix with her boyfriend right before—" Penny stopped midsentence and toyed with the rearview mirror.

"Oh," Judith said. "*Before.*" She stretched out each syllable. "Such a big word in our lives now."

Penny squirmed and tugged at the shoulder strap of her seat belt, flipped an air vent open and then shut again. "Oh, kiddo," she said, her voice wavering. She reached awkwardly across the console and crushed Judith into a quick embrace, knocking her sunglasses askew as she smothered her older sister's face with her coconut-smelling hair. Her long layers looked lighter, almost caramel-colored from a recent highlight. She wore no make-up, and her eyes were pink-rimmed and puffy. Judith realized that Penny had been crying at some point during the morning.

They left the elegant, white-gated neighborhoods of Fairlawn, its professionally trimmed, manicured, and landscaped lawns that matched the residents. Penny owned a new townhouse in the equally affluent neighboring suburb of Bath. Since her last promotion, she made enough money to retire by the time she turned forty, but like the other agents in her company, she lived for her work. Judith had always suspected, though, that Penny was lonely, disappointed she hadn't met the right man yet to start a family with. And at one time, she might have looked up to Judith as having the kind of life she wanted for herself—

husband, children, a beautiful home, the pleasures of traveling, interesting hobbies. However, at that very moment, looking at the profile of her sister's pretty face, Judith realized that Penny probably wouldn't trade a childless single life with her for anything in the world.

Late-morning traffic sped by as they traveled the interstate to the opposite side of Akron. Judith's stomach swelled with motion sickness, and she reclined the seat back to close her eyes. Everything was moving too fast and making her dizzy.

The parking lot of the Acme Click was spotted with only a few cars, too early on a Wednesday morning for many people to be out grocery shopping. Judith gathered her sack of dry cleaning and her grocery list. A light spring rain fell as they ambled across the wet pavement.

"I hope we get out of here before rush hour," Judith said.

"We'll be fine." Penny wiped a raindrop from the tip of her sister's nose. "We'll stay until you get everything done."

Inside the supermarket, Judith gasped for breath as the automatic doors closed behind her. Under the enormous glaring lights and the stares of customers and store employees, the space so big and overwhelming, an agoraphobic panic seized her chest. Close to hyperventilating, she let Penny help her to a bench, where she put her head between her knees to keep from passing out.

"Stay here," Penny said. "I'll be right back. We'll get this over with as quickly as possible." She ran to fetch a cart and drop off the prescription and clothes. At the service counter, Penny pointed out a deodorant smudge around the hem of Judith's black wool dress and a coffee stain down the front of her navy blue suit to a young female employee. Concentrating on getting her breathing under control, Judith waited quietly on the bench and watched as the girl filled out garment tags and searched pockets, finding a pale blue card folded in the front pocket of Peter's black suit. She laid it on the counter, where Penny snatched it up and stuffed it into her purse. Judith knew it was the memorial folder from Lucas's service. She turned away and put her head back between her knees.

Penny pushed the cart patiently down the aisles, in no rush as Judith scrutinized every shelf, indecisive. She loaded the basket with cartons of yogurt, butter, and cottage cheese. No one in their family ate cottage cheese, but she was going to buy three containers of it. She grabbed four packages of bacon and four more of sausage.

"What exactly are you doing?" Penny eyed the multiple stacks of food.

"I'm buying in bulk so I don't have to shop every week. You can't take time off work to chauffeur me around every time I need toilet paper."

Penny nodded as she added four boxes of cream cheese.

In the pasta aisle, Judith loaded bags of spaghetti, manicotti, and macaroni even though Peter rarely ate pasta. When they turned down the cereal aisle, Penny smiled and waved to a young woman struggling to push her heavy cart. The woman waved back and shushed two little girls with matching blond pigtails at her side, bickering over what appeared to be a package of Double Stuff Oreo cookies.

Judith glanced at the children, then the woman, and dropped the box of bow ties in her hand, backing away from the cart. "I'm going to the car." She shoved her wrinkled list into Penny's hand. "Will you finish this for me? I have to go . . . "

"What? Why are you leaving? Judith—"

"I, I have to go."

She pulled her hat down to her brows and scrambled through the automatic doors. In the parking lot, she realized she didn't have the keys to open Penny's car, so she sat on the dirty, wet pavement, leaned against a tire, and waited. The seat of her pants and underwear soaked through, and she shivered in her windbreaker. Penny finally wheeled out the mountainous cart and fished around in her pockets for keys.

"What's happened? What's the matter?" she asked, helping Judith off the ground.

"That lady—" Judith struggled to answer. "That lady with the two girls . . ."

"Who?"

"Ed, his wife . . ."

"Judith." Penny shook her head, confused. "That was Julie Perry. We used to work together. She was our office receptionist before she quit to have kids."

"But, but," Judith stammered. "I thought it was, I thought she was Lynn Kranovich. The little twin girls, the blonde hair . . ."

"Oh, Judith," Penny gasped. "I'm sorry." She pulled Judith's head to her chest. "I . . . her name didn't register. You just freaked and ran out of the store, and I had no idea what was wrong." She tucked wet strands of Judith's hair behind her ear. "I shouldn't have pushed you so hard to get out of the house."

"What'll I do if I ever run into these people?" Judith cried into the slick nylon of Penny's jacket. "I feel like I can't go one more second."

"Hey, hey," Penny said and briskly rubbed Judith's shoulders, kneading her back like a boxing coach psyching up his contender before a match. "Okay, now. Let's just get these groceries. Okay? We're okay now."

Penny released her and turned away to unload the bags, wiping at her eyes and forcing a cough to cover her own sobs.

Calypso Orchid

IN CONTRAST TO HER MINIMALIST, beige-toned office, Dr. Haji looked like some sort of exotic flower in her fuchsia skirt and satin blouse with a multicolored fringed shawl draped across her shoulders. She dipped her head and peered at Judith over her red-framed bifocals. She removed the glasses whenever she had to wait too long for an answer to her question, holding the eyewear in her hand even as they hung around her neck by a gold-and-red-beaded chain. Judith noticed this gesture within a few moments of sitting down once Lindsey's session was over, and it made her nervous, causing her answers to come even more slowly and the glasses to come off more frequently. The therapist's dark skin was unlined and smooth, and Judith thought of an expensive mahogany dining room table her grandmother had once owned. Dr. Haji's black hair, wound around her head in a tightly twisted croissant-shaped bun, shone like a wet coat of paint.

She made notations on Lindsey's chart with a steady hand, her white-nailed fingers moving the pen across the paper. That morning had been Lindsey's first appointment, an introduction really, and there were required paperwork and questionnaires to be filled out. Judith was putting a great deal of hope on Dr. Haji, a specialist in the field of adolescent eating disorders and depression. Lindsey's need for intervention had reached a critical level: forcing her onto the bathroom scale, Judith was astonished to see the girl had lost nearly fifteen pounds off her already small frame. Dr. Haji had come highly recommended by their family physician.

"I think my introductory session with Lindsey went well this morning. I would like to see your daughter once every week for two hours," Dr. Haji said in her rich voice, only the *T*s and *D*s sharply enunciated with her Indian accent. Or maybe Pakistani. The nameplate on the desk read *Dr. R. S. Haji, PhD.* Judith would've liked to ask what the *R* and *S* stood for, what her first name might be, but didn't want to seem rude. She wondered why Dr. Haji wasn't a physician like most Indian doctors in the area, an allergist or cardiologist. It was unusual to find a female Indian clinical psychologist. Judith also noted that she did not wear a wedding ring, and there were no personal photos anywhere in the room.

Judith fixated on the large aquarium against the opposite wall, watching the dozen or so tropical fish swim through the pristine water of the tank, darting around the pink castle and plastic plants. She could just hear the hum of the filter and see bubbles dancing across the top of the water. She once again tried to name the type of flower Dr. Haji reminded her of. She would look it up in one of her rare flower guides when she got home.

"It is my initial assessment that your daughter is suffering from acute depression and a mild form of PTSD—posttraumatic stress disorder," Dr. Haji continued. "You are familiar with this term?"

"Yes." Judith nodded readily and accepted the appointment card handed to her.

"I would not recommend any medication such as antidepressants at this time, because of her recent weight loss. These medications typically suppress the appetite. We will try the therapy appointments for a month or so and wait to see if there are any results."

"Okay." Judith picked at a broken and peeling French-tip nail, painfully aware of the irony in her quick action to get help for her daughter, overriding Lindsey's angry complaints to see the doctor, in comparison to what she had done to help her son, which was nothing. She wondered if Dr. Haji recognized it, too.

"And Lindsey has not been back to school since the incident?"

"No."

"I think that is best. She should not be rushed to reenter a school environment if she continues to express no desire to do so. Perhaps you and your husband could look into tutorial services for her so she will at least be able to finish the school year?"

Judith jotted down *find tutor* on the back of the appointment card.

"And it would be beneficial for Lindsey if you and Mr. Elliott could agree to meet with me every other week after her appointments."

"That would be fine," Judith said as she tore the nail off. "Peter couldn't be here today because he had a very important conference call." She felt a hot blush rise at the sound of such a weak excuse, knowing her husband had shown no desire to reschedule the prior work commitment. Judith wondered if the conference call even existed, if Peter was actually just sitting in his office at home, staring at the covered window.

Dr. Haji opened her door, and they rejoined Lindsey, who was reading a magazine in the waiting area.

"I also suggested to Lindsey that she keep a daily journal to record her thoughts and feelings, a healthy outlet for her strong emotions during this time." She motioned to the red leather book resting in Lindsey's lap.

"Until next week. It was a pleasure to meet you both." Dr. Haji turned back to her office, and her colorful scarf fanned out behind her like a brilliant kite floating in the sky.

JUDITH DROPPED LINDSEY off at the violin shop to pick up some replacement strings and to speak with her instructor about restarting her lessons in a few weeks. Judith had been surprised when Lindsey asked to do this after the appointment with Dr. Haji, and even more surprised and pleased when she insisted on going alone. Judith agreed to pick her up in front of the shop in one hour.

She decided to pass the time at a bookstore across the street, finding herself drawn to the stationery section, lingering over the journals with their elegant covers and cleanly lined pages in pastel colors that filled the back wall of shelves. She thought about what Dr. Haji had suggested for Lindsey, keeping a daily journal where she could release her feelings and emotions into a safe place. Judith had kept a journal once before, her freshman year of high school. The year Virginia had married the first stepfather, the one who lasted only two weeks after their wedding, hit by a passing car while changing someone's tire on the side of the road. A nice man, as far as Judith could tell. She had barely known him.

The first journal, actually more of a diary, had been a small book with lavender paper and dates at the top of each page. She was diligent about writing in it daily and kept it hidden in an old doll case at the back of her closet. There had been a comfort in dumping her problems and worries into something with a giant pink heart on the cover.

From the clearance bin, Judith selected a plain white journal with light green pages bound by a black metal spiral. She returned to the car to wait for Lindsey. As soon as she was behind the wheel, she took the journal out of the plastic sack and opened it to the first page, digging a pen out of the bottom of her purse. She paused for a moment, pondering what to say. Then a string of words formed themselves on the paper under her trembling hand.

May 15

My son is dead and I am writing with a purple fountain pen.

She set the book and pen aside, leaned her head against the chilled glass of the window, and let it come. Finally. It had been three months and one day, over twenty-one hundred hours since

Lucas fired the first bullet. At last, she broke open. Swelled like an angry, torrential river overtaking its banks, drowning everything in its path. Seeing the words in front of her, on paper and written by her own hand, suddenly made it more real in that moment than in the entire past three months.

My son is dead . . .

The nightmare every parent feared, worked so hard to prevent, to ensure and protect against. All the cautionary things she and Peter had done to help themselves sleep better at night. Bike helmets, cabinet locks, outlet covers (weren't they still in the basement, boxed up somewhere?), baby monitors, car seats, curfews. Now, she was living that very nightmare, sinking deeper and deeper, sitting in the parking lot of a strip mall. She wept until her chest burned and her stomach ached, soaking five napkins from the glove compartment.

An elderly woman tapped on the window with the handle of her umbrella. Startled, Judith sat up, wiping her eyes, embarrassed, and fumbled to start the engine so she could get the window down.

"Are you all right, dear?" the woman asked sweetly.

"I'm—I'm fine," Judith stammered.

"You seemed terribly upset, and I was worried." She clutched the handle of her leather purse between her gnarled fingers, and her warm breath smelled of mint.

"Oh, my mother died this week very suddenly." The false story poured from Judith's mouth before she even realized what she was saying. "It was a heart attack. A real shock for our family."

"You poor dear," the woman said, and pressed her bag to her chest. "My husband died of a heart attack ten years ago, and I still remember the shock of it. He was weeding my flower beds and *bam*." She slapped her hands together. "Dropped face first into the begonias. It's hard, dear, but you'll get through it."

Judith nodded and felt her eyes well up again. "Thank you," she croaked.

The old woman shuffled across the parking lot and made her way through the lines of cars until she found her own. A sprinkle of rain pattered against the windshield, and Judith started the wipers. She saw the purple words in her open journal.

My son is dead. . . . Three innocent people were dead. She gripped the steering wheel and screamed, wishing to shatter the windows, the world around her.

May 31

It is five in the morning and I can't sleep. I've stopped taking any pills to get me though the night and the last few days have been really tough. It seems like I doze off for only a few minutes at a time and then I wake up with a jerk, like I was having a nightmare, only I know I wasn't asleep long enough to dream. I'm so tired right now and want desperately to take a pill . . .

Peter is going back to work today and Lindsey will spend the morning at the tutoring center and then the afternoon in a violin lesson. For the first time in over three months, I will be alone in the house and I am very apprehensive. My stomach is in knots and I've got a headache. This feeling reminds me of when Peter returned to work a few weeks after the birth of both our kids. I was nervous and anxious about going solo with a new infant for ten hours straight, and the second time around, scared silly to be responsible for not one but two *kids by myself. But now the question is, What do I do with myself all day? Nothing is like it was, everything is changed and I don't know the way. I am so lost and it's like I can't understand the map I've been handed. I wish I could call Penny and ask her to come over and stay with me, but I know I've got to stop bugging her at work. She's taken off so much time already.*

I know Peter needs to get back to work, too. His boss has been so generous, giving him PTO for the first two months and then allowing him to work from his home office for another month. I can tell he's anxious to go back, ready to get out of the house. He seemed restless the past couple of days, polishing his shoes, organizing his briefcase, washing the cars.

I dread Peter going back to work because I am terrified of being left alone. I'm afraid of people coming to the house. We get hang-up phone calls and angry letters in the mail. Cars still drive down our street regularly, people watching, staring at the house. Sometimes I lie in bed at night and think I hear footsteps coming up the stairs towards our bedroom. It makes me ashamed the next morning when I wake up, alive and unharmed, realizing how concerned with my own skin I really am.

The Roosevelt High School graduation ceremony was last Sunday and I read in the newspaper that there was a special dedication of scholarships in honor of Matt and Mr. Kranovich.

All eyes are on our family right now and I am terrified of what they see.

Civil Liability

A DARK, PEWTER-COLORED MOLD had begun to grow and spread over the bare studs of the unfinished porch, releasing an unpleasant mildew smell. One corner of the plastic sheeting had come untacked and flopped open, permitting a steady breeze throughout the kitchen. The cardboard boxes containing Spanish tiles had warped from exposure to the elements, and the fine coating of what had once been a mixture of sawdust and dirt had turned to a hardened cementlike layer. The normally bright, sparkling kitchen was grimy, the floor needing to be swept, the stainless steel appliances smudged and fingerprinted.

Peter sat at the kitchen table with his morning coffee and the newspaper. The liquid inside the mug had gone cold, and he stared at the same page of the sports section, his eyes fixed and unmoving across the box scores. As he sat, he gnawed at a crack in his bottom lip until it was an open wound, beading blood. Judith entered the kitchen with tangled hair and rumpled pajamas, taking no notice as Peter balled up the paper and stuffed it into his briefcase. Nor did she notice the handful of tissues he grabbed from the bathroom to hold against his bleeding lip. She went to the kitchen sink with a drinking glass and stared through the window as she turned on the tap.

She watched her neighbor, Mrs. Clarkson, walking her dog along the wooded area behind their houses. The hyper little terrier yipped around Mrs. Clarkson's feet and jumped at her shins every few steps, tangling himself in his leash. It made

Judith think of a dog that Lucas had once begged to have, back when they had lived in the brick house by the airport. A neighbor moving to Orlando had given the dog up. Mitzi, a patchy-furred beagle with cloudy eyes and rotten breath. Judith had said no a dozen times, refusing any kind of animal in the house. With the kids in school and Peter at work all day, she knew she would end up being the poor sucker taking care of dear, dying, incontinent Mitzi. However, after Lucas's prolonged begging and pleading, she had relented. She'd understood that he was just desperate for companionship, any kind of friend. Mitzi was allowed into the Elliott household and to Judith's surprise, Lucas had nursed her through the last months of old age until she died in her sleep at the foot of his bed. Poor Mitzi. Judith hadn't thought of her in years.

"Judith," Peter said loudly. "Can you please get the door? I'm late for work."

"Oh, sorry." Judith switched off the faucet and set the empty glass down. Dirty cereal bowls and juice glasses overflowed with the water she had left running. She hurried to the front door.

An attractive young man with two rows of perfect teeth and wearing a crisp polo shirt and khakis greeted Judith, thrusting his warm hand out to her. "Good morning, ma'am. Are you Mrs. Judith Elliott?" he said, pumping her arm up and down until the loose underside skin flapped and swayed like a turkey's neck.

She nodded dumbly, squinting against the glare of sunlight behind him. His eyes were so alive and his voice, with just a trace of Southern twang, was so friendly. She had been virtually alone in the house for days, hadn't spoken with anyone other than one-word exchanges with Peter and Lindsey. Now here was someone interested in conversing with her. She replied in one quick breath, "Yes, I'm Judith Elliott. Would you like to come in for some coffee?"

His hand came loose from hers and the smile dissolved from his face. "I'm an associate from Morris Private Investigation," he said. "I'm here to give you these." He thrust two thin envelopes into her face; one marked *Mrs. J. Elliott*, the other, *Mr. P. Elliott*. "The law firm Epstein, Brown, and Gilbert is serving you papers. Sorry. Have a nice day."

Peter hovered over her shoulder before she could even close the door, the envelopes crinkling as she squeezed them between her fingers. "What did he say that was?" Peter asked, following her into the kitchen, close as a shadow. "Who was he? What did he say that was?"

Judith slid the official-looking document from the envelope labeled with her name and scanned the single-page, full of confusing and foreign words.

Civil action . . . intentional tort . . . just and equitable under circumstances . . . decedent's representatives . . . on behalf of deceased son and loss of consortium . . .

Negligence. $1 million.

"We're being sued," she said, the words sounding distant and garbled in her own ears. "By Karen and Dean Michaels."

"Sued? I don't—" Peter stammered. "Sued?" His voice rose with a shrill edge to it and he knitted his brow into a deep furrow.

"It's a civil lawsuit. One million dollars."

"What does that mean?" a high voice asked from the opposite side of the room.

Judith looked up from the page in her trembling hands and saw Lindsey clinging to the shadows of the hallway.

"Does that mean you and Dad have to pay all that money?" she asked.

Judith sank onto a stool and laid the paper on the counter, where Peter snatched it up. Lindsey wound the excess material of her oversized nightshirt around her fingers, her body lost under the shapeless cotton, her trained musician's model posture now bent.

"I don't know, Lindsey. We need to talk to a lawyer," Judith finally answered.

"If you can't pay the money, will you have to go to jail?"

Peter dropped the paper onto the counter and slipped into his suit jacket with nervous, jerky movements. "I'm late for work," he said, tugging at the starched cuffs of his sleeves. He brushed his hand down the front of his light blue silk tie and froze. Blood, from his lip. He grabbed a wet dishcloth from the sink and furiously scrubbed at the stain.

"We don't have a million dollars, do we?" Lindsey pressed. "Where would you get all that money?"

"Peter," Judith said as he added a dab of hand soap to the cloth. "Peter, we need to talk about this—"

"I'm going to have to change ties," he muttered and yanked the knot loose from his throat. "I'm already late." He brushed past her and up the stairs.

Judith started to say something more but stopped. Instead, she folded her hands and pressed them against her temples, to ward off the budding pain behind her eyes. She looked back at the hallway, but Lindsey was gone, vanishing from rooms just as fast as she appeared. Judith returned the paper to the envelope and located a small, gray business card taped to the inside of a cabinet door. She looked out the window once more, but Mrs. Clarkson and her dog were gone. The yards were empty. Judith picked up the phone and dialed the number to schedule an appointment with Howard M. Pierce, Attorney-at-Law, a name they were now all too familiar with.

JUDITH THOUGHT HOWARD Pierce was a slovenly looking man. His suits, though they were tailored designers, seemed outdated—frayed threads along the seams and thinning material at the elbows, just a hint of fading in the fabric. The knots in his ties were sloppy, and he always looked about two weeks overdue for a haircut. His office matched his appearance: disorganized, cluttered, unkempt. Nevertheless, he was an excellent lawyer and, she knew, a good man.

"Peter, Judith," he greeted, and shook their hands, cupped between both of his rough palms. He stepped over stacks of law books on the floor and poured them each a cup of coffee from the small pot next to his desk. He never sent his secretary after it.

"It's good to see you both again, but I'm so sorry it has to be under these circumstances."

"Thank you," Peter said. "How's your wife doing?"

"Better," Howard nodded. "Much better. She's done with the chemo, and the doc thinks it looks good."

Judith glanced at the rows of dusty picture frames lining his bookshelves, photographs of children in baseball uniforms and graduation caps and gowns, family portraits with him and his wife seated in the center, one snapshot of Howard posing next to a dog, a German shorthair with a dead pheasant between its teeth.

"Why don't we go ahead and have a look, then," Howard said, pulling a pair of smudged reading glasses from his breast pocket. Peter handed him a copy of the petition, and Howard read it quickly. "And it's just the one family so far?"

"Yes," Peter answered.

"Pretty straightforward, here." Howard laid the paper aside. "Not entirely unexpected, I must say. They filed a separate complaint against the school district, too. I spent the morning compiling literature on similar past cases, and to be totally up front with you both, many of these plaintiffs win."

Peter's face remained unchanged, but he twisted the hairs on the back of his hand with his thumb and index finger as he listened to Howard. Judith reached across the small space between them to touch his arm. She felt how rigid his muscles were, even through his suit jacket. He shifted his weight and leaned onto the other armrest, Judith's hand dropping at her side.

"Could you give us a general timeline for one of these things?" Peter asked.

"We could reasonably expect to go to trial within a year," Howard said and sipped his coffee. "They will probably call you both for depositions at some point, maybe six to nine months from now. For today, I'd like to start with your interrogatories. One of my paralegals will do that."

"What's an interrogatory?" Judith asked.

"Just a questionnaire, general information about you and Peter." Howard handed her a sheet of paper from his desk drawer. "And my fee terms for a case like this are three hundred dollars an hour. You can set that up with Marsha at the front desk."

"Fine," Peter nodded. "I'll look at our homeowner's insurance when I get back to the office."

"Yes, I would recommend that." Howard scooted back his chair and stood, shaking hands with Peter again. Judith searched for a place to set her untouched mug of coffee. The cream had separated and settled unappealingly at the top.

Peter paused at the door and turned to Howard. "Don't you think one million sounds like an unreasonable amount?"

Judith had an urge to slap him for saying such a thing out loud.

"No, not in matters such as this," Howard said as his eyes briefly moved to his photos. "How much is too much for the life of a loved one?"

June 10

Served.

We're now being sued. Not entirely unexpected, *as Howard said. The reporters have started calling again since the paperwork was filed. I heard Lindsey answer the phone this morning and tell someone to blow it out her ass. She slammed the receiver down so hard that the plastic cover cracked.*

Since the meeting, I feel like I need to start doing *something to pass the hours of the day, or I might go crazy. I think about doing laundry or picking up dry cleaning, emptying out garbage cans or going down to the basement to resuscitate my violets. Get busy. Start moving. Don't think, which is apparently Peter's new philosophy. He's lucky—he goes to work all day and can forget. He leaves our house, doesn't have to look at Lindsey and me and instead can hunker down behind his desk. He can talk to twenty-five different people about twenty-five things other than Lucas.*

Yet, it's there. I know it's around him at all times. I can see it behind his eyes, in the smell of his clothes, the heaviness in his voice. It sits next to him during every meeting, phone conference, and presentation. It presses against his elbow as he tries to write reports and memos and as he types e-mails on his computer. Still, he won't look at it; he won't talk about it, no matter how often his thoughts stray in dangerous directions from the task before him. I've never seen this in him before, but I know what it is because it lives inside me, as well. Fear. He's terrified. He's flailing for something to keep him afloat in the vast waters that are drowning our family. And that something isn't me. And it isn't his daughter. It's his work.

After talking to Howard Pierce about legal terms, court dates, filed motions and settlements, I now see Peter's saving grace. Denial. Don't think. Don't talk. Don't look too closely. The light will burn your eyes.

Only . . . I am no better. I just look the other way to see the futility of everyday life.

Each time I start a chore, I think of something else that Lucas will never experience. Riding in a convertible. Getting accepted to a college. Sharing a dorm room. Picking out an engagement ring. Each new thing I think of is like ice water injected into my bloodstream. A lifetime of missed moments. Next year, he'll miss the senior prom. Then his class will graduate and start college. And graduate from college. Then wedding announcements will start showing up in the paper with happy faces and Lucas will keep missing it all, left behind, long forgotten by that time. Then again, maybe a part of me hopes he'll be forgotten. Which is worse, which is better?

And I can't stop thinking about Ed, Hannah and Matt. Three people who got out of bed February 14 and thought it was just another day. Maybe Hannah had a quiz she was cramming for. Maybe Matt was thinking about ditching Government to hang out with his football buddies behind the bleachers in the stadium. And Ed Kranovich, who probably kissed his wife and twin girls good-bye for the day. Maybe he was going to call the floral shop and send flowers to the house. Maybe he was going to make his wife a nice dinner, or take her to her favorite restaurant. Ed Kranovich, who told me during parent-teacher conferences in November that Lucas was a bright boy, had so much potential, just needed more confidence. He said that if Lucas could just believe in himself more, he would go far in life. I start to think about them and can't breathe. I get desperate and want to call someone, but I don't know who. Not Penny. She can't handle the emotional stuff anymore. Certainly not Virginia. I've learned in the last month that I don't have any friends.

Last night, I dreamt about the day we brought Lucas home from the hospital after he was born. I saw in perfect detail what he wore home sixteen years ago—a pale yellow sleeper with embroidered ducks all over it. It was pouring rain that day and Peter drove six miles an hour because he was terrified of getting into an accident.

I watched my hands, my twenty-four year old hands, as they swaddled Lucas in a blue fleece blanket like the nurses had shown me and laid him down in his bassinet. Then I sat in the rocker next to him and said, Now what? Is it okay if I eat a bagel?

In the dream, I saw our first house exactly as it had been when he was born—the peach café curtains over the kitchen sink, my silver baker's rack, our old brown leather couch with the rip across the middle cushion. I even watched, in the dream, the same episode of M*A*S*H I had watched that night.

That dream was the best I've felt since Valentine's Day. Those first few seconds when I sat up and blinked, squinting into the dimness of our bedroom for a bassinet that hasn't been next to my bed in over a decade . . . I should wake the baby . . . He'll need his bottle soon . . .

Sticks and Stones

JUDITH JERKED AWAKE FROM A restless sleep, startled by a noise outside. She sat up and patted Peter's empty side of the bed. He must have fallen asleep on the couch in his office again. It used to be that whenever she woke him up for some random thump in the night, he grudgingly stumbled out of bed in his boxers, turned on lamps and hall lights to hunt down whatever thief or kidnapper she was convinced was in the house. But she never woke him anymore, even during the few nights he shared the bed with her. She no longer slept through an entire night— each sound outside, each creak of the house punctured her light slumber. She spent many late hours watching television or writing in her journal. Or just staring into the dark.

Judith rose, drawing the curtain aside to look out the window. A soft rain fell, steady and silent. So far, it had been an unusually damp summer. A car was parked on their curb, the silhouette of a person behind the wheel. Judith had seen the rusty silver station wagon two other nights in recent weeks. Instantly, she was angry, assuming it was a reporter come back to snoop around their house, take pictures, or dig through the trash now that the lawsuit had been announced.

Enough. She didn't care if it was someone there to burn down their house or beat them to death. She'd had enough. *The eyes were everywhere.*

She yanked her robe down, pulling the little white stick-on hook off the door with it. She rushed down the stairs, crashing into a side table and knocking over her collection of hand-painted thimbles, and threw the front door open. She charged barefoot across the cool, soggy lawn, reached the station wagon, and pounded on the passenger window with her closed fist. "What the hell do you want!" she screamed.

A woman jumped and turned, grabbing her throat with a startled hand. Judith recognized the woman's face, illuminated by the streetlight. Caroline Myers. Hannah's mother. Hannah, who had been sitting one seat behind Kristin, hit by mistake, as Lucas was trying to kill the love of his life.

Judith withdrew from the car. She shivered and glanced up and down the street. The neighborhood was perfectly still.

Caroline reached across the seat and cranked the squeaky window down a few inches. "Get in," she said, moving a stack of papers out of the passenger seat. "Just get in."

Judith reached for the handle, hesitated, then stepped back. She feared what Caroline Myers could be there to deliver. Rage. Blame. Punishment. Unexpectedly, she found herself welcoming it. The possibility of words hurled at her, accusations to match the burdensome yoke of guilt draped over her shoulders. She reached for the door handle, knowing she deserved whatever came.

As Judith slid into the empty seat, Caroline leaned forward and hugged the steering wheel, resting her head against the worn vinyl. The car smelled of vanilla and coffee. The back seat was buried under folders and sheet music, wadded-up napkins, and empty fast food sacks. Judith wondered how many times

Caroline had driven Hannah to school or piano lessons in this car. Hannah, shy and soft-spoken, her hair always in a French braid. Judith waited for Caroline to say or do something. Silent minutes ticked by, and Judith fought an itch at the back of her throat to speak, to say anything, no matter how stupid or ridiculous, just to break through the maddening tension. *Just get it over with!* she wanted to scream.

"I had to see your house," Caroline finally said, lifting her head to look beyond the dented hood. "See where he lived."

A low fog drifted over the wet pavement. The world outside became blurry and distant. Judith felt insulated sitting in the car, trapped with a woman who must hate her. She stole a peek at Caroline and her faded corduroy slacks with a baggy red cable-knit sweater, unraveling at the wrists. Her long, dull hair hung over her ears, spilling down from the straight part in the center of her head, a line so meticulous that Judith could see the white of her scalp in the dark.

"Dan doesn't know I'm here. He'd be furious," Caroline said.

Judith nodded. "I'm sorry I yelled at you. I thought you were a reporter. They've been bugging us since the lawsuit."

"They've been bugging us, too," Caroline nodded, then gestured to the house. "Your front picture window is broken."

"Someone threw a rock at it last night," Judith answered, looking at the angry, splintered web of lines just visible in the porch light.

"Guess you're pretty unpopular right now," Caroline said. She opened a black, steaming thermos of coffee and took a long drink.

She looked at Judith for a second, then took an empty Burger King cup from the console, wiping it out with the edge of her sweater before she filled it. Judith didn't hesitate to accept it, gratefully wrapping her cold fingers around the cup. She tipped it back and was surprised to taste a fair amount of whisky in the coffee. She sputtered and choked, gasping for a few quick breaths.

"I keep coming back here," Caroline said. "At night."

Judith swallowed a cough. "Why?"

"I just need to know," Caroline said slowly. "I just need to know that he was a person. A human being. Somebody's son and brother. Not a monster." She lowered her head back to the steering wheel. "I need to hate you, and I need to forgive you, and I need it all at the same time."

Judith took another drink and closed her eyes as the liquid burned its way down her throat and through the rope of anxiety wound around her chest. The words nearly bubbled up. Words she should say, what Caroline wanted to hear, words so heavy, and yet so desperately empty that Judith couldn't get them out.

I'm sorry. I'm sorry. I'm so very sorry.

"She was an only child," Caroline said.

Judith set the empty cup on the dash. She clenched her hands into fists and jammed them into the pockets of her robe, pushing, pushing against the jumpy muscles of her thighs.

"We tried to have another one. Even thought about adoption but never got around to it. Too expensive, anyway."

A sour, queasy feeling began to churn Judith's stomach from the mixture of alcohol and emotion. Anything could come next.

"There were so many kids at her funeral," Caroline continued. "They came in busloads, and there weren't enough chairs. People stood in the aisles, in the hallways, and even out on the sidewalk." She gripped the wheel, twisting the loose vinyl cover between her hands. "Didn't you know something was wrong?" she whispered, a tremor in her voice.

Judith barely moved enough to shake her head once. "No."

"Do you believe in hell?"

"I don't know what I believe."

Caroline sat up. "Hannah used to borrow my clothes," she said, her voice turned distant as if she were absently talking to herself. "I always thought that was so strange for a teenage girl. Don't they always think their moms are so uncool?" She looked at Judith. "It made me feel good when she did that."

"Do *you* believe in hell?" Judith asked. An oncoming car passed slowly, and the women squinted at the bright headlights.

Caroline took another drink from the thermos. "Yes. I'm in it."

The women retreated to silence, neither one daring to look across the great space between them. Judith gathered the hem of her robe. "I'd better go," she said, pulling on the handle to heave herself out of the seat.

"Hey," Caroline said quickly. "I'd like to come back again."

Judith paused, and the open door bumped against her hip. "I'll watch for you."

July 1

Two nights ago, I met Caroline Myers. We sat in her car and talked. It was the strangest encounter. I'm not exactly sure what to say or feel about this and I can't for the life of me figure out what she wants. She said she might come back so now I don't sleep at all, getting up, looking out the window, waiting, waiting . . .

Last night on TV, Diane Sawyer interviewed some famous doctor about the psychology of school shooters and parental accountability. He said that these kids who commit violent acts will give off distress signals beforehand, cries of help, little signs along the way as to what they're thinking about doing. He referred to Jeffrey Dahmer and how he killed animals as a young boy. God help me. My son is being discussed in context with cannibalistic serial killers.

And there was a psychological profile:

Loner. Doesn't make friends easily. Difficult relationship with parents. Not active in extracurricular activities. History of being bullied, picked on, or treated like an outcast.

I immediately thought of Toby Doyle. That name hadn't crossed my mind in a few years, although during a long period of my life it seemed like that was the only one I could think of. Toby Doyle . . . Brings up a lot of old feelings inside me. I can still see the gap between his front teeth and the faded blue and silver Dallas Cowboys coat. The rattail haircut, the menacing red ski mask he wore on cold days.

Toby Doyle, the neighborhood bully who lived three doors down from our brick house by the airport. He threw baseballs at dogs—old, crippled-up Mitzi included—and chased cats down with his bicycle. He called his mother stupid and told her to shove it when he got in trouble. He coughed phlegm up in his mouth and spit it into little girls' hair on the playground. He played a game called Odds or Evens, where he would walk up to another kid, yell 'Odds or evens!' then yank out a handful of their hair. He was a little SOB and it surprises me that he wasn't the one being discussed by Diane Sawyer and her psychologist.

With Lucas, oh, with Lucas, Toby was ten times worse. He called Lucas terrible names—Wussboy, Mongoloid, Carrot Head, Pussyface. He'd push Lucas down the stairs at school, or knock his lunch trays out of his hands, corner him at recess and pummel him until he cried. He stuck gum in Lucas's hair, threw water at the crotch of his pants and prank-called our house. From sixth grade until we moved to Fairlawn last year was one long stretch of misery during the school months. Luckily, Lucas got summers off when Toby went to stay with his dad in Dayton.

During those Toby Doyle years, Peter and I faced the same problem over and over every September. How do we handle this? What should we do about it? The school was never any help, no matter how many detentions or in-school suspensions they gave Toby. Talking to teachers, the principal—worthless. Some of them were every bit as scared of Toby as Lucas was. Mrs. Doyle—also worthless. A single woman too busy with her revolving door of boyfriends to discipline her own kid. I can remember waiting helplessly each day as Lucas got off the bus to see how he looked. His body language told me whether or not it had been a bad Toby day. His defeated posture, the drag or trudge of his feet, sometimes scratches on his face or arms. We tried professional mediation, peer counseling and this dopey role-play therapy with hand puppets the school shrink suggested. Once, I even cornered Toby in his driveway and offered him a hundred bucks to leave Lucas alone and keep his mouth shut about the money. He gladly accepted cash payment on a handshake agreement and bought himself a new bicycle. Nevertheless, within weeks, he was right back at Lucas, worse than ever. So, I "accidentally" ran the bike over when it was parked near the street one night. I never told a soul.

Unfortunately, we were back to logging useless complaints at the school, with the transportation department and district superintendent. Back to leaving unreturned messages with his mother.

Peter finally lost his patience. Not with Toby, but with Lucas. Peter said enough was enough and that Lucas just needed to fight back, to start standing up for himself, figuring out ways on his own to take care of the problem. By this point, Lucas didn't have any friends. He was shy and pale and freckled, too small for sports, and spent most of his time playing with his sister or reading comic books. Everything Peter didn't want for his son. He didn't want his boy to cry in seventh grade PE because he was hit in the face with a dodge ball. He didn't want Lucas to fake stomachaches and sore throats so he could stay home from school. He didn't want his *younger daughter to be the one to stand up for her brother at the bus stop, to hear her yell at the other kids to go to hell or she'd kick them in the ass. I know Peter wasn't trying to hurt Lucas, he just wanted better for him. But sometimes wanting better only makes things worse.*

I know Lucas ended up blaming himself, thinking he was weak and a disappointment to his dad. Now, I know I should have done so much more. Put Peter and Lucas into counseling together. Maybe there would've been some kind of legal action we could've taken against the district or Mrs. Doyle. I could have even pulled him out of school and enrolled him somewhere else. I was so quick to do it for Lindsey (because she's a girl?), but, for Lucas, I did nothing. Peter and I did nothing.

Just wait and see, we kept saying. Toby will outgrow it. Just wait and see, Lucas will learn to deal with it. And it didn't matter in the end. We moved before his freshman year of high school. Problem solved. No more Toby Doyle.

But what we never saw coming was Matt Michaels.

Our inability to help Lucas, the failure of our "wait and see" philosophy were exposed by Matt Michaels. Just wait and see. We saw all right.

I think about Lucas, my sixteen-year-old Lucas, finding beer cans in the yard, eggs thrown at his car, getting into shoving matches and verbal confrontations at his locker, more prank phone calls and

name calling, and what he must have felt like—Toby Doyle all over
again. I think about that day in the classroom, when Lucas walked
in with a handgun tucked into the back of his jeans. A sixteen-year-
old held the weapon, but a ten-year-old pulled the trigger.

Diane Sawyer asked last night what I've asked myself a million
times: where do the parents fit into all of this?

Prozac and Tequila

THE MUGGY SUMMER AIR WORKED through Judith's thin pajama pants and shirt as she crossed the yard to Caroline's car. For a week following their first meeting, she had waited for Caroline to return, finding herself awake and at her bedroom window every night, monitoring each car that passed the house. She'd watched with the same feeling of dread and anxiety as the first night they met but finally gave up, assuming Caroline wasn't coming back. Until this night, when once again the sound of a car door woke her.

Inside the confined space of the station wagon, Judith smelled alcohol right away, knew by Caroline's slouched posture that she was drunk. The air was already thick with cigarette smoke; Caroline produced a new pack from her purse and tore away the cellophane wrapper with unsteady hands.

"It's fucking hot out," Caroline said. "Our damn air conditioner is broken." She handed Judith a half-empty glass flask. "You should've dressed cooler," she said, gesturing to Judith's drawstring pants and full-length shirt.

"I'm fine. I'm always cold no matter what the weather is like."

"That'll keep you warm," she pointed to the flask as Judith took a long swallow. Tequila. The fiery liquid snatched the air out of her lungs.

"You wanna know something funny?" Caroline asked with a mild slur. "I've been fat my whole life, but in the last few weeks I lost seventeen pounds. Who knew all this would be a miracle diet?" She rubbed her eyes and looked at Judith. "You lost any weight?"

"A little." She thought about Lindsey on the scale at Dr. Haji's office every week, standing backwards so she couldn't read the numbers. *Okay, Lindsey, down less than half a pound this week. Looking better . . .*

"I don't know where you had any to spare. You been skinny all your life?"

"My mother never gave me a choice." She could hear Virginia's voice in her head, words that had been drilled into her and Penny since puberty: *Being slender is the best fashion accessory a woman can have.*

Caroline dropped her head back against the seat so that her jugular was exposed at an unnatural, ninety-degree angle. "I quit my job today. I was a teacher. Did you know that? I was a music teacher. Been giving private piano lessons in my house for over fifteen years." She fumbled a cigarette from the pack, lit it with the car lighter. "My therapist tried to talk me out of it. Dan tried to talk me out of it. Said it was too soon and I would regret it after I started to feel better." She took a drag and cracked the driver's side window. "Ah, fuck it," she murmured.

Judith swallowed another mouthful and was surprised at how smoothly the hard alcohol was now going down, how much she took to the taste and the fuzzy edges it created. "Why did you quit?"

Caroline turned her head to look at Judith, a single tear making a long slide down the side of her cheek. "All I do is dream about her. Playing the piano. Bach, Chopin, like little music boxes in my head."

She took the flask from Judith's hand and shook it. "This and a prescription of Prozac are the only stuff that make the music go away. I'll never touch a piano myself again."

Judith dropped her chin to her chest and pulled the cuffs of her sleeves over her hands, tucking them under her armpits. It was getting difficult to breathe inside the small space between the two women.

Caroline wiped her face and tried to flick her cigarette out the barely open window, but the clump of ash tumbled down the glass and landed on her leg. She seemed not to notice, staring out the window at the Elliotts' house, clearly lit by the full moon. In shadow, the massive windows looked like gaping mouths.

"You have a really beautiful house," Caroline said. "Very fancy. Dan and I used to drive around these neighborhoods, just to see how the other half lived. We're seeing a therapist now. Did I tell you that?"

Judith shook her head.

"How about you and Peter?"

"No. But we're sending Lindsey."

"Oh, right. Your other child. The *spare*."

Judith stiffened. She'd been expecting this. The lashing.

"How convenient you still have another one around," Caroline said.

Judith took in a deep breath and tried to gather her words, but this did not work—they scattered like marbles dumped onto a floor. "Caroline, you have to know how sorry—"

"Sure, sure. Of course you're sorry," she interrupted and waved her hand. "You still have a daughter alive and I don't, so of course you're sorry. What else are you going to be?" She stubbed her cigarette out against the window and threw the butt onto the dashboard.

"I'm sorry," Judith whispered.

"Your kid shot and killed mine!" Caroline yelled. "Stop saying you're fucking sorry and just tell me why! Why did he kill her? Why did my daughter have to die? She never hurt anyone. She never did anything to your son!"

Judith reached for the door handle and yanked, but it stuck. She jerked it back and forth until the latch finally gave, and she tumbled out of the car onto the grass.

"Oh, sure! Run away!" Caroline flung the flask over Judith's head, and the glass shattered on the sidewalk, tequila splattering and staining the concrete the color of caramel.

"What do you want me to say?"

"I just want to know why!" Caroline screamed and pummeled her fists against the steering wheel. "Why! Why! Why!"

"I don't know why!" Judith screamed back. From someone's backyard a few houses away, a dog broke into protective barks, and Mrs. Clarkson turned the light on over her porch, pressing her nose against the front door window.

"Yes, you do," Caroline sobbed. "Yes, you do. You're just scared. Too scared to take a good look at yourself, because of what you might find."

"What does it matter at this point?" Judith asked, still sprawled on the ground, grass stains streaked across her knees, her voice and face defeated. "What good would it do anyone now?"

"It matters to *me*. I at least deserve some answers." Caroline sniffed. "And you know, I didn't sue anyone to get them."

Judith wiped at her cheek with the back of her hand. "It won't bring any of them back."

Caroline started the engine, gunning the gas a few times to keep it from dying.

"I'm not asking you to give me a list of all the things you did wrong. I just need to understand." The tires squealed as the car tore away from the curb.

"I just need to understand, too," Judith echoed to the darkness, long after Caroline was gone.

July 27

Today, Virginia took me out to lunch after another meeting with our attorney. She also spent the afternoon cleaning my house. She scrubbed toilets, waxed floors, dusted woodwork. Apparently, she was bothered during her last visit by the clothes in the corner of the kitchen, since the laundry room could no longer hold another pair of dirty jeans or boxer shorts. She also wants to repaint my kitchen. It's brown, she told me. It's called cinnamon, I tried to point out. No, brown, and according to her, drab. She brought paint samples. Buttery Yellow. Pale Tangerine.

When my mother comes bearing decorating ideas and wearing one of her coordinated pastel jogging suits, I'm no match. I will end up with a kitchen the color of birthday cake frosting. Virginia Campbell is an indomitable force with embroidered flowers on her shirt. If she were just a stereotypical overbearing Jewish mother or a fanatically devout Catholic, she could pass for mildly charming with a certain kind of predictable annoyance. But she's neither Jewish nor Catholic. Not even a run-of-the-mill Methodist. Just a born-again shopper. A faithful member of the Church of Dillard's Department Store.

I am sitting by a little stream at Sand Run Park with a cup of iced tea, decompressing after being with Virginia for three hours. It's very quiet and peaceful here—not many people around since it's a Tuesday afternoon and it's so hot out. The sky is a perfect, calm blue and I am sitting next to a little stream under the shade of oak and tulip trees. If I close my eyes, lie back onto the soft cushion of creeping Charlie and not think, I can play a game of Pretend. I can almost convince myself that everything is okay. Everything is normal and unchanged. Lucas is at home in his room sketching on a canvas or finishing his geometry homework. Lindsey is at symphony rehearsals or talking on the phone to her friend Amy. I am preparing for the next AVS conference and Peter and I are making dinner plans with some couple from Goodyear or reserving tee times at the club for Saturday morning. We're all okay. I'm still Judith from <u>Before</u>.

Then the wind changes or someone jogs down the trail and I come back. Open my eyes to see the beauty of the clear water and the summer season and think, no, you are Judith <u>After</u>.

I'm furious with Lucas right now. I sit here and think that he'll never experience a summer afternoon again, hear thunder rolling in ahead of a storm, go ice-skating, ride a bike trail. The lists . . . the lists never stop haunting me.

I'm angry that he was so stupid. Stupid enough to throw his life away for a girl who treated him like trash and still gets to go to the mall on weekends and swim at the lake on hot summer days. Stupid, stupid boy.

Now I can't stand it here, the beautiful scenery and sounds of birds chirping in the trees above me. I can't stand smiling. I can't stand laughing. I can't stand eating. I can't stand breathing. I want to kick the glass out of windows, drive my car into a tree, stick my hands into a roaring fire. This hurts so much that I want to peel the skin from my body and scratch my bones.

I just want to sleep until it is time for me to wake up and die.

The Late Show

PETER DROPPED HIS SUITCASE AT the back door and unloaded it, sorting out a pile of shirts for the dry cleaner and throwing the rest of his dirty clothes into the laundry room. He looked tired after a five-day trip to Houston and Dallas. His face seemed longer and thinner, with stubble along his jaw line; his shoulders were now defined more by bone than muscle. Judith stirred a pot of bubbling soup at the stove, leaning against the counter as if she might topple over without it. Lindsey sat at the kitchen table finishing an English paper. The large chandelier above her was dark, and she hunched over her work in the fading light, her nose inches from the lines on the notebook paper.

"Hi, Dad," she said softly from behind her pale veil of hair. "How was Texas?"

"Oh, fine. Fine." Peter barely glanced over his shoulder as he read a list of telephone messages tacked to the bulletin board next to the door. He reached out to hang his keys on a hook but missed, and the heavy ring clattered to the floor. He didn't bother to bend over and pick it up.

"What's for dinner?" He directed the question to Judith's back but she didn't answer or turn around. "What's for dinner?" he repeated.

"What? Uh, corn chowder and bread," she said.

He retrieved a bottle of wine from the rack in the dining room and a crystal glass from the china hutch. After uncorking the merlot, he examined the glass he had selected, holding it up to the light from the window, turning it in circles.

"This wine glass is cracked," he finally said.

"What?" Judith turned around with the ladle in her hand, dripping a line of soup across the floor and her stockinged feet.

"It's cracked," he said. "Right there. A hairline crack at the base." He pointed to it with the glass still raised so Judith had to look up and squint.

"Oh. Yes, I see," she nodded.

"This is one of our Riedel stemware."

She stared blankly at him.

"The set of four we bought on our trip to New York?" he continued. "Your sister broke one glass last Christmas, and then another got shattered during the move. Now this one. There's only one left."

Still, Judith blinked. The soup started to bubble and smelled burnt.

"Never mind," he muttered and tossed the glass into the trash. "It was just a very expensive set of crystal. The best we owned. Can't we take care of anything around here?"

Judith shrugged and turned back to the stove, pulling three bowls from a cabinet. She ladled the soup out of the pot as if it were very heavy and difficult to lift. Peter sat down at the table with a pile of unopened mail and spooned up a few hot mouthfuls, engrossed in a letter from their car insurance company. He flipped on the overhead light, and at once their ashen, fatigue-lined faces were spotlighted. Lindsey squinted but continued to write in her notebook, her bowl and spoon untouched, pushed a few inches away. Judith did not encourage Lindsey to slide the bowl back and at least try one bite. She thought of the long conferences she had suffered through with Dr. Haji and the nutritionist, discussing various techniques to get Lindsey to eat again. She ran them through her mind, the lines of dialogue the doctor had coached, but the words failed her as she watched her daughter shrink further away from the bowl. The therapy wasn't helping.

"I sold his car today," Peter said, looking up but not making eye contact with Judith, instead staring at the space just behind her.

"What?" she asked, shaking her head in confusion.

"I sold—" His composure slipped, the tip of his nose and rims of his eyes turning red. "The police released it from impound." His hands trembled as he buttered a piece of bread, then went back to his letter, the paper quivering in his grasp. Lindsey had stopped writing, her pen frozen in midair; she watched her father gulp the wine.

Judith wadded up a napkin between her cold hands. A high-pitched ringing filled her ears, and she clenched her eyes shut against the sound. She couldn't think about what Peter had just said, couldn't decipher the words.

"Did you pick up my dry cleaning?" His voice was calm again, hands steady. He had yanked away the unpleasant topic of conversation, like a magician pulling a cloth out from underneath a table set with dishes, the china and vase of flowers left standing untouched.

The dry cleaner. Judith couldn't switch the train of her thoughts fast enough to keep up with him. From Lucas's car to the dry cleaner. She needed a moment to think, to process what Peter had just said, but he wasn't allowing her the time. He was staring, waiting for an answer. The dry cleaner. She shook her head and croaked out an answer. "Yes. I did."

The pain in her head deepened just thinking about it. She had been using the same cleaning business, run by a Korean man named Mr. Lin, since they'd moved to Fairlawn. Mr. Lin spoke minimal English but was always friendly to Judith and inquired regularly about her family. Today, he had asked about her kids.

"How you son an' you daughter?" Unaware of Valentine's Day.

She had been paralyzed, rooted to the floor. Mr. Lin asked if she were okay, did she need to sit down.

Out of her mouth had come a clumsy, breathless tumble of words. "My son recently passed away in a car accident. A drunk driver hit him. I didn't want him to get a license so early. Sixteen just seems so young, you know, but we gave in. He was a good driver and in so many after school activities that sometimes I felt like a chauffeur. He passed the driver's test with a high score, only missed one question. Wouldn't you know it? It was about Ohio drunk driving laws."

Mr. Lin removed his apron, came around the counter, and offered her a tissue to wipe her eyes. He placed his hand on top of the plastic bag then, nudging it towards her. "You take home. No pay today. So sorry 'bout boy," he said.

Judith had fled the store, running from Mr. Lin's tender voice, running from the blatant falseness of her story, the bag of clothes on the seat beside her a reminder of her lies during the entire ride home. Oh, how much she wanted that story to be true. If he had to be dead, if they had to lose their son, why couldn't it have been in an accident or to an illness? Something without fault or blame.

"Judith," Peter said sharply, and her eyes snapped open. "I asked you a question. What is this?" He thrust at her a thick manila envelope marked *Summit County Sheriff's Department.*

She refocused her glazed eyes and took the envelope. "It's the Sheriff's report. Howard Pierce wants us to look it over for the lawsuit. I tried to tell you last week but you—"

"I don't want to read it," Peter interrupted, the muscles around his mouth tightening.

"But Howard said—"

"I don't want to read it!" He shoved his chair away from the table. Lindsey cowered further over her writing, rounding her back into a protective shell.

Judith slid her uneaten bowl of soup into the middle of the table next to Lindscy's. The envelope grew heavy against her palms, and she couldn't stop herself from picking at the glued flap until it was free, bending up the small silver prongs and sliding out the smooth sheets of paper. Peter grabbed his wine glass and left the room. She flipped through the pages, scanning the words and sections of handwritten notes, an interview with Lucas's friend from school: *Sheriff Klass: Did you give your dad's gun to Lucas, or did he steal it? Did you show him how to load it and fire it? Did he tell you what he was going to do? Travis McDonnell: No, sir, I swear I didn't know nothing about what he was going to do. We practiced firing my dad's pistol in the backyard but I put it back when we were done. I didn't know he stole it. I swear I didn't give it to him.*

There was a list of the items from his locker at school—*package of Big Red chewing gum; box of colored pencils; white Nike high-top tennis shoes, size 9; blue canvas backpack.* A transcript of the 911 call the school secretary had made from under her desk. *This is Roosevelt High, and we just heard gunshots from down the hall and screaming, and kids are running out of the building. Please send someone—Mary! Get down! Get down! Oh, God, please hurry!*

Judith could barely breathe, could no longer hold the pages in her hands, and they drifted to the floor one at a time. Peter ignored her as he returned to the kitchen and banged around, running water in the sink, scrubbing pots, putting away the leftover food, muttering to himself. Lindsey gathered her notebook in her arms and approached her father, one tentative step at a time, moving around her mother, around the scattered pages of the report as if they were a puddle of mud to avoid.

"Dad?" Lindsey said in a tiny voice. "Do you want to look over my paper?"

Peter ignored her, jamming dirty silverware into the washer. "I can't keep doing this, Judith. This agony every day. I have to get back to some form of normal life."

"Mrs. Sullivan said it's due tomorrow."

Peter squeezed past Lindsey to get the bottle of dish soap from under the sink. "What? Who's Mrs. Sullivan?"

"My tutor." Lindsey repositioned herself, sliding her body between Peter and the dishwasher so that he would have to physically move her. Judith watched Lindsey's painful choreography for her dad's attention, how he navigated around her, creating his own dance steps of avoidance. He finally just drained his glass and left the room with the bottle of wine in his hand.

Judith knew she should go to her daughter. Get up off the chair, take three steps and pull Lindsey into a comforting, reassuring embrace that said they would eventually be okay. That they would survive, they would get through this. *Yes, Lindsey, you can still have birthday parties and sleepovers. You can still go shopping at the mall and rollerblading in the park. It's okay if you find yourself laughing again, and it's okay if you still need to cry.*

But Judith did not say anything. She did not know if she could muster enough convincing confidence in her voice. And Lindsey was not to be fooled. She had witnessed the circus act in the kitchen. No matter what her mother said, she would know better.

Judith did nothing. Lindsey walked away, said nothing.

SOMETIME AFTER MIDNIGHT, JUDITH WAS still awake, sitting alone in the dark chill of the family room in the basement. Her body was stiff from sitting curled up on the couch, watching infomercials selling exercise equipment. Her face was puffy and damp from crying. Lucas's car. Gone. No discussion. With every passing day, she and Peter tripped over more and more things they didn't talk about. *Don't look at the light . . .*

Someone touched her shoulder and startled her. Peter stood behind the couch. "Can't sleep?"

Judith wiped her cheeks and nose with a corner of the afghan she was wrapped in. He sighed and switched off the set, tossing the remote onto the coffee table where it landed with a loud clap.

"Are you coming to bed?" he asked.

She nodded, followed him upstairs, and climbed between the sheets, grateful to suddenly feel tired enough to sleep.

Peter rustled around his side of the bed. "Tim McCann called yesterday," he said to the darkness. Only the sound of their breathing had been filling the space between them. "He and Brenda wondered if we were still going to Atwood Lake in the fall."

Tim McCann. Peter's college roommate. Best man at their wedding. Hadn't called since the funeral.

"I think we should go. Take Lindsey and get away for a few days," Peter said.

Judith watched streaks of light flash across the ceiling as cars passed outside, thinking about the trip to Atwood Lake less than a year ago. Just the previous autumn. Their last vacation with Lucas.

ON A WARM NIGHT IN October, everyone had sat around the lakefront cabin they shared every year, watching the sunset over the gold and crimson treetops. Lindsey had brought her violin and given a short concert.

"You play like a professional," Brenda McCann told her, applauding with the other adults as Lindsey curtsied, her bow in one hand and violin in the other. Lucas was sullen and slouched in a chair off by himself. He leaned his head back and closed his eyes as if boredom might put him to sleep. He had sat through so much of his sister's applause, and for the first time it occurred to Judith that it might bother him.

Brenda left her seat to inspect Lindsey's violin, asking questions and handling the instrument as if it were a fragile vase. "Oh, I wish I would've stayed with the flute in high school," she said, tossing her pretty blonde hair over her shoulder. "But I got more interested in boys than music," she laughed.

Brenda was Tim's second, more youthful, wife. Most of the adult conversations with the childless McCanns revolved around their stock portfolios, their fabulous house, and fabulous trips to Europe. Brenda liked to use the word *fabulous*.

"Lindsey was last year's Youth Symphony Concerto Competition winner," Peter said, lighting a cigar. "She wants to study music after high school." Smoking, something that came up only around Tim McCann.

"She needs to study in London," Tim pointed his Stogie at Peter. "Oxford or Cambridge. And get her into a good music school now, before it's too late."

"How do you like Fairlawn, Lucas?" Brenda asked.

Lucas rolled his eyes and propped a foot up on the coffee table. "It's fabulous."

Brenda turned hastily back to the girl. "So, Lindsey, are you excited about starting a new school in the fall?"

Lindsey nodded, the skin along her neck and around her ears flushed from the attention. "Yeah, I'll go to Hyatt Middle School, and Lucas goes to Roosevelt. He hates Fairlawn, but I love it. My room is huge."

Brenda smiled. "I graduated from Roosevelt High."

"When? Last year?" Lucas smirked from the corner.

Judith suppressed a giggle that bubbled up in the back of her throat; Peter shot Lucas a look of warning with pursed lips and narrowed eyes.

"I love school. I can't wait for it to start," Lindsey chimed, oblivious to the awkward moment. "I already made a friend at the pool this summer. Amy. She lives four blocks from my house."

"Are you playing football this year, Luke?" Tim asked.

"It's Lucas. And no. I'd rather eat paint than play sports."

Peter opened his mouth to say something but drained his wineglass instead.

"Well, when me and your dad were in school, sports were a big deal." Tim turned to Peter. "I don't get these kids who think that sitting in front of a computer screen playing video games is exercise."

"I never play video games," Lucas said, picking at his fingernails. "I don't even own a computer."

"I do!" Lindsey said raising her hand as though she were already in class.

"Lucas is actually a very good artist," Judith said, attempting to salvage the conversation. "He takes these lessons—"

"Why don't we take our drinks out onto the patio," Peter interrupted, emptying the last of the wine from the bottle into his glass. "Enjoy the Indian summer."

As the group formed an obedient line behind Peter, Judith noticed Lucas, still glumly sitting in the corner alone, a dispirited expression in his eyes. She got it then, really understood just by looking at him, that her son was desperately unhappy.

ANOTHER SET OF HEADLIGHTS cut through the blackness of the bedroom and stopped, lingering in front of the house.

"Judith?" Peter whispered, the lights illuminating his face for a few seconds.

"Hmm?" She rolled onto her side with her back to him and wrapped a loose thread from the edge of the sheet around her finger.

"What do you think? About the vacation?"

"I don't know. I need to think about it."

"What do you need to think about?" He sat up, partially tugging the comforter off her body.

"I don't know if I want to go," she said.

He exhaled loudly through his nose. "Well, I want to. I want to get away. It'll be good for us."

Judith wound the thread tighter and tighter until the tip of her finger throbbed.

"We're going," Peter finally said. "Tim and I already made the reservations."

"You did what?"

He didn't answer, instead punched at his pillow to fluff it before he lay back down. Within a few minutes, he was asleep, snoring softly. Judith had an urge to take her own pillow and smother it over his face until the snoring stopped. She snatched the extra blanket from his side of the bed and went to the spare bedroom.

SHE PEERED OUT THE window from the hallway and saw the station wagon, the outline of Caroline's head and shoulders behind the wheel. The flame of a lighter flashed, then a cigarette tip. Judith went into the spare bedroom and pulled the shades before crawling into bed. She was too tired to see Caroline Myers tonight. It had been a long day, from the dry cleaner to the dinner table to the tense conversation about

Atwood Lake. Her head throbbed and her dry eyes ached with a desperate need to sleep. Exhaustion was so deep in her bones that her body hurt.

She watched the glowing red numbers change on the digital clock next to the bed—five, ten, fifteen minutes. She begged her mind to allow her to drift off, to pretend she had not seen the rusty station wagon, did not know Caroline Myers sat alone with her half-empty bottle of whatever she was drinking, waiting, waiting. After twenty minutes, Judith got back up and walked downstairs, not bothering with a robe or slippers.

Caroline's eyes were shut and she was massaging her temples when Judith approached the open passenger side window.

"Hi," Judith said, but did not move to get inside the vehicle.

Caroline straightened, and flecks of ash from her burning cigarette floated around her face. She swatted at them and left a small smudge on the tip of her nose. She reached across the seat and opened the door for Judith.

"I'm not getting in," Judith said, shaking her head. "I can't. I'm sorry. I'm too tired to do this." She wrapped her arms around herself and shivered. "I can't keep doing this. I'm already drained. It's too much."

Caroline extinguished her cigarette in a cup of coffee.

"I think you should stop coming here." Judith stepped away. "Just go home."

"Please get in," Caroline said quietly and dropped her head. "I haven't been drinking. Please. I won't tear into you this time. I promise."

Judith hesitated. A small breeze rustled her pajama pants and filled the inside of her nightshirt, cooling her bare breasts and sending goose bumps over her skin. She closed her eyes and inhaled, wishing she could run away like a petulant child. Or lock herself in her room and hide under the covers. No more facing Caroline night after night, or Peter or Lindsey or lies to Mr. Lin and anyone else who asked how her family was doing. She just wanted to sleep. But there was that sound in Caroline's voice, that need Judith could not walk away from. She opened the door and slid into the seat.

Caroline held out a small box. "Donut?"

Judith selected a chocolate crème-filled long john. "We're getting death threats."

"What kind of death threats?"

"Letters in the mail."

Caroline was quiet for a moment. "You know," she said. "I've been thinking about a cousin I have in Indiana whose son died in a car accident when he was seventeen. He fell asleep at the wheel driving home from a date one night and crossed the center median."

"That's terrible." Judith picked off the last of the rainbow sprinkles.

"He died almost six years ago. Tina's still so messed up," Caroline said. "At Hannah's funeral, she told me I'd never get over it. That I'd just learn to work around this giant mound of pain. Just learn how to get the laundry done and the beds changed while my heart continues to bleed until the day I die." She laughed bitterly to herself. "Pretty bleak, huh?"

Judith stared out the window. "It doesn't really feel like living anymore, does it? I don't know what this is."

"Tina says it's the mothers who are last."

"What do you mean?"

"When everyone else has moved on with their lives, other kids have graduated, gone to college, gotten married, it's the mothers who are left still remembering. The last ones in line left clinging to photos and drawings and scraps of life that mean nothing to everyone else."

Judith tried to swallow a bite of pastry down her constricted throat.

"My point is that I knew you'd understand. You and me, we're in the same place." Caroline fingered the keys hanging from the ignition.

"But we're not the same," Judith said. "Your grief isn't a place of shame." She thought of Peter at the kitchen table with the fountain pen the day after the shooting.

On behalf of the Elliott family, we want to extend our deepest sympathies to the victims and their families. Words cannot express our profound sorrow over this tragic and shocking event.

Caroline offered Judith a sip of coffee from her mug, this time just straight coffee. "You know, I can't talk to Dan about this. It hurts him too much to even mention Hannah's name. And my friends, the rest of my family, forget it. They can't look me in the eye. But you," Caroline said, her gaze burning into Judith's, "you got in when everyone else was getting out." She sighed and lit a cigarette. "Isn't it something like over fifty percent of marriages end in divorce after the death of a child? Where did I read that recently?"

Judith considered the remainder of her donut, pockmarked where she had removed the sprinkles. Caroline suddenly turned up the volume on the radio, smiling. "Oh, I love this piece. It's Bach. Hannah played it in a recital when she was ten."

Caroline closed her eyes and drummed her long white fingers through the air over an imaginary keyboard. Judith watched her fingertips as they brushed the dash and pictured Hannah with the same hands. Perfectly grown and manicured for piano keys, directly connected by a cord that ran from the fingertips, through the brain to the ears. Judith saw how that connection had been severed for Caroline, the loss of the music without her daughter.

The song ended. Caroline reclined her seat and lay flat with her hands folded over her chest, looking up at the sagging ceiling fabric. "I've always wanted to own a convertible," she said. "Take it out at night with the top down, let the wind tear through my hair. And then I'd park it somewhere to count the stars and talk with the moon." She exhaled in a broken, choppy sigh, one eye spilling a thin tear that glistened under the streetlight. "I guess I can do whatever I want now. But I don't want to do anything."

Judith dropped the remainder of her donut into the box and got out of the car without saying anything more.

She was ready to sleep now.

August 17

I'm sitting in the little chapel down the street from our house. It's cool and dark in here and I'm writing by the slivers of light from the stained glass windows. It feels like I've descended into a cave when the heavy doors close behind me, a transport into the mild, peaceful womb of this place. If I move in the pew or drop my pen on the floor, the insignificant sound echoes off the concrete walls and is carried up into the sweeping ceiling. I have an urge to yell something, for my voice and the sound of my sadness and hurt and anger to be magnified to the size I feel it really is. That would probably bother someone, though, and I would be asked to leave. And I want to come back.

An old woman just sat in the pew ahead of me. She is praying the rosary with her eyes closed, a soundless chant rippling over her lips. She is neat and well kept, hair perfectly curled like she's just seen the beautician this morning. A pink scarf holds her coif like a tender cotton candy bandage with a tiny bow clipped to the base of her hairline. I want to tuck in the tag of her dress, which pokes up like a banner and spoils her otherwise tidy appearance.

I love how churches smell and feel. Like standing between the thick branches of a Christmas tree. A scotch pine. I went to church a few times with my friend Angela Armstrong when I was in high school. Her family was Episcopalian and Angela always wore a special coat that was just for church. Her mother had ordered it from the Sears catalog and it was beautiful—blue velvet with big gold buttons down the front and a satin-lined hood. Her family started taking me to church with them shortly after my father died. The pretty hymns and long prayers were like a poetry reading with communion, sitting shoulder to shoulder with all those dressed-up people, surrounded by flickering candles and breathtaking stained glass. It was comforting. I felt refined and special, like I was part of something exclusive and important. Then I got caught smoking a cigarette behind the gymnasium at school with Angela and another girl (I don't remember her name) and I was never invited back to the Dover Street Episcopal Church.

I never lost that feeling of comfort inside a church, so when I passed by St. Margaret's today while on a walk, I had to stop. Had to come in and sit under the pictures of Jesus being hung on the cross, prop my feet up on the little floor benches or kneelers, or whatever they're called, because I couldn't help myself.

The old lady just put her rosary away and lit one of the candles in the little alcove off the chapel. She's clasped her hands together again and I wonder what it is she's praying about now. She's been here awhile so she must have a lot on her mind. I wonder if she'll feel better when she leaves, feel relieved of whatever it is she brought with her to the church. I wish something as simple as prayer could do that for me.

We never took our kids to church, never exposed them to any religion or to God and Jesus, the apostles and all that. Now I can't help but think that maybe, if we had gone to church, even sent the kids to Bible school once in a while, maybe Lucas wouldn't have done what he did. But, if I allow myself to believe in God, in the possibility of Heaven and the soul and all that, then I will also have to believe in Hell, accept the possibility of my son burning in punishment for all eternity. I can't think about that. It's just easier for me not to believe in anything. Dead is dead. I don't have the strength to consider anything else.

Maybe church could've helped him, I don't know. I feel crazy, like a skipping record, spewing out the same sound over and over. What if we'd done this? What if I'd done that? What if we'd held him back in first grade like we talked about? What if we'd tried harder to solve the Toby Doyle problem? What if we'd given him an earlier curfew or not let him date until he was seventeen? What if I had only asked if Travis McDonnell's parents would be home that weekend in February? What if I'd just knocked on his door one day after school or some Saturday morning and said 'Lucas, let's talk. . .'

I'm crazy with the what ifs . . .

But the insteads are my reality. Instead, we sent him on to second grade even though he was so far behind he could barely read or write. Instead, we watched him suffer at the hands of a total thug, reduced to hoping the situation would just get better when we ran out of solutions. Instead, we allowed him to get involved with an older, more experienced girl, too fast for him. Instead, I never thought to ask if the McDonnell family ever left their son and his friends unsupervised for an entire weekend, never asking what the boys did over at his house, never tried to get to know Travis or his parents. Instead of knocking on his door, I went shopping with Penny or played tennis at the club or spent hours in the basement with my violets, tending, babying, giving my undivided attention to plants and not my son. I did his laundry, cooked his meals, nagged at him to do his homework and thought that was enough.

That night in the garage, what if I'd done something, anything, instead of just standing idly by . . .

What if I'd knocked on his door just one time and he'd answered?

Visitation

THE LANDSCAPE WAS CARPETED IN vibrant greens from a day of rain showers and mild sunshine. Peter squinted at the passing road signs and rummaged through his shirt pocket for the eyeglasses he'd left on the kitchen counter. He adjusted the windshield wipers, tugged at his seatbelt, fiddled with the radio. Judith looked over her shoulder at Lindsey in the back seat. She was leaning with her forehead pressed to the window, shoulders hunched toward her chest. A dozen long-stemmed white roses lay across her lap. She unconsciously rubbed a callus on her finger, a darkened, hard lump on the pad of her left index, proof of the long hours she now spent practicing her violin. She was shrunken—pale skin, sharp elbows, and knees on a frame that was mostly arms and legs.

Whatever Lindsey was thinking didn't show on her face. She had learned to remove whatever she was feeling from the exterior of her body. Nothing on the outside to reflect what might be going on inside. It used to be that she was one big burst of emotion, a great flourish of joys and sorrows with hand gestures and facial expressions. She had thrown herself into whatever she was doing with such dramatic passion that most people knew enough to just get out of her way. But as Judith watched her daughter knead the callus with her thumb, *rub rub rub*, she realized that Lindsey had been stripped of normal teenage girl things: giggles and annoying language, tying up the phone, passing notes in class to her girlfriends.

Peter turned the car down a long gravel drive that wound through towering pine trees, their long needles dripping water onto the roof of the car with small plunks. The vehicle rolled to a stop, and Peter gathered his jacket and an umbrella. He cleared his throat, staring at Judith and Lindsey.

"Ready?" he asked and attempted a smile, but the question had come out too loud, too abrupt.

They walked across the slick lawn, Lindsey and Judith arm in arm under their own umbrella, weaving a path between the other markers. They slowed as they neared the barren mound of dirt, the new headstone streaked with rainwater, then stopped.

"Oh, God," Peter uttered under his breath.

Judith stared at the etched headstone. ELLIOT was crossed out with green spray paint, and below it, in horrid, gangly lettering: MURDERER. All around the gravesite were empty beer cans and bits of garbage. The flowers from the overturned stone vases had been ripped and strewn about. A scorched patch of grass darkened the earth around the marker, littered with cigarette butts, and a large orange construction flag stuck out of the exposed dirt.

Judith stepped closer to the grave and dropped the umbrella, arms limp at her sides, her body swaying as if she might faint. She knelt to the mound, her knees sinking into the soft, muddy earth. The rain pelted her back and head, chilling her skin through her clothes. She reached for a wet, crumpled fast-food sack and carefully smoothed it across her thighs.

"Mom?" Lindsey asked, putting a hand on Judith's shoulder. "What are you doing?"

She began to pick up the trash around her—an apple core, candy wrappers, pieces of soggy newspaper—and dropped them into the sack. She worked in silence, filling the smelly bag slowly.

Peter drew Lindsey under his umbrella, nudging her towards the car. Lindsey continued to watch her mother for a few hesitant steps, then dropped the flowers at her feet and let her father lead her away.

Judith crawled through the muck, picking, gathering, and stuffing the bag. She set the vases upright and retrieved the roses Lindsey had dropped, dividing them up, six on each side of the headstone. She grasped the thick metal rod of the flag and pulled, but it had been hammered deep into the soil. She braced her feet on either side, sinking further into the mud, and pulled again, but was unable to get a firm grip. Her hands slid up the rusted metal, leaving burnt orange-colored streaks across her palms. She dropped back to her knees, plunged her hands into the ground, digging, digging, pawing, throwing handfuls of mud over her shoulder like a dog scavenging for a hidden bone. She tunneled a small hole around the rod and pulled again. This time the flag came free. She stumbled and fell onto her backside, splattering mud. A flock of birds startled in the tree above her and flapped their wings, squawking in alarm.

She reached for her striped umbrella, abandoned upside down next to the grave and collecting water, and stuck it into the hole left by the flag. They had buried him with a set of paints and brushes and a blank canvas. She didn't want his colors to run.

Judith dragged herself to the headstone. She licked her mud-encrusted thumb, bitter and gritty, and rubbed at the paint in futility. She closed her eyes and leaned against the cold stone, the hard lines of the etched words pressing into her shoulder.

Lindsey had tucked a wallet-sized photo in his front pocket, a picture of the four of them at their old house when the kids were still in grade school. They were sitting on the glider swing in the back yard on a summer evening. They had been swimming at the beach all day, everyone getting sunburned. Later, they would barbecue hot dogs on the grill. She and Peter had sat down on the swing together, laughing about something, and soon Lucas and Lindsey had jumped on, wrestling, picking, giving each other bunny ears. Penny had grabbed a camera. Judith wondered if Lucas would have picked that very photo to be buried with, had he been given a choice.

Judith struggled to her feet and kicked off her ruined, muddy shoes, leaving them under the tree. She trudged back to the car and slid into the front seat next to Peter. His forehead was pressed against the steering wheel. Lindsey sat with her chin to her chest, shaking and weeping soundlessly, wiping her nose with a napkin. Judith shivered in her wet, sullied clothes, mud clumped in her hair, streaked across her face, and caked on her hands. She reached for a napkin from the glove compartment.

"Judith—" Peter said, but she put a hand up to quiet him.

"Just . . . just give me a minute," she breathed. "I just . . . need . . ." She leaned her head back against the seat and squeezed her eyes closed, thinking about the covert funeral planning. No memorials, no religious service. Not even an obituary. They had found him anyway. Still being ridiculed and bullied, even six feet under the ground.

"We should—" Peter's breath caught in his chest and his eyes filled with tears. He moved his lips, trying to finish the sentence, to create a sound with the air from his lungs, but then gave up and started the car.

ꙮ

JUDITH STOOD OUTSIDE Lucas's bedroom door, her hand poised above the burnished knob. She had not yet washed the grime from her hands or face, and her skin felt taut, cracked. She leaned towards the oak door, inhaling the polished wood smell, rubbing her cheek across the smooth surface. Peter was banging pots around in the kitchen, and Lindsey's aching violin music wafted from the other side of her door down the hall.

Judith needed to go inside, to rest her eyes upon the only remnants of him in the world. It was time. She took a deep breath and turned the knob. The door creaked and swung open. The room beyond smelled stale, stuffy from being closed up for so long. Months, since the day after. *After*. That word again. Like one half of the bookends to her life. Bronze-cast: *Before* and *After*.

She bent, lightheaded, and put her hands on her knees for a moment, then stood and inhaled. It was *him*. His scent, his cares, his life. Or what his life had been, hanging on the walls and in the closet, heaped on the floor and cluttered over the desk. It was *him*, and she could almost reach into the void to touch his flesh. She ran her hand across the tangled sheets of his bed, the flannel pajama bottoms tossed over the back of a desk chair. She took his pillow, a dent still pressed into the center from where his head had rested, buried her face into the soft cotton, and began to cry, leaving dirty fingerprints and dark circles from her tears.

"Enough!" Peter yelled and wrenched the pillow from her hands. Surprised, Judith stumbled forward, still trying to hold on to the cloth cover, but she lost her balance and fell to her knees.

Peter hurled the pillow against the closet door and grabbed a cardboard box left behind by the sheriff's department the day of the search. He pushed Judith, still crumpled on the floor, out of his way and began tossing items into the box—clothes, papers, books—anything he could reach.

"Peter!" Judith gasped. "What's the matter with you? Stop!" She leapt up and grabbed his arm, trying to pry the box from his hands. They both yanked on opposite sides until a gash tore down the center of the cardboard, sending random objects across the room. Judith dropped back to her knees and scrambled to scoop the contents into her arms. An empty pop can, spiral notebooks, chewed up pens. "You ruined it!" she sobbed. "It was how he left it, and now you ruined it!"

"You've lost your mind," Peter said, red-faced and panting. "The police moved every—"

"Get out! Get out! Get out!" Judith screamed, and flung the remains of the box at her husband.

"What is wrong with you two?" Lindsey cried from the doorway, her violin in one hand, bow in the other. Her face was contorted in fright and confusion.

"Go back to your room," Peter barked.

"I hate this house!" Lindsey said, crying.

"I said go to your room!" he yelled.

"I hate you!" she screamed, smacking her bow against the doorframe and snapping it in two. "I hate you! This is your fault! He did this because of you! Because of that night in the garage!"

"Lindsey, shut up!" Peter pointed a shaking finger at her. "Don't you ever talk to me like that again!"

"I don't care!" she sobbed. She ran down the hall and locked her bedroom door behind her. Peter kicked the cardboard box out of his way as he stormed out of the room. In a moment, the front door slammed, rattling windowpanes throughout the house. The engine of his car revved, and he peeled down the driveway.

Judith continued clutching the items to her chest, cradling them as she would a fragile newborn baby. She looked around the room again, the mess and chaos, and saw what her son had created. Whether or not by intention, they had become like spinning tops, twisted between his fingers and dropped onto the hard floor, turning furiously out of control until their momentum dwindled, sputtered, and then stopped altogether, dizzy, disoriented, desperately changed. She felt certain that her son would feel not sadness at the uncontrollable motion he had created for his family, but pity.

August 26

I am sick in bed today. I thought it was the flu—low-grade fever and nausea—but I saw the doctor yesterday, and he said I have an infected fibroid tumor. Now he's talking surgery before Christmas. For the meantime, I've been lying in bed over the past forty-eight hours, sipping chamomile tea that Lindsey brings me, staring at the ceiling.

Peter hasn't been home in eight days. Traveling for work. Meetings, conferences, whatever. I'm not sure where he is at on any given day. Dallas? Houston? Chicago? He said he'd leave the names of his hotels on the bulletin board but he didn't, and he never answers his cell phone. I tried to call him after my appointment with Dr. Menlo yesterday, and then realized I had no idea where he was or how to get hold of him. I had to call his secretary to find out. She said, with an awkward cough, that he was in Denver for a seminar. I hastily thanked her with a flimsy excuse for why I didn't know where my own husband was. When I called his room, he didn't answer the phone and hasn't returned my messages. I am furious with him. Even though I know he's doing this because he hurts so much, I'm still mad because I don't have anyone else to be mad at and I'm tired of being mad at myself. I'd like to unload on someone else for a change. If not my husband, then the next person who crosses my path will do.

Sometimes, when Peter lies down in bed next to me at night, when he thinks I'm asleep because I pretend to be asleep, he cries. Very softly, making these half-sobbing, half-sighing noises that nearly break what's left of my heart. His gasps jostle the bed and he sniffles like a little boy afraid of the dark. I can picture the long slide of teardrops down his face onto the pillow, the small wet circles that form there. I have done this so many times myself. Still, I cannot touch him. Even though I want to reach over, wipe the streaks off his cheeks, and put my hand on his heaving chest, I never do it. The crooked place in my heart stops me, punishing him for all the nights he let me cry alone when I was the one who needed him.

I wonder what he's thinking about when he cries. Maybe he's reliving the trip alone to the funeral home to pick out a casket. Brass or silver handles? How about a satin lining? Or maybe he thinks about towing Lucas's car from the police station to the used car lot where he sold it, after he'd had to go through it to remove Lucas's belongings. CD cases, empty McDonald's cups, dirty gym clothes wadded up in a duffel bag. Or is he thinking about that first night when he went to the coroner's office . . . seeing our son laid out on a metal table with a sheet over his lifeless, cold body, the doctor pulling the cover back and Peter saying something like 'Yes, it's him . . .''

I have no words for that. No words at all.

Comebacks

IT WAS JUDITH'S BIRTHDAY. The third day of September, and she was forty years old. A forty she had never imagined. She sat alone in the formal living room, in an overstuffed chair positioned in front of the picture window, watching passing cars and pedestrians enjoying the late summer day. She had always pictured forty as battling wrinkles and gray hair with a spontaneous trip to Europe. Shopping sprees in Paris. After so many years of thinking about that dreaded age, it had finally arrived, and she did not care. In three days, it would be Lucas's seventeenth birthday. It was a new school year. He would've been a senior.

The telephone rang. Virginia, offering to take her out for sushi with Penny, but Judith declined. No cake, please. No candles. No wrapping paper and shiny bows. She wanted to be left alone in her chair. Peter was in Tulsa until the end of the week. Lindsey was at a violin lesson and would then go to the library to do research for a history paper, which was fine with Judith. She just wanted to sit in the quiet and watch the parade of her neighbor's cars. There were the boat-sized Cadillacs and Oldsmobiles for her elderly neighbors, the lumbering SUVs of the childless professional couples, minivans equipped with televisions playing cartoons to keep carpools of other people's kids quiet for the eight-and-a-half-minute drive from the elementary to Culver Street. The Lincolns and Lexuses were the highly buffed sedans of the suit-and-ties like Peter, golf bags probably stowed in the trunk alongside unread copies of financial books and biographies and spare packages of clean white shirts. A parade of people Judith didn't know. Strangers. Even Mrs. Clarkson, out for a walk with her dog, the little terrier taking his traditional Tootsie Roll-sized crap on the Elliott's yard. Stupid dog probably couldn't squeeze a single turd without the sight of their red front door.

Birthdays past, Judith had bought new party dresses and had her nicest pieces of jewelry cleaned, jewelry she wore only on special occasions—a diamond tennis bracelet with matching drop earrings, an emerald pendant with her wedding date inscribed on the back, a gift from Peter for their tenth anniversary. When she turned thirty, he'd flown her to Maui for a week, rented a private bungalow; they toured the island in a Jeep, at leisure. Looking back, they seemed to have been a couple that shone most on holidays and anniversaries, making their greatest efforts for the marriage in correspondence with annual dates on the calendar. The remaining boxes of the month were left neglected the rest of the year, or penciled in with the business of other interests.

Judith wasn't angry with Peter for not being in town for her birthday. After all, she hadn't even been conscious during his forty-first back in March, that first excruciating month. A funny thought occurred to her. What did she usually buy for Peter on his birthday? She couldn't remember. She combed her brain for a single memory of a gift—a shirt, a watch, some sort of new wallet. Oh, yes. A tie. She had bought him a red silk Christian Dior tie recently, *before*, but she couldn't place what the occasion had been. Nor did she recall the store, or the day she would've purchased the tie. Gone. Another bit of information lost through one of the many holes taking over her brain so that every time she gave her storage center a good shake, more memories leaked out like water through a colander.

The mailman strode up the sidewalk, whistling to himself as he deposited a handful of envelopes into their box next to the front door. "Good Afternoon, Mrs. Clarkson," he called down to the street as the old woman returned from her walk. The terrier burst into a fit of ferocious yaps. "Fucking dog," he muttered, unaware that Judith was standing just on the other side of the opened window, laughing to herself.

She retrieved the stack and flipped through bills and advertisement flyers as she wandered into the kitchen, her bare feet padding across the chilled tiles, stepping into a sticky spot and absently rubbing the bottom of a dirty foot against her pant leg. Around the time of her thirty-seventh birthday, she had gone through a bit of a midlife crisis. It was the first time in her life, up to that point anyway, that she'd ever experienced depression. A constantly disappointed, letdown, where-is-my-life-going depression. She and Peter had argued for six months straight about the children, their friends, how much time Peter spent at work, whether or not it was time for her to get a job. But what would she do at thirty-seven? She'd never worked a day of a professional job in her life. She even went so far as to accuse Peter of having an affair. She knew damn well he wasn't; she had at least that much insight into her marriage, but just the act of accusing him, shouting the words at him as if she believed it, had given her a level of satisfaction she'd never expected. If she created an unfaithful husband, then she'd have a reason to feel sad and depressed.

Weeks of this empty fighting between them went on, long bouts of not talking to each other, going to bed angry and waking up angrier. Then one afternoon, Judith had come across a website for the African Violet Society's annual convention. It was the answer she had been waiting for. A purpose. A *something*. It had been that easy. Now, three years later, she was right back where she had started, only worse, lost and wondering what she was supposed to do with the rest of her life.

She filled a glass from the tap and sipped the water as she sorted the stack of mail on the counter: junk mail into the garbage, bank statements into the bill basket. She halted, her body gone frozen, the glass suspended in her quivering hand, tiny ripples shuddering through the water. On the bottom, a thin white envelope with curly, soft writing across the front. Return address: *Kristin Danforth*.

Judith dropped the envelope and backed away with her hands outstretched for protection as if a snarling dog were threatening to bite her. *Kristin*. Judith had not seen the girl since New Year's Day, the last time she'd visited the Elliott house as Lucas's girlfriend, and it had proven to be an embarrassing afternoon. Judith had come home earlier than expected from a lunch date with her sister, while Peter and Lindsey were at a matinee. Lucas was supposed to be at the mall with Kristin; they had been dating a couple months at that point. Judith liked Kristin well enough—a bubbly, attractive girl with long blond hair and bright pink nail polish. She was a junior, same grade as Lucas, but nearly a year older. Held back in first grade, she had explained. They were in an independent art class together, and Lucas had painted an oil portrait of her.

After their lunch, Penny had dropped Judith off at the end of the drive. As she entered through the front door, she heard soft music coming from upstairs, and it occurred to her then that Lucas's car was in the driveway.

She had knocked. She hadn't waited for an answer, but she *had* knocked before opening his bedroom door. Although she'd seen nothing specific, just flashes of skin and flying arms and legs, it was enough. And Lucas's loud cries, *Jesus, Mom! Shut the door!*

After scrambling down the stairs, flushed from shock and embarrassment, Judith waited tensely at the kitchen table while Kristin, with downcast eyes and tangled hair, scurried outside to Lucas's car. While Lucas, taking his time to get dressed even though he knew his mother was downstairs waiting on him, had seemed proud, almost defiant when he leaned against the counter with his arms crossed over his chest, half his shirt left unbuttoned. Judith launched into a lecture about pregnancy and diseases and getting into physical relationships too fast. She talked without taking a breath, nervous and uncomfortable, while her son was the one who seemed totally at ease. His only response, Judith remembered as if he were speaking at that moment: *I love her. I would die without her.*

Judith picked up the envelope, tore it open, and unfolded the lined paper, covered in the same feminine cursive, written in pink ink.

> *Dear Mrs. and Mr. Elliott,*
>
> *I wanted to write to you a long time ago but didn't know what to say. I am so sorry for your loss and I think about your family all the time. I hope you know that I cared very much for Lucas—*

Judith crumpled the paper between her hands and squeezed. A sudden fury shook through her arms and hands, a rage towards Kristin Danforth that she hadn't acknowledged until that moment. She rose from the floor and rummaged through the junk drawer full of pens, rubber bands, and scrap paper. She found a book of matches and struck one, holding it to a corner of the paper until the flame ate its way up the print, through Kristin's hollow, empty words, burning down between Judith's fingers. The smoke alarm went off in the hallway. She dropped the smoldering ashes into the sink, flipped the faucet on, and used the sprayer to douse the remaining embers, leaving a black, charred mess in the stainless steel basin.

TWO HOURS LATER, AN empty bottle of Peter's bourbon lay abandoned at her feet where she sat slouched in the chair in front of the window. She shrugged the blanket from her shoulders and sat up. She felt like going for a drive.

The neighborhoods were quiet in the dwindling day as she cruised up and down the streets of Fairlawn. Windows glowed with the soft blue flickering lights of television sets playing summer reruns or the news. Judith remembered the way to Kristin's house even in her inebriated state. She had picked Lucas up once when his car wouldn't start, had shaken hands with Mrs. Danforth and her greasy-looking boyfriend. They lived in a small ranch house just slightly larger than the Elliotts' garage. It was a stark white box, really—no shutters, no porch, no color on the trim. Judith slowed the car, watching the dark outline of a body pass behind the gauzy curtains covering the front window. Kristin was probably in her bedroom, on the phone to a friend, twisting the cord around her fingers as she talked. Or working on an algebra assignment while sitting cross-legged on her bed with the stereo blaring. Playing with her hair. She always played with her hair.

Judith recalled the attractive girl sprawled across the Elliotts' couch in the basement, watching movies with Lucas on the weekends, her head resting on his lap. She remembered the sound of Kristin's giggle from his bedroom after school, the smell of her perfume on his clothes when Judith did the laundry. It was hard to say what had happened between them. Lucas had never given Judith the details. Kristin probably just got tired of him, bored and ready to move on to something new and more exciting than Lucas and his oil portraits and paintbrushes.

Judith didn't know how or when the break-up happened. She only saw Lucas after. He'd come home early from school one day shortly after the holiday break. She had been making a chocolate cake for one of Lindsey's orchestra fundraisers when he stumbled through the back door with a bloody T-shirt pressed against his nose.

"Oh, my god! Lucas, what happened?" She dropped the hand mixer and helped him to a chair.

"Got in a fight," he said, his voice nasal from the pressure of the shirt.

"Here, let me see." She gently pulled his hand away. "With who?"

"Matt Michaels. He's a football player."

"Why on earth?" She dabbed at the blood with a wet paper towel. His jacket had long stains down the front, and his knuckles were red, scraped raw in some places.

"He's Kristin's new boyfriend."

She'd drawn away and seen Lucas fighting back tears, biting his lip and blinking hard. "Her boyfriend? I didn't know you two had broken up."

He ground the heel of his hand into his watery eyes.

"I'm going to report this boy to the police," Judith had said.

"Don't bother. Won't do any good." Lucas had winced as she felt along the bridge of his nose.

"This explains who egged your car yesterday. We should call your father."

Lucas had grabbed her hand and held on as if he were dangling over a cliff. "No! Please don't call him. He already thinks I'm a big pussy. He'll just bust my balls about it."

"We can't let these boys get away with this kind of harassment and assault."

He'd lowered his head and clasped his hands behind his neck, sagging into the chair with a long, broken breath. A fat tear slid down the bridge of his nose and hung at the tip for second before falling onto his shirt, mixing with the blood.

"Oh, Lucas. I'm so sorry. I won't say anything to your dad if you don't want me to."

JUDITH'S CAR BUMPED OVER THE curb, and she nearly clipped a mailbox as she strained to look at Kristin's house. She accelerated out of the neighborhood and felt the hot waves of anger tearing through her bloodstream again, fueled by the last warm effects of the alcohol. She suddenly wanted to know what Kristin had done with the portrait Lucas had painted of her. Did she stuff it into the back of her closet? Put it out with the trash? Or was it still hanging on the wall, her own face created by his hand, staring down at her every night while she slept?

Judith drove on to Caroline's street a few blocks away, squinting at the house numbers until she made out 1522 Hazleton Drive. There it was. A light gray split-level with a breezeway leading to the one-car garage. Judith stopped at the end of the driveway, stared at the dark windows. This was where she lived. The hedges needed trimming and the grass mowing, but otherwise it looked like a perfectly comfortable home.

Judith wished Caroline would walk by a window and see her, come outside and get into her car for a change. She needed desperately to talk to someone. Her head pounded and her eyes burned. She should never have drunk all that bourbon. She should never have gotten behind the wheel of a car. She should never have let Lucas go out with an older girl. She should never have kept his secrets from Peter. She should never have let him walk out of the kitchen the day of the bloody nose without doing something more.

I wish those assholes were dead.

Judith opened the car door to vomit onto the street.

I don't want anyone else but her. Ever.

She had never talked to Lucas about the hang-ups or violent threats left on the answering machine. She'd pretended not to see him pick up the empty beer cans from the front lawn every morning before his father left for work. She had told herself time would take care of it. Everything would blow over. Just give it a little longer. *Just give it time . . .*

But February had arrived, bringing Matt's broken windshield and those awful minutes in the garage that Judith had not yet allowed herself to think about. Lucas had spent a weekend at his friend Travis's house while his parents were out of town, one week before Valentine's Day, while their gun cabinets were left unlocked.

September 4

Last night I drank a little too much. Okay, let me rephrase that. I got SHITTY DRUNK. I turned forty yesterday, a big birthday even without everything else. Thursday is the sixth. But I can't think about Thursday yet. I can only think about today. Today is Tuesday. First, I have to get through Tuesday.

So far, Tuesday has not gone well:

I woke up early (it was still dark outside) behind the wheel of my car. It was parked, quite crookedly, in the empty parking lot of a Home Depot, engine still running (how did I not run out of gas?). I have no idea how long I was there, how I got there or how I wasn't arrested.

After dragging myself home to sleep for a few hours, I had to get up and take Lindsey to an appointment with Dr. Haji. Well, the appointment ran long and Lindsey was really upset when she came out of the office. Dr. Haji asked to speak with me in private for a few minutes. Great. I was, shall we say, not at my best by that point. Approximately thirty seconds into Dr. Haji's discussion, my state of health deteriorated rapidly.

I barfed all over her patent-leather shoes.

Then, on the drive home, I ran a stop sign and some guy driving a FedEx truck hit us. Not very hard, he wasn't going that fast, but fast enough that the passenger side air bag deployed and sent Lindsey into hysterics. About an hour later, she broke out in a mysterious raging case of hives. I called Dr. Hammond and he thought she was probably having an allergic reaction to the powder and particles from the airbag. I'm about to head out in the (now dented) car to get her some antihistamine. No more bourbon for me.

I just finished making about ten phone calls of apology—our insurance agent, Dr. Haji, the FedEx man, the FedEx man's boss, Howard Pierce (with whom we had an appointment this afternoon and I forgot) and my neighbor, Mrs. Clarkson. Apparently, I clipped her mailbox at some point last night.

How is it I managed to single-handedly create so much messiness in one day?

So far, I'm not liking forty much . . .

Belated Birthday

JUDITH DODGED THE WATER SHOOTING from Mrs. Clarkson's lawn sprinkler as she walked out to Caroline's car, trying to anticipate the range of wetness in the dark by sound only, the *cht cht cht cht, pshh, cht cht cht cht pshh*, circling between the two houses. She stepped in a soggy patch of grass, water squishing. It seemed ridiculous to water a yard in late September, so close to the onset of cold weather and with rain predicted in the next few days.

As Judith neared the car, she heard Caroline laughing to herself. Something about the woman's appearance seemed odd. Her coiled hair was stuffed beneath a white baseball cap with multicolored rhinestones studding the bill, and by the clear light of the moon, Judith could see that her face was sunburned, the skin across her nose and cheeks a bright, painful red unusual for this time of year. Once inside the car, she noticed that Caroline's shoulders, bare in a yellow tank top, were also blistering. However, she appeared unbothered as she giggled through a crumbly bite of oatmeal cookie, catching the morsels in her hand cupped below her chin.

"What's so funny?" Judith asked, her smile stiff and confused.

"I saw the funniest movie the other night," Caroline said. "There was this guy and his friend, and they were on this road trip, and all these things went wrong, and it was just so funny."

Judith smiled again and shrugged her shoulders, perplexed. A car full of teenagers sped by, the stereo pounding, the music mixing with their loud chatter and laughter. It was a warm autumn night, full of noisy bugs and barking dogs and kids out well past their curfews, everyone and everything not sure what to make of the lingering summer weather. Judith's wet, sockless feet began to chafe in her tennis shoes, and she wished she had slipped on a pair of sandals or just gone barefoot. For once, her feet were sweaty instead of numb.

"I can't remember the last time I rented a movie," Caroline continued, fanning her face with a paper plate she picked up off the floor. "Oh! And I baked!" She opened a plastic container and presented a dizzying array of cookies and chocolate treats stacked between sheets of wax paper.

"It was so nice to get back into the kitchen!" she exclaimed. "I went a little overboard, so please, take these." Caroline dropped the container onto Judith's lap but only after taking a handful of chocolate chip cookies and gingersnaps.

"Then, yesterday I spent the day at Lake Erie," she said with her mouth full. "It was heaven. Hiking and swimming and lying on the beach. Just total peace and quiet."

"Sounds nice," Judith said, eyeing Caroline's crimson skin. She snapped the lid back over the cookies and stared quizzically. "You seem . . ." Judith struggled to find the right word to describe Caroline's alterations.

"I know!" Caroline interrupted. "I feel really good. This has been a good week, you know?" Caroline finished another gingersnap in two bites. "I've been doing so much thinking lately and finally feel like I've got a plan and something to look forward to."

"What kind of plan?"

"A life plan!" Caroline made a drum roll with her hands on the steering wheel. "Big things for me and Dan, I tell you."

Judith rolled her window down to let in a breeze. Caroline seemed to generate a heat of her own in this new hyperactive state.

"First," Caroline held up her index finger. Her short nails were painted a bruised blue, all ten fingers looking as if she'd slammed them in a car door. "We're going to do a little redecorating in the house. Some new paint, curtains, maybe even gut the bathroom, I don't know, we'll have to see how the money plays out. Then, we're taking a vacation. I mean a good one. Vegas or Florida or San Francisco."

Judith listened in silence, watching Caroline's jerky hands. Caroline opened a bottle of iced tea and took three long gulps before handing it over. Judith tipped it to her nose, discreetly sniffing for alcohol, but there was none. She glanced around the interior of the car for extinguished marijuana joints or suspicious bottles of pills.

"Okay, now, the next step will be a big one." Caroline took her cap off and perched it on top of the gearshift like it was a tiny mannequin head. Rhinestones sparkled in the moonlight. "We're going to take in a foster child. I've given this a lot of thought. We're a loving couple with a nice home, plenty of room. Certainly the time. We'd be perfect." She looked at Judith, wide-eyed and expectant, almost frantic with her breathlessness.

Judith felt the pressure of a response, the right response that Caroline seemed to be desperately seeking in that moment. She managed a weak smile that felt unconvincing. "What does Dan say about all of this?"

"Oh, Dan will come around," she waved her hand, dismissive. "It's a lot to take in, you know? But it'll be good for us. He'll come around." She nodded.

"Have you told your therapist?"

Caroline fidgeted with the strap of her top, then was momentarily distracted by two stray cats chasing each other down the sidewalk, screeching. "I haven't told her yet. I'm getting all my ducks in a row first, you know?" She leaned forward and squinted through the windshield as the cats fought their way up a tree.

Judith stared down at the plate of cookies, at the little dots of colorful candy baked into the dough. She cleared her throat. "Don't you think you're pushing yourself a little bit? Maybe forcing yourself to do some of these things too soon?"

"No! Oh, no," Caroline vehemently shook her head. "I'm ready. If there is one thing this whole ordeal has taught me, it's that I have to stop pissing my time away. You have to seize every minute, because it just might be your last."

"It's only been seven months. That doesn't seem fast to you?"

Caroline retrieved her cap from the gearshift and yanked it down over her hair. "Really," she said sharply, turning away from Judith to look out the window. "I'm ready." Her voice dropped to a whisper. "I don't know what else to do."

"Maybe you should just give yourself a little more time to figure it out—"

"So what did you do this week?" Caroline's voice was loud and perky as she flopped back against the seat, rocking the car slightly.

Judith sighed. It was Saturday. She had survived the week. Her fortieth birthday, the disastrous day after, telling Peter about the minor accident when he got home, and Thursday. She had survived the wrenching, exhaustive twelve hours of Thursday. She had waited for Caroline, needing desperately to talk all week, to just sit in her company. Then to Judith's relief, Caroline had finally come. Only she had shown up with sparkles and cookies and *life plans*.

Judith felt a sudden sense of loneliness and disappointment, of being left behind, the only girl at school not invited to the party. She wanted Caroline to be desolate for as long as she was. There was a comfort shared between them in their suffering, but with Caroline's new *life plans*, Judith was left to suffer alone. She had no *life plans*.

"Oh, nothing much," Judith answered softly. "It was my birthday."

"Well then!" Caroline clapped her hands together and handed over a second box of cookies. "Happy birthday, kid."

Take It Back

THE NEW CELL PHONE WASN'T working. Or Judith hadn't programmed it right. The instruction booklet was pressed flat on the table in front of her. She stabbed at the buttons, random numbers and sequences that she knew weren't correct, but at this point she felt it was worth trying any combination, even if only to get an error tone. That way she'd know at least some aspect of the phone worked. Penny leaned over her, the end of her ponytail falling onto Judith's shoulder and tickling her neck and ears. She brushed it away with annoyance.

"You have to get back to the main menu," Penny said, and snatched up the box to read the back. The bulky recharging cord fell out, clattering on the tabletop.

"I'm trying," Judith said, squinting at the small screen on the front of the phone. "I need glasses."

"Or better instructions," Penny muttered.

"Might I remind you both that our lunch reservations are in an hour," Virginia called, her voice muted; she was leaning deep into the refrigerator, sorting through the shelves. "Judith, this mayonnaise expired three months ago." She set the jar on the counter. "And it's never been opened."

Judith laid the phone down and rubbed her eyes. "Mother, might I remind you I can't go to lunch with you today. Lindsey has an appointment with Dr. Haji at two."

"Oh. Then why are we waiting around for you?" Virginia planted her rubber-gloved hands on her hips. She wore a flowered apron to protect her pale blue blouse and tan wool trousers as she attacked the kitchen. Her gray-blond hair was swept back with a pearl comb that matched her teardrop earrings and the pearl buttons down the front of her white cardigan, which she had carefully folded over the back of a chair before she began cleaning.

"I told her I would stop by to help her with the new phone," Penny said, exasperated. "Don't you ever listen to me?"

"I listen to you, Penny. I'm just being conscientious about the time."

Judith shrugged and tossed the phone back into the box. "Don't worry about it."

Lindsey shuffled into the kitchen, carrying the plate of food Judith had earlier set on her desk for lunch as she worked on a math assignment. The ham sandwich had only a couple bites out of it, and the pudding cup was unopened.

"Hey, kiddo," Penny said, eyeing the uneaten food. "Want to go to lunch with us? Any where you want."

"No, thanks," Lindsey answered, filling a glass of water from the jug in the refrigerator.

"Lindsey," Judith sighed. "We agreed that you would eat—"

"Judith," Virginia interrupted. "Is your air conditioning on? I know it's October, but I'm positively boiling in here. It must be eighty degrees outside." She fanned herself with a dishtowel. "It's miserable, and my hair is going to frizz."

"Maybe you're having a hot flash," Penny smirked.

"I don't get those," Virginia replied, an offended clip to her voice.

"Yes, the air is on," Judith said.

"Then why is it so hot in here?"

"Because of the enormous hole in our wall." Judith closed her eyes and propped her head up with her hand.

"Why don't you just finish that blasted porch? What are you waiting for? It's such an eyesore," Virginia said, wiping her brow with a napkin. "Tell Peter to get a hammer and a box of nails and get to it."

Penny snorted. "Oh, right. Peter and tools. Good one, Mother."

"We'll get around to it," Judith murmured. She opened one eye and watched Virginia tug on the hem of Lindsey's baggy T-shirt. Judith took a sharp breath. She recognized the T-shirt. It had belonged to Lucas.

"This looks like a boy's shirt." Virginia shook her head and tucked Lindsey's hair behind her ear. "You should really dress more feminine. You're such a pretty little thing. I was tiny and petite like you at your age."

Lindsey stepped out of her grandmother's reach and flicked her hair from behind her ear so it once again hung over her face.

"We should go," Penny said, handing Virginia her overstuffed purse. "I'll come back later, and we'll figure the phone out." She kissed the top of Judith's head.

"I don't understand young girls today," Virginia complained. "No one seems to want to dress like real ladies anymore . . ." Her voice faded as Penny slammed the door closed behind them.

"Lindsey," Judith said, turning to face her daughter. "Why don't you change your clothes before we leave for your appointment with Dr. Haji?"

"I don't want to see her today," Lindsey said. She leaned against the table and scratched the top of one bare foot with the other.

"Why not?"

"I don't know. I just don't want to."

"Your sessions with her are important."

"Yeah. Important for me or important for you?"

Judith withdrew, surprised and speechless. She stood to face her daughter. They were the same height now, but it was obvious Lindsey would be tall like her father. Lucas was the child who had been short, like his mother.

"You need to go," Judith said, staring at the graphics on the front of the shirt—Salvador Dali clocks melting from a tree branch. Lucas had won the shirt in a drawing contest. It had been his favorite.

Lindsey dumped out the remainder of her water and trudged upstairs to change. Judith began sorting the outgoing mail, sticking stamps on a pile of envelopes she would drop at the post office while Lindsey was in session. She glanced over a letter from her AVS chapter, a reminder of their next meeting and the upcoming yearly convention in Mansfield. She studied the registration form, regretful for a few moments, thinking about the rows of abandoned pots in the basement, the crispy brown leaves of her dead plants littering the floor, years of hard work and meticulous attention gone. Pieces of her recent conversation with Caroline played through her mind . . . *a life plan* . . . *pissing my time away* . . . *seize every minute* . . . and her feelings of abandonment and loneliness returned, creeping off the letter and onto the skin of her hands with the sensation of a spider crawling up her arm. She had no right to deny Caroline any attempts to move forward, to try and put her life back together. But the bitter feeling was still there; the spider would scurry about her body no matter the effort she made to flick it away.

It was too late to register for the AVS convention this year, but maybe it was time to at least get back to her flowers and plants, get her mind occupied, like Caroline said. It wouldn't really change anything; Judith wasn't that optimistic, but perhaps the days would spin past faster and she would find herself tired at night, ready to fall asleep when she laid her head on the pillow instead of lying awake, thinking, always thinking. It was as if, once the lights went out in the bedroom and she was left to the darkness and the sound of Peter's snoring (when he was at home), her brain became cued to study her regular list of worries. It was an established list now, the same five items she mentally checked off one by one after ample rumination:

1. *Lindsey: eating and school*
2. *The lawsuit: upcoming depositions and monetary repercussions*
3. *Appointments with Dr. Haji: difficult Q&A sessions*
4. *Going out in public*
5. *Peter*

She often devoted entire journal entries to the first four worries on the list, narrowing down the specifics of exactly what bothered or upset her, forming subcategories of main categories. Organizing her worrying process probably hadn't been what Dr. Haji had had in mind when she suggested Lindsey keep a journal, but it was a comforting habit now for Judith. If she let go of the worries, of the organized list, then she wouldn't be ready for the bad moments, wouldn't be emotionally prepared. At least this way, she expected them to show their scary faces at any moment, and so she peeked around every corner before proceeding. Except for Peter. Number five, the last on the list. She had yet to subcategorize him, to define what exactly was her worry. All she felt sure of was that he needed to be on the list.

The front doorbell rang. Judith tucked the envelopes into her purse on her way out of the kitchen. She swung the door open without checking the window first; a gust of wind swept a handful of dried leaves into the foyer with a sound like tiny animal claws clicking across the floor. A young girl in a white shirt and denim overalls stood on the front bricks.

It was Kristin. Exactly as Judith remembered her—pink lip-gloss, heavy black eye liner, and nervous, fluttering hands.

"Oh! Hi, Mrs. Elliott." Her high voice sounded scratchy, and she cleared her throat. "I, I was going to call first, but then we were, like, in the neighborhood, so we just stopped by."

Judith's heart beat furiously behind her ribs, her legs watery, threatening to give out beneath her. She couldn't swallow, couldn't blink. Kristin Danforth on her front porch. Valentine's day came hurtling back. Judith could see a tiny scar, a pinkish white line at the tip of the girl's left ear. Her only scar.

Kristin wrung her hands together, the skin around her knuckles turning white. "This has been, like, the worst thing in my whole life. Even worse than when my mom had breast cancer, and I, I just wanted to tell you and your family how totally sorry I am. I really am so sorry."

Judith let her eyes drift over Kristin's shoulder to a car parked on the curb with the engine running. It was an older sports car of some kind, black, with a teenage boy behind the wheel. He lifted a bottle from between his legs and took a long drink.

"Um, I don't know if you got my letter, but this is why I wrote to you." Kristin held out her hand. "To give this back."

In the center of her soft, creamy palm lay Lucas's class ring. The sapphire stone was dull, smudged with fingerprints, and the gold band still had blue thread wrapped around it, fitted for Kristin's thin finger. Judith held her breath and reached out, dreamlike, to take the ring, her arm extending slowly, fingers closing around the metal, warmed from being clutched by the girl.

"I thought you would want it back," Kristin whispered. "I, um, never got the chance to give it back to him." She choked on a small, high-pitched sob and looked down at her worn sneakers, shoving her hands into her pockets.

Judith turned the ring over and over, her fingers gone stiff and cold despite the warm day. She traced the engraved letters of his name, the outline of an artist's paintbrush and pallet, the numbers of the year he would've graduated. She shifted her gaze back to the girl, taking in the tanned arms, the sunglasses perched on top of her head, and then to the young man behind the wheel of the car. Possibly a new boyfriend.

"Uh," Kristin squirmed. "I, I gotta go. Ben's waiting for me."

Ben. He had a name. And the two of them had somewhere to be. They had plans for the day.

Judith's mind flashed to that day in January: Lucas's torn shirt and bloody nose. The hateful notes and insults scrawled across his locker. The break-up. Matt and his buddies. Toby Doyle. All heavy and weighing down his slumped shoulders, carried in the blue backpack along with the gun on that final day, one month later.

Kristin—pretty, healthy, breathing Kristin. Going somewhere fun with her new boyfriend, riding in a car with the windows down, hair flying and sunlight on her face. But for Lucas, never again. For him, there would be no more lazy days cruising around in a car, afternoons eating ice cream at the mall, or catching a late movie on a weekend night. Judith swayed and lost her balance, grabbing the doorframe to steady herself.

"Are you okay?" Kristin asked, moving to offer help.

As the months had passed, Judith's thoughts had never lingered for very long on Kristin. Only as long as was necessary. There was so much else to consider and worry over: Lindsey's weight loss and emotional apathy, her own deepening disconnection from Peter, the lawsuits, the disorienting imbalance of grief and shame. Now, faced with her, Judith realized, and with little surprise, she hated this girl. One small part of her acknowledged the cruelty of the feeling, but it also made an overwhelming sense: had there never been a Kristin, there never would have been a Valentine's Day. This girl was to blame.

Judith leaned forward so they were eye to eye. "I wish his aim had been better," she whispered, and slammed the door.

Peppermint Questions

JUDITH WAS UNDERDRESSED IN THE cool office, wearing a short-sleeved blouse, linen slacks, and sandals. Goosebumps broke out on her arms, and her toes felt icy numb. Outside, the Indian summer heat measured eighty-five degrees; in the office, it felt like Alaska. Dr. Haji appeared comfortable in a yellow blazer and matching silk slacks, her red toenails peeking out from a pair of open pumps like ten maraschino cherries. She perfectly complemented the exotic surroundings of her office, the shelves and tabletops bursting with bright flowers and lush green plants, a canary perched on the branch of a tropical tree, deep in the jungle.

"Dr. Hammond sent over a copy of her last weigh-in," Dr. Haji said. "Looks like she lost another two and a half pounds?"

Judith nodded, straining to get a glimpse of the fax sheet in the doctor's hand.

"And you're still working with the nutritionist?"

"Yes." Another two and a half pounds. Judith dreaded the weigh-ins. She knew her daughter wasn't getting any better. Yesterday, she had found clumps of Lindsey's hair in the shower drain.

"She reported no social activities again this week," Dr. Haji said.

"That's not correct," Judith raised a finger. "She went to her violin lesson and to a movie with my sister."

Dr. Haji scribbled a quick sentence on the file sheet and capped the end of her pen. "I meant socializing with peers, other children her own age."

Judith curled and uncurled her cold toes, working to get circulation back. She eyed the lighter, discolored spot in the otherwise dark carpet near the door, the scene of her last embarrassing visit with Dr. Haji.

"I would like to discuss Lindsey's argument with her father this morning," Dr. Haji said, shuffling Lindsey's thick file lying open across her lap. "What was the disagreement about?"

Judith hesitated before answering. "Didn't she tell you about it herself?"

"Yes, but I would like to hear your understanding of it."

"They had a fight about school." Before Peter had left for the airport that morning, he'd asked Lindsey if she'd filled out her fall class schedule, reminding her that the deadline for registration was fast approaching. Lindsey had erupted into a meltdown.

"Mr. Elliott wants her to go back to school in August?"

"Yes."

"As a freshman at Roosevelt High?"

"Yes."

"And why do you think your daughter is resistant to attending Roosevelt?"

Judith rubbed her hands up and down her arms to warm her mottled skin, and then under her pant legs, feeling a fine growth of bristly hair. She was off her usual shaving schedule. She stared at the sparkling brooch pinned just above Dr. Haji's left breast. It was a cluster of rubies and diamonds in the shape of a ladybug.

Dr. Haji removed her glasses. "Mrs. Elliott?"

"What? Oh, well, that's pretty obvious, isn't it?"

"Mmm-hmm." Glasses back on. "And what are your feelings on the situation? Do you agree with your husband that Lindsey should start high school at Roosevelt?"

"I don't know. We hadn't really discussed it until this morning. I don't blame her for not wanting to go, but what alternatives do we have? Four years with a tutor doesn't seem like a very good idea."

"Has Lindsey communicated to you any interest in a music school instead of public school? A type of educational institution with a primary focus on music?"

Judith sank into the crevices between the couch cushions. "No. She's never mentioned it to me." She knitted her brows together. "Are you suggesting we move?"

"Well, that's something you need to discuss with her and with your husband. But it might be an option to consider. I understand she's quite an accomplished musician for her age. There are some wonderful music schools throughout the country that would probably be thrilled to enroll her."

Judith opened her mouth to say something, but Dr. Haji moved on, reading from another note on the chart. "Lindsey also tells me that a young girl recently visited you at your house. A few days ago, yes?"

Judith blinked stupidly. She was not aware that Lindsey had overheard the exchange with Kristin. She cleared her throat, her mouth suddenly dry and pasty.

"This was your son's former girlfriend?"

Judith nodded. She glanced around the office, seeking distraction. The aquarium had been drained, the fish gone. Pink rocks and a glittering castle sat at the bottom of the dry tank, the plastic plants tipped over on their sides.

"And this was an angry confrontation between you and the girl?"

"We weren't yelling at each other or anything," Judith answered, looking back at the doctor.

"But you are very angry with this girl?"

Judith adjusted her position on the leather sofa, creating a whooshing sound beneath her. "I was angry that day."

Dr. Haji nodded, staring over the tops of her bifocals, one finger pressed into the side of her cheek. "Your son was very despondent over their parting, yes? And there was some difficulty with a group of boys because of this girl?"

Judith began to shiver. Apparently, Lindsey and Dr. Haji had talked about more than school.

Lowering her voice, Dr. Haji spoke slowly. "Lindsey mentioned some business with a broken windshield and involvement with the police."

Judith fished around in her purse until she found an old piece of hard candy in one of the side pockets. She tore off the wrapper, the crinkle of the plastic harsh in the silence between them. She popped the peppermint into her mouth.

Dr. Haji closed the chart and set it on the coffee table. "Mrs. Elliott, I need to know the details of this incident. Lindsey is very troubled by this event and has not yet been able to discuss it."

There it was. Gently laid out before her, unfolded like a delicate piece of old lace with yellowed and fragile threads. The one question, the one dark memory she had been unable to bring herself to face. Judith stared down at her hands, her white palms, listening to the tired sound of her own breathing, the flutter of plant leaves as more freezing air rushed from the wall vent. She closed her eyes, thinking about how the garage door had rumbled closed that night, sealing them together, only a small cast of light from the harsh bulb overhead illuminating their faces, their four hopeless faces. The concrete had been wet, slick with melting snow from the car's tires. The puddles had smelled earthy, pungent. The echo of their loud voices off the stark white walls had split her eardrums. *Stop! Don't hurt him!*

"Mrs. Elliott?" Dr. Haji's tone remained soft and gentle.

Judith scrambled to her feet and clutched her purse to her chest. "I . . . I'm sorry. I've got an appointment across town. I've really got to go." She bumped into an end table and mumbled another apology.

She opened the door and pulled Lindsey up by her wrist from a waiting room chair. Lindsey dropped the magazine she had been reading. The heavy oak door slammed behind them. Judith swallowed the peppermint candy in her rush; she hacked and coughed as Lindsey pounded on her back until she could breathe again. Waiting for the elevator, Lindsey studied her mother's face.

"What happened in there?" she asked.

Judith stabbed the down button for the third time, still coughing, eyes watering, grateful that she was unable to answer her daughter's question.

October 22

Driving home from Dr. Haji's office today, I saw an older silver Honda Civic, a teenage boy with light reddish hair behind the wheel. I had a moment, a frozen second that stopped my heart. An incredulous, ridiculous moment of feeling, that maybe, oh, Lord, was that him? Could this be an awakening from the months of nightmare? But then the car passed and I got a good look at the boy's face, tanned skin and long nose, and the moment was gone, just as quickly as it had come.

It is nearly Halloween and still nice outside, sunny and everyone's lawns still green. Soon it will be November and the days are running out when I can think, 'Oh right, last year at this time, exactly one year ago today, Lucas was doing this, our family was doing that, he was in a watercolors workshop, he bought his car, he went to the Homecoming dance on his first date . . .'

Come February, those thoughts will be done forever.

Dr. Haji . . . I wasn't prepared to answer questions about what I said to Kristin and I was angry with her for asking. And embarrassed. I'd been caught by my daughter and my daughter told her therapist and her therapist confronted me. What I said was wrong and uncalled for and I didn't mean it. And I certainly didn't mean for Lindsey to overhear it.

I seem to be mad at everyone. I've been highly emotional these past few weeks and, I'm not stupid, I mean emotional in a nongrief *sort of way. I mean irritable in a put-out, put-upon, mistreated sort of way. My outburst at Kristin aside, I feel just plain old bitchy. It's a petty kind of irritability; the checkout girl at the supermarket didn't double bag my canned goods, a telemarketer called after nine PM and the postman dropped a letter into one of my potted begonias on the front porch where it got wet and some of the ink ran. Probably an accident, but it still pissed me off and I called his supervisor to complain. I'm like one of those desperate women in the commercials for PMS medication.*

Maybe it's the start of menopause. Or the fibroids. Or a permanent change in my personality—God forbid. Or maybe it comes back to the grief talking in foreign tongues. So how am I supposed to recognize the difference? And what do I do about it?

I was not ready to talk about Lucas and the windshield and all that. All That. *I can hardly even bring myself to say what* All That *even is. And such two tiny little words—*All That*—to blanket the enormity they stand for. What I wanted to say to Dr. Haji, what I have yet to say to myself, is that I don't want to talk about* All That.

Because All That *is more painful, more shameful for me to talk about than what Lucas did on Valentine's Day. I can't go back to that night in the garage, not yet. I'm not ready to revisit those moments. We were not those four strangers in the garage. I don't know who those people were but they were not my family.*

She, *standing in the doorway of the garage, watching, was not* me.

Atwood Lake

AN AIR OF FORCED ENJOYMENT hung thickly in the cabin. A strained happiness, stretched like a rubber band from one side of the room to the other, ready to snap at any moment. Tim and Brenda McCann smiled like porcelain dolls, their lips and teeth frozen, feigning ease with their present company. Determined to prove that they were faithful friends and, despite their earlier lack of support, that they could offer comfort and fellowship to Peter and Judith during their time of family crisis.

Talk over the last twenty-four hours had been kept mostly to golf games, the NFL season, and stock portfolios. The only mention of Lucas and Valentine's Day had been in the form of brisk hugs from Brenda and shoulder squeezes from Tim as they had solemnly greeted the Elliotts at the cabin door, both saying, "You've been in our prayers." But since then, Tim had discussed at great length the new line of software he was developing for his company as Brenda showed off a photo album of the weddings she had designed and coordinated over the last year. Judith recalled a similar album from their previous visit. The sparkling brides and bouquets were starting to run together.

"You see, each wedding should have a distinct look and feel," Brenda explained over a picture of table centerpieces. "Not a theme, mind you, but an individual sense of style that is really tailor-made for the bride." Judith smiled as if she were a potential client of Brenda's discussing fabric samples and cake toppers. *Smile, nod, smile, nod. Oh, beautiful. I love that one.*

Their four-bedroom cabin faced the sunset over Atwood Lake from the top of a small hill, partially hidden by the brilliant autumn canopy of mature oaks and American beeches. A dirt trail led from the front door straight to the gentle, lapping waves of the shoreline. Brenda woke each morning before six to hike the trails, shower, and have food on the table before eight. The fridge was stocked with enough food to last for weeks; the breakfasts alone—piles of eggs, honey-smoked bacon and sausage, loaves of homemade whole grain bread, baskets of muffins—were enough to feed a hungry regiment. Fun and relaxation were proving to be more demanding than Judith had remembered. Tim and Brenda were tanned and fit in ways only childless couples could be, well rested and up on all the latest good movies and novels. But Judith was exhausted after just a day and a half. She also sensed the fatigue in Peter by his deep sighs while he shaved or when he picked up a fork at the table, the pronounced lines creasing his forehead.

Judith and Peter had not been in each other's prolonged company for some time. She had counted the days in her head as she had lain next to him in bed the previous night. Since the afternoon at the cemetery. His business travel had become more and more frequent, and whether legitimate or invented, she did not ask and didn't think she wanted to know. The drive from Fairlawn to the lake had been quiet, only the talk radio chatter filling the space between them. Peter had kept his attention on the road while Judith watched the scenery. Lindsey slept the entire trip with her iPod headphones tucked into her ears, her goose-pimpled skin tightly wrapped in an afghan against the chill.

Since their arrival, Lindsey had spent most of her time listening to music or reading a book in her room or on a blanket by the water. Her presence among the group was awkward and uncomfortable, a parallel to Lucas's last year. Lindsey's silence was as solid as a sixth guest; her long absences to take a walk or canoe ride without notifying anyone had already caused two disruptions in activities to hunt her down.

On the second afternoon, the four adults played eighteen sweaty rounds of golf, dipping frequently into the cooler of beer perched on the back of the McCann's cart. They trailed into the cabin single file, staggering from exhaustion and alcohol. Lindsey had been practicing her violin but quickly laid the bow and instrument in their case when the group noisily entered the cabin. As the adults stowed their equipment, wiping their red faces with towels and discussing plans for the evening, Lindsey shuffled the pages of sheet music she'd been studying and dismantled her music stand. Judith started to apologize for their loud intrusion, but Brenda interrupted.

"Oh, I need a shower!" she exclaimed. "I smell like a locker room. I never expected it to be so warm! Remember three years ago when we stayed here with an inch of snow on the ground and Tim wrecked the Beamer when he slid into a tree?"

"So everyone is agreed, barbecue at the clubhouse for dinner," Tim announced.

"Are you wearing a dress, Judith, or khakis?" Brenda asked.

"Dress," Judith answered and scratched at a sun rash on the back of her neck just above her collar. She had worn her hair tucked into a ball cap, leaving that sensitive patch of skin exposed.

"I think we should catch the comedy show after dinner. Does that sound fun?" Tim asked.

"Absolutely," Peter agreed. "How about it, Lindsey?"

She shrugged her shoulders as she snapped her black violin case shut.

"Do you want me to iron your blue dress?" Judith asked her.

"Whatever." She dropped onto the couch and slid her headphones back into her ears. She curled into a small ball and pulled a blanket over herself, even though she wore slacks and a long-sleeved shirt, and closed her eyes, turning the volume up until Judith could faintly hear the strains of the music. She thought of the symphony trip Lindsey had taken last year over Labor Day to Six Flags. She'd eaten four hot dogs on a dare and ridden an upside-down roller coaster twelve times in a row.

Peter reached down and lifted one of Lindsey's earpieces, leaning in close. "Be ready by six."

Lindsey didn't open her eyes. "Whatever," she said, and tilted her head away from him.

❧

JUDITH WATCHED HER DAUGHTER IN the buffet line. Even with endless bowls and platters of food, everything from barbecued ribs to hot dogs to dripping slices of watermelon and a giant carrot cake decorated with cream cheese frosting and candy pumpkins, Lindsey selected only a small scoop of potato salad and half of a plain hamburger. She surveyed the choices in front of her with obvious discomfort and appeared pained at the thought of having to eat the two meager items lost on the oversized paper plate in her hand with Brenda two steps behind. *So that's your secret to staying so slender. Lucky girl . . .*

Once their group circled the sea of striped umbrellas for a second time, they finally located five available chairs and crowded around a glass-topped patio table near the edge of the activity. They had a lovely view of the sun setting over the lake, turning the treetops the color of fire. Tim and Brenda ordered more cocktails and chatted with Peter about their annual ski trip to Aspen. He listened with the seriousness of a business meeting, intense and focused on every word, asking the right questions at the right time, keeping the conversation in constant motion. He allowed nothing to slow down or linger too long in unplanned places.

How much did you pay for your Lexus? How's your 401K this year? What was the name of that crazy roommate you had freshman year at Kent? What's the square footage of your house? How many years have you been in Cincinnati now?

Judith quickly fell behind the swift changes in topic and abandoned her attempts at polite chatter. She had already drained three glasses of wine and ordered a fourth by the time she finished her dessert. She couldn't stop watching Lindsey pick at the tiny mound of potato salad on her plate, moving it from one side to the other, spreading it out until it looked as if it were the last bites she couldn't finish instead of the small amount she hadn't even tried. Judith's mind wandered, and she thought about the last visit with Dr. Haji, what Lindsey must have said to the doctor about the night in the garage. She thought momentarily about the new and improved Caroline, probably working hard on her big *life plan*.

"So, Judith, think you could retire in Fairlawn?" Tim asked, sending his unsatisfactory single-malt scotch back with the waiter for the third time. Judith, oblivious, had not heard the question and shrugged absently.

"Oh, Fairlawn is such a nice area," Brenda said. "I have a friend who just moved to Bath." She was drinking a fruity beer and made her lips like a donut hole each time she took a drink from the bottle so as not to mess up her lipstick.

"Judith's sister bought a new condo in Bath about the same time we moved," Peter said. "There's so much new construction going up out there."

"How is your sister, Judith? Is she still dating that architect?" Brenda asked.

"No," Judith answered, drowsy from too much wine too fast. "They broke up last year."

"We hate Fairlawn," Lindsey said suddenly. "We're moving."

Tim and Brenda glanced back and forth at one another.

"What are you talking about, Lindsey?" Peter said, laughing nervously. "We're not moving."

"We can't stay. Everyone hates us."

Tim and Brenda fiddled with the napkins in their laps and took quick drinks from their glasses. Flicked imaginary bugs off their arms.

Peter set his fork down. "Lindsey—"

"And we're being sued. For millions of dollars."

"Enough!" Peter slammed his beer glass onto the table. An older couple sitting behind him glanced over their shoulders and discreetly scooted their chairs a few inches further away. Judith tried to put her arm around Lindsey, but the girl slapped it away, bumping the table and rattling the melting ice in the glasses.

"Peter, man—" Tim began.

"It's nothing," Peter cut him off. "We're fine. Our lawyer said it won't come to anything. We just can't dwell on the bad things . . ." His voice trailed off, and he picked up a napkin to wipe his brow, which had become covered in tiny beads of sweat.

Judith watched her husband as he ran his fingers through the sides of his hair, as her daughter wrapped her arms across her stomach and withered into a tiny ball of paper skin and brittle bones. She poured herself another glass of wine and looked across the lush grass and crimson treetops to the glittering water of the lake. A calm day with no wind, perfect for a sunset sail.

JUDITH WASHED THE MAKE-UP OFF her face, bending over the sink with a lathered cloth and warm, running water. Wispy strands of her hair, which had fallen loose from her clip hours ago, stuck to the sides of her wet face. One diamond stud earring came loose and fell into the basin, slipping down the drain with the water before she could catch it. She was drunk. Maybe she would throw up. She sat on the toilet lid and leaned her head against the cool porcelain of the sink's edge. The earrings had been a gift from Peter many Christmases ago. How fitting. She splashed a handful of water over the back of her burning neck. She hadn't thought she would need sunscreen in early November while they golfed. She would blister and peel. She always peeled.

She pulled a thin, cotton nightgown over her head and dropped her gold watch into her jewelry bag. She heard Peter cough from the bedroom. He was angry with her because she'd gotten so drunk at dinner. Dropped a martini glass. She'd been no help with Lindsey. She told stupid, nonsensical stories. She'd fallen down a hill after the comedy show and skinned her knee, making an ass of herself in front of their friends and everyone.

Their marriage had become like a parent-child exchange. Maybe it had been that way for a while. She hated lectures, the disapproving glares and comments when she was late for a lunch date, when she lost her car keys, when she laughed too loud at a movie. It was that cold knot in her stomach, anticipating the scolding. He never yelled but said just enough to make her feel small and childish, as if she'd been grounded for getting a bad grade. So far, between her drunkenness and Lindsey's outburst, the trip to Atwood had brought nothing but disquietude for Peter.

When she came out of the bathroom, he was still awake, stretched out across his side of the bed with a knit blanket casually draped over him from the waist down. Judith slid under the covers with as little movement as possible, trying to spare her upset stomach. The smooth, crisp sheets felt good against her hot skin, and she pressed her head into the cool pillow.

Peter jostled the mattress as he moved behind her, close to her back with his breath against her tender neck. He slipped an arm over her waist and pressed himself to the skin of her inner thighs. She held her breath and bristled at his touch, even though she hadn't felt it in so many long, silent months.

"Don't," she whispered.

He pulled his hand away. "What?"

"Peter, please," she answered and drew the sheet up closer to her chin.

He grabbed her shoulders and flipped her onto her back, pinning her to the mattress.

"Look at me!" he said, sweating, long drops sliding down the side of his face like tears, eyes wide. She had never seen him like this—desperate and out of control. She couldn't stand to look at him. She clenched her eyes shut and turned her face to one side, into the pillow.

He maneuvered himself atop her, dropped his face down into her hair. "I just want to feel normal again." He grabbed her breast and squeezed until she squirmed and cried out in pain. Their struggle knocked the headboard against the wall, rattling the framed sailboat print hanging above their heads.

"Peter!" Judith gasped. "Stop! This isn't going to help anything." She gulped down a breath of air; most of his weight was on her chest. "We'll never be normal again."

At that, he released her and sat up on his heels, trembling and staring down at his hands open and resting like dead weights on top of his thighs. Judith lay motionless, watching the man she had married, shared children, a home and a life with, as he began to sob silently. There had been love and tenderness once, hadn't there? In years past that now felt so far and distant, he had held her hand whenever they rode in the car, had always rubbed her feet at the end of a long day. They had laughed at the same corny jokes. Had shared a love of greasy Chinese take-out. She remembered first meeting him, in an off-campus bar, how commanding his presence was when he'd entered the room. Tall, athletic, well dressed. That sexy look of cool unconcern. She had wanted to run her hands through his thick, dark hair, so wavy and soft looking. She thought about the sweetness of their wedding night, curled up together in a room very much like this one on Lake Erie, whispering to each other about plans and dreams until morning.

But from the endless, destructive reach of February 14, everything had been reduced to aching silences, hurtful looks of blame and anger. The drive and ambition that had drawn her in the beginning now were turned against her. Because of his ever mounting expectation and demand for perfection, she had become a disappointment. Their family had become a disappointment. He had set them all up for failure. She knew, tangled in the sheets of their confrontation, that the slow decay of their marriage had begun long before Valentine's Day.

Peter stood, snatched his robe off the chair, and wrapped it around his torso, tightly knotting the belt. "I'll sleep on the couch," he said. "We'll leave first thing tomorrow."

He slammed the door on his way out of the room, and the sailboat print fell to the floor behind the bed and shattered.

November 16

This morning I was stalked when I went to a Jiffy Lube to get the oil changed in my car. While waiting, I walked across the street to a bookstore, just wandering around in my usual daze. Then I noticed this man watching me through the display windows. Next, I went next door to a coffee joint and bought a cappuccino. There he was again, hovering outside the windows and checking me out. I started to get really freaked and almost said something to the cashier but she was just a high school kid small enough to stuff in my purse.

I thought I'd make one more stop just to be sure I wasn't being stupid or overreacting. I left the coffee place and walked a block to a flower shop on the corner. Sure enough, he followed me. He really did look threatening—black leather coat and jeans with combat boots, long hair pulled back into a ponytail with something like eight earrings stuck in various parts of his head. I asked the old lady in the flower shop for their phone to call the cops but she said it was out of order because they were installing a new line for credit card machines. Figures. Of course, I forgot my cell on the charger at home. Wouldn't have done me any good—still don't know how to use it.

I decided to make my way back to the Jiffy Lube where there were lots of other big men. Men with wrenches and tire irons and greasy, scary hands. My stalker would be outnumbered. I walked out of the flower shop, trying to stay calm. The guy was immediately two steps behind me. The street was completely empty and I thought if I *screamed no one would hear me. I slipped my hand into my purse for the little can of pepper spray I keep on my key ring.*

The guy tapped me hard on the shoulder three times and said "Excuse me." Well, I just went ape shit and started screaming "Fire! Fire! Fire!" like they tell you on all the talk shows because if you yell "Rape!" no one will come help you. I yelled and whipped around with that pepper spray and nailed him right between the eyes. I have never heard a man wail like that in all my life! He fell to the ground gasping and holding his eyes crying, "Oh, help me! Jesus, help me! I'm blind! I'm blind!" That's when I saw the camera and the notebook with a WTNB sticker on the front clutched in one of his hands.

Oh, crap. He was a reporter. Double crap. I got on my hands and knees and tried to see if he was okay but he wouldn't even let me look. Leave it to a man to be such a baby. "Don't touch me!" he yelled. "I only wanted to ask you a few questions! Jesus! My eyes! My eyes!"

Okay. So I went back to the coffee place and used their phone to call an ambulance, the guy still refusing to let me get near him while we waited for the paramedics. As it turned out, he started asking the police to arrest me. My potential rapist tried to get me thrown in the can. He lay on a stretcher in the back of the ambulance and whined like a little boy, trying to get me brought up on charges. I don't think the paramedics felt very sorry for him, though, after I told them who I was and that he was a reporter who'd been following me up and down the street. They were really quite nice to me about the whole incident.

Reporter guy decided he might live after the paramedics basically kicked him out of their rig. As it turned out, my aim wasn't so great. I hit him mostly in the forehead so only a few drops got in his eyes. Once the ambulance pulled away, the crowds of people had gone back to their respective places of employment, we were left alone on the street again. I offered to buy him a cup of coffee as an apology and he accepted. He shook my hand and told me his name was Jeffrey, and into the little coffee joint we went.

He said, as his eyes continued to water profusely, that he'd been sent by his boss to ask me about the civil suit. Apparently, it is now public, and Karen and Dean Michaels have formally filed against the school district, as well. I told Jeffrey that I had no comment. Nothing to say. All that trouble—nearly losing his eyesight—and he still didn't get squat from me. He said he'd been covering our story since Valentine's Day but this was the first time he'd seen any of us up close. He thought I looked pretty normal. Thanks, I said. He walked me back to the Jiffy Lube where my car was ready. We shook hands and I wished him luck. He wished me the same.

Something occurred to me after I left the mechanic's shop. For an entire morning, while running errands and during my would-be assault, I hadn't thought about Lucas and Valentine's Day once, or Peter or Lindsey or Caroline or Dr. Haji—all the things and people that I feel are constantly pulling me in different directions with all their problems and questions and issues. So, it has begun. The magic of time. How it plays with your mind through mundane, ordinary tasks, diluting the sharp edges of pain and sadness, even if for only a couple of hours. I greet it with a feeling of relief, but also tremendous guilt. How can I be so selfish as to put everything out of my mind for two whole hours? I should be carrying this with me every second of every day for the rest of my life. Why should I be able to enjoy a cup of coffee again or go window-shopping during a leisurely stroll? Or have the nerve to find humor in what happened this morning, chatting with Jeffrey the reporter and wishing the mechanics a nice day? I smiled this morning. I giggled this morning

I'm left feeling terrible.

I am sitting in my gynecologist's office waiting for more test results and blood work and scans. I'm bored. All of Dr. Menlo's magazines are three months old and every perfume sample has been torn out of them. I'm glad that I at least remembered to bring my journal. I could be here for hours.

I feel like week after week is taken over by appointments with doctors and conferences with attorneys and sessions with Dr. Haji, the nutritionist, the tutor, and the violin instructor. The last of my window herbs died this week.

I seem to have acquired the bill paying and money management in our household. This is a big change, an enormous, gigantic change. Bills, insurance, investments—always, ALWAYS Peter's domain. I never had any part in it, no questions asked. I'm ashamed to even admit that for many years, he gave me a credit card limit and cash allowance each month. I couldn't have guessed how much money was in our savings account or what banks we had accounts with. These days, he's never home and doesn't even seem interested anymore. He just lets the unopened envelopes pile up on his desk. So unlike him. I repeatedly remind him and he tells me he'll get to it, tomorrow, Saturday, next week. I stopped pestering him and just moved the bill basket to my desk in the kitchen. Then I brought the financial records from the filing cabinet, and the lock box of legal documents. I don't even think he's noticed. When Howard's secretary calls the house, she now asks for Mrs. Elliott. When our financial advisor schedules a meeting, he checks it with Mrs. Elliott. When the doctors, teachers and therapists send mail about our daughter, they address the letters to Judith Elliott.

Who knew I had two feet on which to stand . . .

We've taken to sleeping in separate bedrooms since the trip to Atwood. He moved his clothes and personal things into the spare bedroom the day we got home and I didn't discuss it with him. I stuck an extra pillow onto his empty side of the bed because the enormous space left between the wall and myself feels as if it may swallow me whole. Maybe he's seeing someone else. I wish he were seeing someone else. It would be easier if I could blame all of this on another woman, a young twenty-something with long legs and an ass of granite. But I know it's not an affair. His reasons for moving into the spare room are far more complicated and sad and I don't know how to chip away at this impenetrable wall between us. I'm starting to see that we didn't have the right tools to begin with. And if I were angry with him, if I were furious at his disconnection and gestures to shut me out, then maybe I could feel hope for us. But I'm not angry. I'm not bitter or furious or upset with him. I'm apathetic. I'm sad.

Most of all, I'm just tired. *And that makes me* scared.

Even So . . .

IT WAS AFTER FOUR IN the morning, and Judith was attempting to revive one of her violets. She bent over her potting table in the basement, an empty bag of soil at her feet. The florescent grow light hummed reassuringly along with the soft music playing from the stereo. She had not bothered to protect her hands with gardening gloves, and her skin was black from the knuckles down, dirt caked under her broken fingernails. She buried the roots of the struggling plant in fresh soil and tamped it down in a new ceramic pot, giving it liquid vitamins from a dropper. She had been unable to sleep, feeling restless and fidgety as if she had drunk too much coffee before bedtime. Peter had a chest cold, and she could hear his coughing and nose blowing every few minutes. The smell of his vaporizer bothered her, even a floor away. She hated the smell of menthol.

Judith removed her apron. She wiped her hands on a rag, brushing off the front of her pajamas with a clean towel. Reaching into her breast pocket, she plucked out a white capsule, a sleeping pill from her stash in the bedroom, and swallowed it dry. Most nights she tried to fall asleep on her own without them but usually gave up after suffering through a few late hours.

As she turned off the stereo, she heard the sound of Caroline's car, the familiar hollow rattle and sputter of a muffler about to fall off. She waited until all was quiet outside again, then switched off the lamp, leaving on only the ultrawhite warmth of the grow light.

As she stepped outside, her skin prickled in the December air. It had finally turned cold, but still no snowfall for the year. Judith crossed her arms over her chest for warmth and looked up at the starless sky, pregnant with clouds and the possibility of the year's first storm. She crossed the hardened ground to Caroline's car, which was parked crookedly and a good foot away from the curb. The windows were fogged over. Caroline greeted Judith with a hacking cough as she got in.

"Are you sick?" Judith asked.

Caroline nodded, wiping her nose with a tissue. "Head cold." Her voice was raspy. "I've had it since Thanksgiving. Turkey tasted like shit."

"Peter's sick, too. But he won't go to the doctor, so he'll probably end up with bronchitis."

Caroline opened a thermos that smelled of herbal tea. She then produced a travel-size bottle of whisky from her purse and added a couple of splashes to the tea. "Clears my sinuses," she said, then noticed Judith's hands. "Your fingers are dirty."

Judith looked down. "Oh. I tried to repot a plant. Say, how much of that have you already had tonight?" She knitted her brows together. "By the looks of your parking job, I would say more than enough to clear your sinuses."

"Spare me," Caroline rolled her eyes. She coughed and spat into her tissue. By the streetlight Judith could see that Caroline's tan was gone, faded to a sallow color. She had pulled her hair back into a sloppy bun and wore a tattered T-shirt over a pair of men's pajama pants with a paisley print that reminded Judith of her father on Sunday afternoons with the newspaper. Caroline's eyes were puffy and her movements slow, pained.

"You haven't been around for a while," Judith commented. "I wasn't sure if you were ever coming back."

"Well, here I am," Caroline said distractedly as she traced a hairline crack in the windshield. Her finger followed the jagged line down to where it met the dashboard. Judith had eventually made up her mind that Caroline was done with her for good, no more nighttime visits with her new life plans. Her own Thanksgiving had been misery. An uncomfortable dinner with Peter, Lindsey, Virginia, and Penny, noticeably lacking conversation over dry turkey and lumpy mashed potatoes that Judith had scorched in her rush to finish the dinner on time. She had overslept that morning, taking too many pills the night before, battling her old habit that hadn't reared its head since last spring. But at least she'd gotten through the holiday. One down.

"So," Judith pressed, craning her neck to look Caroline in the eye.

"So what?" she snapped.

"Never mind," Judith waved her hand. "You came here. So if you want to talk, then talk. I can't read your mind."

"What? What do you want me to say?" Caroline shrugged, spilling her tea on the seat between them. "Can't you guess? Can't you tell? I bottomed out after Thanksgiving. The holidays, you know, knocked me on my ass. Christmas just around the corner, and it all builds back up. I feel like I'm back to square one." Caroline closed her eyes and pressed the warm thermos to her forehead. "The last time I saw you, I had all these things I was going to do and—and who was I kidding? I was talking like an idiot. I'm nothing but a big jackass."

"You're not a jackass," Judith said quietly. "You were doing what you had to do to get by." She thought of the bottle of sleeping pills, hidden in her bedside table, her own heels dragging at the depressive thought of Christmas, digging in until the skin on her feet ripped open and bled.

"Even so," Caroline sighed. "I still feel like one." She looked out the window at the drops of ice-laced rain that were starting to dot the glass. She screwed the cap back on her thermos and tossed it into the back seat, drinking straight from the little whisky bottle.

"The foster care people turned me down," she said over the pecking sound of the falling sleet. "It's only been six months, they kept saying. Too fast; I still needed time to grieve. They felt sorry for me. It was humiliating. And Dan, he treated me like I'd gone crazy." She rolled the window down a few inches and stuck out her fingertips, letting the water run down to her wrist and the tiny crystals fill her palm. "I was so angry with him. We had this terrible fight, and I moved all of my things into the basement."

"What was the fight about?"

Caroline wiped her hand on her shirt and rolled the window back up. "Because he completely dismissed me. Because what I was saying was important to me, and he wouldn't listen." She lowered her head and sighed. "And I was mad because he was right. The foster care people were right. I was a fool. It was too soon."

"Ten months," Judith said. "Sometimes it feels like ten years. Sometimes ten days."

Caroline snorted. "My therapist said I was rushing myself through the grief process to avoid feeling the pain and doing the real work of healing. She billed at least three extra hours over that one."

"It's probably normal, what you did."

"God, listen to you," Caroline said. "So insightful. Maybe I should pay *you* for my therapy."

Judith laughed, but a fraudulent feeling passed over her as she listened to Caroline's honest self-examination. She had barely acknowledged an awareness of her own grief, bubbling just below the surface under her deliberate control. Like a boiling pot of water she could lift the lid off of for a split second to release the steam, just enough so it wouldn't spill over, scalding everything around it.

"I just . . ." Caroline twisted the bottle between her hands. "I just wanted to be done with it and move on, you know? To be through the worst of the pain and on the other side feeling good again. Guess I thought I could force myself to feel better. But who was I kidding, right?" Caroline offered a drink from her bottle.

"No, thanks," Judith shook her head. "I've managed not to catch Peter's cold, and I don't want yours."

Caroline sneezed and fished another tissue out of her purse. "I think I caught this one from sleeping on that cot in the basement. Well, I don't ever actually sleep anymore."

"If you agree with what Dan said, then why are you still in the basement?"

"I don't know," Caroline shrugged. "We don't know what to say to each other anymore."

Judith nodded. It occurred to her that she could tell Caroline about Peter's move into the guest room, about his transferring his clothes into the spare closet while she had been at an appointment with Lindsey and Dr. Haji, so that when she returned home and went to the closet to put her shoes away, she was met by a void that seemed to echo with hurt, angry accusations. She could tell Caroline that when Peter sat down to eat dinner that evening, she had said nothing. What good would it do, admitting this out loud? She and Peter had become separated by more than just a bedroom. Confessing this to Caroline wouldn't help or change anything.

"What did you first like about Dan when you met him?" Judith asked.

"His glasses," Caroline answered as she reclined her seat back and stared at the ceiling.

"His glasses?"

"Yeah. He had these little gold-framed spectacles that made him look so smart, like he had the answer to every question in the world. I found it wildly sexual."

Judith laughed.

"What about you and Peter?"

"Oh, gosh," Judith sighed and laid her seat down, even with Caroline's. "Well, he was good-looking, of course, but it was his attitude. The way he carried himself. He was so confident. I guess I thought he would have all the answers, too." Judith stared at the dome light above her head and reached up to touch the dingy felt liner. "And maybe I wouldn't have to come up with any on my own."

Caroline reached into the back seat for a sweater, pulling it across her chest as she nestled deeper into the seat with a yawn. Her eyelids drooped, and her voice sounded sleepy. "She would've been sixteen last month," she mumbled. "Sixteen years seems like such a tiny piece of my life, but yet it was my *whole* life."

A small chill crept over Judith's bare arms and legs. Steady drops of rain pelted the car, sliding like teardrops down the windows. She glanced over at Caroline and saw that she had dozed off, making small *phht* sounds between her parted lips. Judith sat quietly for a long time, listening to the tap of the rain and Caroline's steady breathing. She tugged the cardigan up to Caroline's chin and slipped the whisky bottle from her limp hand, cracking the window to pour out the remainder of the liquid. She stretched out in the seat, lulled by the sound of the rain and cozy air of the vehicle, her sleeping pill finally taking effect. She closed her eyes just as the sun started to come up, and she knew she should go back inside before Lindsey and Peter awoke. Even so, she and Caroline could sleep just for a while.

Defensive Wounds

PENNY WENT AHEAD OF JUDITH to open the door to Dr. Menlo's office as Judith took an easy step up the curb and rested for a moment, the pain in her abdomen subsiding to a mere ache once more.

"Watch the patch of ice, here," Penny warned, pointing to a glassy spot on the sidewalk.

Judith had awakened that morning to the worst pain of her life other than childbirth and phoned her gynecologist, who told her to come in immediately. She'd then called her sister out of a meeting to come pick her up. Peter was overseas until who knew when, hopping from one Asian country to another, introducing a new product or rubbing elbows with other important suits, or something along those lines. She tried his cell phone twice and hotel room once, with no answer, and finally decided to leave him a message after she'd seen the doctor.

Inside Dr. Menlo's office, Penny slid Judith's coat and purse off her shoulders, careful not to inflict more pain, and hung them on the rack next to her own. A perky receptionist greeted them, everything about her perfectly round—her eyes, face, and softball-shaped breasts under her shirt. Even her handwriting was symmetrical curls and circles.

"You must be Mrs. Elliott," she said.

"Yes, I called ahead," Judith panted, pressing her forearm over another shooting pain.

"I just need you to fill out an updated information sheet for our records, and the doctor will see you," the woman beamed.

"Here, I'll do it." Penny took the clipboard. She held out an arm to steady Judith, lowering herself into a chair.

"What's your social security number?" Penny asked.

"Just get out my wallet." Judith closed her eyes and leaned her head against the wall. "It's on my driver's license."

"Did you get hold of Peter?" Penny asked as she filled in lines and checked boxes.

"No."

"How about Virginia?"

"Yes. She picked Lindsey up and took her to her house."

"What's Peter's social security number?"

"I have no idea."

"Don't you have it written down somewhere?"

Judith exhaled irritably. "Isn't it on the old forms they've got filed away somewhere?"

Penny thumbed through the papers. "I don't see it. Is it printed on your checks or anything?"

"I don't have it!" Judith snapped.

"All right, for Christ's sake," Penny muttered. "Here, sign this." She handed the pen to Judith. Penny's cell phone rang, and she unclipped it from her belt to read the incoming number. "I have to take this," she said, stepping outside for privacy.

Judith shifted in her seat, trying to finish the last form but unable to concentrate through the pain. Penny had signed the wrong year at the top of the page and Judith scratched it out. It was January 8th. A new year, the other side of the Christmas holiday. Actually, there had been no holiday at all. Judith had been ill the weeks before and after Christmas, symptoms from the tumors, and had remained in bed under heavy painkillers most of that time. She found that she secretly welcomed the pain and illness, an excuse not to get out of bed and face the calendar, the happy shoppers crowding the malls, the colorful strands of lights in windows and along rooftops, twinkling, reminding, always reminding.

No one in the house had bothered to bring the tree up from the basement to assemble and decorate, or hang stockings over the fireplace, or string garland above doors and around the banisters, as Judith had done every previous Christmas. She hadn't taken over the kitchen with her stainless steel bowls and hand mixer to make tins of peanut clusters for the neighbors or plates of white fudge to hand out at AVS meetings. No blooming Christmas cacti trimmed with red velvet bows for Peter's coworkers or Lindsey's violin instructor. No greeting cards were sent out with smiling Elliott family members seated in front of the fireplace dressed in color-coordinated sweaters, and only a dozen or so snowmen greeting cards and yearly update letters had arrived in their mailbox those weeks between Thanksgiving and Christmas. A dismal feeling had descended over their household following November 27th, draining the rooms of light and fresh air, matching those first black months after Valentine's Day.

Judith glanced wearily at a young pregnant woman sitting across the room reading a fashion magazine propped up on her immense belly, the laces of her canvas tennis shoes missing to accommodate her swollen feet and ankles. Judith couldn't help but smile when the magazine quivered under the sudden movement of the woman's abdomen.

A small television set in the corner of the waiting room flickered, playing a local morning news show with the volume turned off. A tearful man and a woman holding what looked to be a school photo sat in front of a backdrop of downtown Akron. Judith sat up and leaned towards the set, squinting at the familiar faces, her heart rate quickening. *Karen and Dean Michaels.*

Judith struggled out of the chair and moved closer to the television, clutching the clipboard to her chest, and turned the volume up just loud enough for her to hear it. Her wallet slid from her lap, and she left it dumped open on the floor. The picture in Karen's hand was Matt's yearbook photo. He wore a red-and-white varsity football jersey—number twenty-one—and a broad, confident smile on his handsome face.

"He was a good boy," Karen was saying. Her skin appeared washed out under the harsh camera lights, and she spoke softly, barely audible even with the microphone clipped to her shirt.

"I taught him how to throw passes," Dean said. He put his arm around Karen and patted her shoulder with his oversized hand. "We always practiced in the back yard. Ever since he was a little kid."

"And where were you on the day of the shooting?" the female host asked. "What were you doing when you heard the news?"

"I was at work," Karen answered. "I went to the elementary school as soon as I heard it on TV. I called Dean, and he met me there. We were terrified, waiting for the buses to unload. One after another, and still no Matt. Finally, the last bus left, and Dean had to force me to go home. Later that night, someone from the sheriff's department came and told us."

"But we already knew by that point," Dean added.

"And now you are pursuing a civil lawsuit against the parents of Lucas Elliott, the student who committed the shootings?" The hostess knit her brows together as she flipped through a stack of white index cards.

"Yes," Dean nodded. "But it's not about the money. We feel like we owe it to Matt to do this. The Elliott boy never had to face justice for what he did, and we think the parents should take some responsibility."

"It's just so hard for us to understand how someone could do something like this," Karen said. "I still can't believe it even happened—" She covered her mouth with a shaking hand, too choked up to continue.

"The parents need to be accountable for what their boy did," Dean said. "This was cold-blooded murder, and our child senselessly lost his life at seventeen."

"Have you spoken with the Elliott family since the shooting on Valentine's Day?"

"No," Karen and Dean both shook their heads firmly.

"Nothing since that general statement they released to the press the day after the shootings," Dean continued, sounding bitter. "And now they've lawyered up, so we'll probably never get the answers we want."

"How could two parents have no idea that their own son was troubled enough to go on a murderous rampage?" Karen cried behind her tissue. "How? Where does that kind of evil come from?"

Judith blinked hard, sank back into the chair, and pressed her clenched fist to her mouth. She dropped the clipboard onto the end table next to her, where it bounced and clattered between the chair and the wall. The pregnant woman lowered her magazine and stared as the receptionist asked Judith if she needed a cup of water.

A rush of air preceded Penny as she hurried back into the office. She tucked her phone into her pocket and looked at her sister. "Judith," she said, gathering their belongings, the spilled wallet, the clipboard. "The nurse just called your name."

৵৩৯

JUDITH LAY ON THE HARD examination table, shivering in a stiff paper gown, her bare knees bent and clenched together. She stared up at the dotted squares of the ceiling until she lost all sense of distance and perspective and focus. Karen Michaels's words echoed in her head.

That kind of evil. That kind of evil.

She vaguely heard Dr. Menlo as he lifted her feet into the stirrups, explaining his every move while the nurse kept telling her to relax. She laid her hands over her flat belly, running her fingers along the faded, pocked lines zigzagging just above her pubic bone. Stretch marks, from her pregnancy with Lucas. She had carried him low, always feeling as if she might wet her pants when she sat down or laughed too hard. Peter had called the unborn baby String Cheese, after the food she craved most over those long nine months.

Dr. Menlo's voice was a distant drone. ". . . tumors have spread to the uterus . . . more aggressive treatments . . . high chance of surgery . . . possible hysterectomy . . ." He lowered her feet out of the stirrups and pulled a sheet up to her waist, then scribbled out another prescription as he talked.

That kind of evil.

"Just take it out," she interrupted, her voice sounding flat and defeated to her own ears. The doctor stopped writing and tried to hand her the prescription slip, but she waved it away.

"Just take it out."

She knew exactly where that kind of evil came from.

Under the Knife

"WAS THAT YOUR DAUGHTER?" THE nurse asked, pushing Judith in a wheelchair down corridors deep into the guts of the hospital. Judith watched the rectangular overhead lights pass by like the painted dashes of a highway.

"Yes. Lindsey. She stayed with me last night. And my sister," Judith answered, tugging the hospital gown discreetly over her knees. She wished someone had offered her an extra blanket for the ride.

"That's nice. Your girl looks just like you. Only taller," Terri smiled. "And she's so skinny!" Her small talk and holiday jewelry annoyed Judith. Even though Christmas was over, the nurse wore a pair of tiny red bell earrings that tinkled with every step and a mistletoe pin on her lapel that beeped the chorus of "Here Comes Santa Claus," which she'd triggered accidentally while helping the semidrugged Judith into the chair.

"Okay, this is your stop." Terri parked the chair behind a curtain, and Judith slid into an empty bed to await her turn in the operating room. A line of patients waited ahead of her, like an assembly line at a factory, running one by one down a conveyor belt.

"How long will it be until I go in?" she asked.

Terri adjusted the flat pillow behind Judith's back. "A little while yet. We're pretty busy today, as you can see."

Judith shut her eyes and turned her head away as Terri inserted a needle into her arm for an IV. "Just a little something to help you relax for now until the anesthesiologist comes by to speak with you." Judith's skin around the needle site burned with cold. A chill spread through her chest and down her arms as if she had broken through a thin layer of ice into the water below.

"I usually have a pretty strong reaction to anesthesia, so I don't need very much," Judith said, peeking at the needle taped down to the crook of her arm. "I get sick to my stomach really easy."

"This isn't anesthesia yet." Terri hung a plastic bag of clear liquid on a metal rack next to the bed. "It's the good stuff beforehand. Makes you all warm and fuzzy." She winked and walked away.

Judith smoothed the rough sheet and thin blanket out over her legs. She was still cold, shivering now, her nose running. She looked around at the other patients, some sleeping, some reading, the rest pensive and nervous, just as she was. Across from her, Christmas decorations were still taped to the wall—cutout snowmen and reindeer, red stockings overflowing with candy canes and presents, a red-cheeked Santa Claus hanging crookedly by his waving hand, his left side having come unstuck.

Soon it would be February, the date always looming so huge and loud and unavoidable no matter how much she tried to look away. She thought about what she had been doing one year ago on this day, the tenth day of January. She actually remembered— ordering furniture and shelving for the new sunroom. She had gone to the outdoor furniture store on that Monday, then purchased a new violin case for Lindsey, who had come home early from school with the flu, after she had dropped her old case and broken the handle on the way to the bus stop. Lucas had spent the night studying for an exam at Travis's house. Peter had surprised her with the tickets for their cruise with his work colleagues. The cruise they had never taken.

She had telephoned Peter last night, catching him in his hotel room at an odd hour with the time difference. He wouldn't make it home in time for the surgery—an afternoon meeting he just couldn't miss. He would catch a flight the following morning and be home the day after. Their conversation had been short and confusing due to a bad connection. Before hanging up amid static and loud crackling, Judith had thought she heard Peter say that he loved her.

"What?" she had yelled into the receiver. "What did you just say? Peter? I didn't hear you. What did you say?" But the line had gone dead. He'd already hung up. The possibility of his saying that he loved her, even if in a moment of guilt or homesickness, made her ache for him to come back and sit at her bedside through this. It had been so long since she'd heard those words. Too late now. Just one more bad connection between them.

Judith was getting dizzy, feeling the first twinges of nausea. She rolled onto her side and pulled her knees up close to her chest, tucking the cumbersome IV tube under the blanket with her. She could almost fall asleep, drop off into the murky confusion overtaking over her mind. She blinked, her lids weighty. Where was she again? Suddenly, she envisioned hazy people all around her, staring, accusing, demanding apologies and acknowledgments of guilt. Their faces came into swimming focus—Lynn Kranovich and her little twin daughters, matching red bows neatly tied in their hair. Karen and Dean Michaels, holding armfuls of photos as they wept angry tears. And there was Caroline, playing an invisible piano on the edge of the bed, Dan trying to pull her away, to make her stop.

Judith swallowed a sour lump in her throat and blinked to make the faces go away, but they were only replaced by more people, other parents of school shooters, welcoming her into the sad, shameful club in which they all had memberships. *We understand*, they mouthed to her. *We are all failures of the worst kind. Our children are murderers.*

Something brushed against Judith's arm and startled her. "Okay, we're ready," the nurse with the singing lapel pin said as she bent over and laid a hand on Judith's shoulder. "Are you all right?"

Judith tried to untangle herself from the blankets and IV tube. She wanted to flee the hospital and the city and the faces, to run away from her life. She didn't want to be Judith Elliott anymore. She wanted Judith Elliott to go back to the big, empty house on Culver Street to serve her prison sentence and leave her alone. "How did I let this happen?" she croaked, her throat closing.

"Oh, honey. Don't cry. This is a routine surgery. Dr. Menlo is one of the best surgeons around, and we'll take good care of you."

Judith grabbed for the metal side rails, the frayed edges of the blanket. She was going to throw up.

"Okay, okay," the nurse said, handing Judith a plastic vomit basin. "Just take a deep breath."

Judith cupped her hands over her heart, a steady *thump thump thump* against her palms. If only each night she could scoop it out, empty it of all the sorrow, guilt, and pain that filled it, *drip drip drip*, throughout the day. How much more would it hold? Not much more, surely. Maybe they could take her heart along with her uterus. Slice it out artery by artery, pull it away from the existing tissue until it was like a soft red tomato free of her body that she could place in a box and send to those little twin girls with a note that said, *Please. I've nothing else to give you.*

She was wheeled through a set of swinging doors into the operating room and hoisted onto a table. Dr. Menlo stood at her side as she shivered, trying to speak to him, but her voice failed. The anesthesiologist extended her arm onto a cold tray and prepared the mixture that would send her into oblivion. He seemed like a dark angel, just outside her line of vision. She turned to look at him, and he smiled reassuringly. With her free hand, she cradled her heart once more. A stinging tear slid down her cheek.

That kind of evil.

"We're ready, Judith," Dr. Menlo said. "Take a deep breath and count backwards from ten."

Wait, she tried to say. She wanted to talk to the faces, the sad, angry faces still staring at her over Dr. Menlo's shoulder.

"I'm sorry," she managed in a whisper. Just two tiny words. So simple, yet so much.

"Don't apologize," Dr. Menlo answered, thinking she was speaking to him. "Lots of people get nervous before surgery."

Thump. Thump. Thump.

"Just take it out," she murmured, drifting, drifting.

"Everything will be okay, Judith," someone said over her as the lights dimmed and swirled like cream spreading in a cup of coffee.

Ten, nine, eight . . .

✧✧

JUDITH AWOKE TO THE SOUND of women's laughter. She opened her eyes and licked her dry, cracked lips. She tugged at the neckline of her hospital gown, which had pulled tightly across her neck while she slept. The room was dark but for the glowing buttons on the IV machine. She tried to sit up, but the excruciating contraction of her tender abdominal muscles sent her back against the pillow, gasping for breath.

The laughter erupted again outside her room, and the slit of light under the door was interrupted by the shadows of two sets of feet moving back and forth. Now the door opened a crack.

"Okay, see you tomorrow, Tammy," a nurse called over her shoulder, and entered the room. Judith turned her head away from the harsh light of the hallway.

"Just checking vitals again," the nurse said, still smiling from the exchange with her friend moments before. "You look better today. We'll get you something to eat and maybe up and walking around a bit after breakfast."

"What time is it?" Judith asked, her voice hoarse. She groped for the control at her side and raised the head of the bed a few inches.

"A little after six AM" The nurse switched on a small overhead light and wrapped a blood pressure cuff around Judith's arm, pressing a cold stethoscope to her skin. She watched the gauge on the wall behind the bed and squeezed the pump until Judith's fingers tingled.

Reaching for a cup of water with her free hand, she was startled to see Peter curled up on a vinyl pullout chair, sound asleep. His suit jacket hung neatly on the back of the chair, and his suitcase and polished black shoes stood at attention in perfect alignment by the bathroom door. He stirred, drawing the bile green hospital blanket over his face to block out the light, uncovering his stockinged feet, toes twitching. His limbs spilled over the cramped chair, and, even asleep, he wore a look of discomfort.

"When did he get here?" Judith asked.

"I don't know. He was here when my shift started a few hours ago." The nurse removed the cuff and made some notes on Judith's chart. "You missed your daughter and sister. They left about a half hour ago."

"Breakfast sounds good. I'm starving," Judith said.

"I think I could round something up for you," the nurse said, winking as she left the room.

Judith turned on the television and flipped through the channels, stopping at a local weather report. More flowers had arrived at some point while she slept. A tasteful vase of lilies from her mother, a potted plant from Peter's boss, and a dozen yellow long-stemmed roses, no card but surely from Peter. She glanced through the reading material stacked on her bedside table—the morning newspaper, already dismantled and read by someone else, a current edition of *AVSA Magazine,* a mystery novel Lindsey had selected for her.

She picked up the book and found her journal underneath, a black pen stuck in the metal spiral binding. She opened the cover, running her fingers over the messy, hasty swirls and scribbles of her own handwriting. Words, thoughts, momentary pieces of herself she barely remembered writing down. Some of the pages were wrinkled with spilled drops of coffee and smudges of food, maybe pie filling or pizza sauce. She flipped back to the first page and counted the entries, fifty-two in all. The first entry, in purple ink, only one line. Another, in red ink, over eight pages long. Random items were hidden among the pages, stuck between her words: a sales receipt to a gardening store; a note from Lindsey's music teacher reminding Judith to please pay for her new lesson book; at the very back, a bookmark that Lucas had designed for her as a Mother's Day gift a few years ago. He had sketched in colored pencils a string of lavender violets around the border with *MOM* through the center in elegant calligraphy. She had stumbled across it while leafing through a book on flowers she planned to donate to her local AVS book drive. The marker had been stuck between pages eighty-eight and eighty-nine, long forgotten. Nearly lost forever in the inadvertent possession of a stranger.

Someone knocked on her door, two tentative, barely audible raps. "Come in," she called, restrained, trying not to wake Peter.

The door yawned open, a shaft of light preceding the visitor. Kristin Danforth stepped into the room, hesitant, peeking around a bouquet of carnations and two red heart-shaped balloons tied to the vase clutched in her hand.

"Mrs. Elliott?" She stopped just a few feet inside the room, a safe arm's length away from the door. "Um, I won't bother you or anything, but I seen your name on this delivery down at my mom's shop." Kristin paused for a gulp of air, and Judith realized she'd been holding her breath as well.

She cleared her throat and gestured to the ledge below the window. "Just put those over there, please."

Kristin nodded and walked to the window, her sneakers squeaking on the tiled floor. She wore only a sweatshirt and jeans, no coat, gloves, or hat, and the tips of her ears were red. She arranged the vase, turning the balloons forward so the 'Get Well Soon' printed across the front showed.

"Kind of early for a delivery," Judith commented.

'Oh, I . . . I know. I'm sorry. I was helping Mom close the shop yesterday and seen the order ticket. I wanted to bring it myself before school—"

"It's okay," Judith interrupted. "I'm glad you brought it."

Kristin's shoulders lowered, and she smiled with visible relief. "My mom didn't want me to come 'cause, you know, about last time. But I, like, really needed to tell you something."

Judith put a hand up to stop her from going any further. "Please. I need to say something first. I owe you an apology. I should never have said what I did to you that day." Her voice wavered, and she took a moment before continuing. "It was unfair, and I didn't mean it."

Kristin stared down at her hands as she picked her nails, unable to look at Judith. She bit into her bottom lip, fighting back small, convulsive sobs, then finally started to cry. She made tiny, kitten-like sounds, tears running down her face and smudging her mascara, a few drops clinging to the end of her nose before falling onto her white shoes.

"I didn't think he'd, like, take it so hard when we broke up," she cried. "I mean, I thought we were just having fun. I know this was my fault," she shook her head. "Right before Valentine's Day, he called me really late one night. He told me that he stole a gun from Travis McDonnell's dad and that he'd been practicing, learning how to shoot it. He goes, 'I'm gonna do something big, and Matt Michaels and his friends will regret ever messing with me.' But I, like, didn't take him serious or nothing. I just thought he was showing off or trying to scare me into getting back together or something." She crossed her arms over her chest and started to cry again. "If I had told somebody what he said, none of this would've ever happened. And I kept it a secret this whole time. I didn't even tell my mom or the police or anybody 'cause I knew everyone would blame me."

Judith felt suddenly cold, exposed, unprotected. Kristin also shivered, tucking her hands up inside her sleeves like a turtle's head retracting into its shell. She looked so young, fragile. A little girl. She *was* just a girl. Just a kid, careening through life with the carelessness of adolescence. Judith thought of herself as a teenager, pretty and aloof, unaware of her power with the opposite sex. She thought of boys she had dated, names and faces now fuzzy or lost completely, a few steady boyfriends whom she had loved, kissed, slept with, and broken up with—sometimes for valid reasons, sometimes no reason at all.

Like everyone else close to Lucas, Kristin was changed forever. Judith had denied this fact until now. She had not thought about other people beyond herself and Peter—friends, teachers, neighbors—who might blame themselves in some way for what happened, questioning lost moments, split seconds. *I should have, I should have . . .*

Judith was moved by Kristin's courage in facing her and owning what she believed was her responsibility. Judith thought of her own secrets, far heavier and more profound than what Kristin had been carrying, and her cowardice and shame about saying it out loud when Dr. Haji had questioned her.

"It wasn't your fault," Judith whispered. "No one blames you." She paused until Kristin looked directly at her. "I don't blame you."

Kristin wiped her face with the cuff of her shirt, leaving dark streaks across the white material. "Thank you," she said. "I guess I'd better get going. My mom's waiting for me." She gestured over her shoulder to the hallway and smiled. "I think she's been listening. Enjoy your flowers."

The door clicked shut and she was gone.

Judith struggled out of bed, pulling herself up by the rails with difficulty, and shuffled to the window. She turned the bouquet of carnations, searching for a card, but there was none. Looking out the window to the parking lot below, Kristin walked hand-in-hand with her mother, her back straight, ponytail swinging.

February 14

Today it has been one year.

I woke up at six-thirty this morning and it started. This obsessive thinking about what Lucas was doing at every passing minute exactly three hundred and sixty-five days ago. The breakfast table and the blueberry pancakes. Loading the dishwasher. That momentary pause in doorway, his eyes, his expression. Maybe he was trying to tell me something before he left. I can't stop thinking about what had been going through his head as he drove his sister to the middle school. Lindsey, the last person in our family to see him alive, told the sheriff that he was quiet. They listened to a Led Zeppelin CD. She said she dropped her violin case as she got out of the car so he helped her carry her books to the front door of the school. The last thing he said to her was, "Take care of yourself, Linds." She punched him in the shoulder and told him to piss off. She had thought he was making fun of her, teasing like older brothers do.

And what was I doing when he entered the high school? At 8:03 I was probably still reading the paper at the table with a cold cup of coffee. Or greeting Wanda? I remember that I sat for extra minutes that morning, enjoying the aftereffects of the pleasant meal our family had just shared. At that moment, I remember, I was happy. *Even now, I can't comprehend what Lucas was about to do as I sat on my ass in my bathrobe feeling* happy. *At nine o'clock, when second period English II began, I think I was writing in my planner, some stupid list like a thousand others I've written,*

thinking they were so important, so critical to get done. Worry
about my plants, the next show. At 9:40, I was in the shower while
Lucas was being excused from class so he could get a gun from the
backpack in his locker. As I washed my hair and shaved my legs,
he hid in a bathroom stall and loaded the gun with five bullets. And
why five? Why not only three—for Kristin, Matt Michaels and
himself? And why do I even wonder about that?

By the time he walked into Mr. Kranovich's classroom at 9:51 and
pulled the gun out of the back of his jeans to fire the first shot into
Matt Michael's forehead, I was probably standing at the mirror
brushing out my wet hair. Rubbing a little gel through the roots
when he turned and fired at the teacher, hitting him in the chest. Mr.
Kranovich had tried to stop him. Ed Kranovich, a husband and
father, but on that day, a teacher trying to save the other kids in his
classroom. As Kristin sat screaming in her seat, I plugged in my
hair dryer. And when Lucas shot the bullet that missed Kristin but
instead struck Hannah Myers in the throat, I was turning the dryer
on and flipping my hair upside down.

So, in the last seconds of my son's life, when he was still breathing
and blinking, when he was turning the gun on himself, putting the
barrel to his temple and pulling the trigger, I'm guessing I was blow
drying my hair. Fluffing and combing as my little boy splattered his
brains all over the same chalkboard on which Mr. Kranovich had
been outlining Macbeth *only minutes before. I keep thinking, did I*
feel something? Anything, at the very moment the gun discharged
into his skull? A jolt? A current or cold sensation that something
bad was happening to one of my children?

But I know there was nothing. I was simply blow drying my hair.

And I can't stop thinking about that chalkboard. Did someone take it down and replace it with a new one? Or did they just send the janitor in to scrub it clean? Who was sent to do the grim task of washing away my son's blood?

A minute and a half was all it lasted. Ninety seconds.

Peppermint Answers

IT HAD RAINED THAT WEDNESDAY, one week before the fateful Valentine's Day. Peter had overslept and was late for an early meeting, so the morning was rushed, frantic. In their disorganization, Lindsey had almost missed her ride to school. Judith had argued on the telephone with the builder about installing a sink in one corner of the sunroom, haggling over plumbing lines and drainage pipes. No one had noticed Lucas out in the garage, digging an old wooden baseball bat from his little league days out of the plastic chest stowed behind the mower.

Just after three in the afternoon, Judith had been assembling a new heat lamp for her violets, trying to ignore the banging and hammering of the construction crew when the telephone rang. The assistant principal from Roosevelt calling about Lucas. He'd gotten into some trouble. Could she please come down to his office? Judith checked her watch, annoyed by the interruption in her schedule. Lindsey's violin lesson ended at four, and she had an orthodontist appointment to get her retainer adjusted at four-thirty. Judith telephoned Peter, tracking him down through his secretary at a late lunch meeting downtown. A tense discussion ensued, who needed to be where with whom and by what time. It was finally decided that Peter would reschedule his afternoon appointment and go to the school to talk with the principal.

Judith went about her errands: chauffeuring Lindsey around, picking up dry cleaning and then Chinese take-out for dinner. She was surprised to find that Peter and Lucas weren't back by the time she got home, nearly six in the evening. She and Lindsey ate on the floor downstairs in front of the television, a treat not usually allowed during family mealtime. By seven, Judith was worried. She tried Peter's cell phone, but it was turned off. Finally, a quarter after, she heard the familiar grind of the garage door opening. She waited on the back steps, watching the car pull into the bay, rainwater dripping off the tires, steam rising from the warm, wet hood. Though the car was parked, Peter and Lucas remained seated inside. She could see that Peter was upset by his sharp body language—flailing hands, jerky head movements, a fist to the steering wheel. He opened the door, and at once his words echoed throughout the garage.

"And you'll pay to fix it with your own money."

"What happened?" Judith asked. She slipped on a cardigan and stepped down onto the bottom step, the cold seeping through her thin socks.

"I can't talk about it right now, I'm so pissed," Peter snapped.

Judith exhaled, exasperated. "Well, where have you been?"

"We've been down at the police station for two hours," he yelled. "Your son was charged with vandalism."

"Vandalism? Of what?"

"He smashed up some boy's windshield in the high school parking lot with a baseball bat." He waved his hands at Lucas, who remained in the car, shoulders concave and head drooping, his shaggy hair falling over his eyes.

"Whose car?"

"Some kid named Matt Michaels. His parents wanted to press charges," Peter snatched his briefcase from the back seat and slammed it on the roof. Lucas jumped at the noise.

"Matt Michaels," Judith repeated to herself, picturing Lucas and the bloody nose. *He's Kristin's new boyfriend . . .*

"I had to call Howard Pierce to come down to the police station and help us out. He got the charges dropped, and it won't go on his permanent record."

"What did the school say?"

"In-school suspension for two days starting tomorrow." Peter shook his trench coat out with two hard snaps before draping it over his forearm. "I don't know what's gotten into him. He refused to apologize to the boy's family. He copped a shitty attitude with everyone at the police station. How could he be so stupid? How could you be so stupid?" he repeated, leaning down into the car.

Lucas flung the passenger door open and kicked it shut, rocking the entire vehicle. He stalked towards the house with his jacket balled up under one arm.

"Where are you going?" Peter said. "We're not done talking about this."

Lucas ignored him and continued walking.

"I said come back here!"

"Fuck you," Lucas muttered under his breath.

"What did you just say?" Peter stepped around the car, his eyes widening. He reached out and put a hand on Lucas's shoulder, but Lucas slapped it away. Peter grabbed hold of his shirt collar, but Lucas spun around, dropping his bag, and shoved his father square in the shoulders. Caught off guard, Peter reeled backwards into the side of the car.

"Lucas!" Judith gasped.

Peter regained his footing and lurched towards Lucas, grabbing a fist full of his T-shirt and twisting it until Lucas's heels rose off the ground. "Don't you ever do that to me again!" Peter shouted, the ends of their noses mere inches apart.

"Peter! Let him go!" Judith threw her arms between their bodies to break them up.

"Fuck you!" Lucas yelled, his face contorting into tears. He hit at Peter's forearms with his small hands, weak swats that made futile slapping noises. Peter pushed him into a rack of tools hanging on the wall, lifting him higher until his toes brushed back and forth across the concrete. They knocked a snow shovel over, and it clattered to the floor.

"You don't talk to me like that!" Peter bellowed, purple veins bulging at his temples. Lucas kicked and struggled to break free, but Peter only held tighter, pressing his forearm across Lucas's chest and throat.

"Stop! Don't hurt him!" Judith cried, pounding on Peter's back.

"What's happening?" Lindsey called over the noise, frightened, confused, watching from the open doorway.

"Go to your room," Judith ordered, rushing up the stairs. She seized Lindsey's arm and tried to force her back into the house, but the girl clung to the doorframe.

"What's happening? What's happening!" she screamed. "Make them stop!"

Judith found herself rooted—unable to turn away, unable to watch, unable to shelter Lindsey or stop Peter and Lucas from hurting each other. This was a nightmare family, not her own.

"Go ahead and kill me," Lucas cried in a strangled voice. "I don't care."

Peter released him and staggered sideways, looking at his son as if he'd just seen him for the first time, just awakened to realize what he'd been doing. He clenched his eyes shut, chest heaving, and bent slightly with his hands on top of his knees. Lucas crumpled to the floor, holding his reddened throat and coughing, tears running down his cheeks. Minutes passed in the returned quiet of the garage, the four of them immobile, breathless, unblinking. Outside, the rain picked up and pounded against the roof, sheeting the windows, smearing the darkness outside.

Lucas jumped to his feet, grabbing the shovel from the floor. He hoisted and swung it with an animalistic roar at his father. Peter jumped sideways, the scoop of the shovel whistling past his head, inches from his scalp. It slammed into the windshield of the car, splintering the glass with a sickening crack. Judith and Lindsey screamed as Peter grabbed his chest like he was having a heart attack, stumbling onto the top of the lawn mower, staring open-mouthed at his son.

As if he had done nothing out of the ordinary, Lucas gently propped the shovel against the wall. He dusted off the seat of his jeans and retrieved his jacket from a puddle of water under the car, brushed his disheveled hair off his forehead with a trembling hand, and walked unsteadily past Judith into the house. Lindsey followed close behind him, separate bedroom doors slamming shut moments later.

Peter limped over to the steps and he sat down. The back of his white dress shirt was soiled and had come untucked. He examined a scrape on the underside of his arm for a few seconds, poking it with his finger, then dropped his face into his hands. Judith, still frozen in the doorway, watched his head sag as he was overcome with sobs, shoulders trembling as he rocked from side to side. The timed overhead light clicked off and their shadows converged into a long dark stretch across the floor, the broken glass of the windshield still crackling like a campfire.

She turned away and went back into the house, closing the door behind her.

DR. HAJI DID NOT WRITE as Judith recounted the night in the garage. She laid her pen down, removed her glasses, and closed Lindsey's chart. She looked Judith directly in the eye the entire time. No interruptions for questions or comments. She just listened.

Once Judith had reached the end of the story, she felt drained, her limbs heavy, her movements lethargic. And she was thirsty. She never remembered to bring a bottle of water with her to the appointments. After a moment, Dr. Haji went to her desk and produced a bag of wrapped peppermint candies from a drawer. She dumped it out into an empty crystal dish on the coffee table between them, gesturing to Judith as she helped herself to one. They sucked on the hard candy in silence before Dr. Haji finally slid her glasses back on.

"Did you ever speak with your son about what happened?" she asked.

Judith lowered her head. "No."

"Your husband or daughter?"

"No," she whispered.

"And how do you feel about that now?"

Judith removed the peppermint from her mouth and held it between her fingers, thinking for a moment. "I'm ashamed. It was the biggest mistake I've ever made. Doing nothing."

"How do you think your husband feels about it?"

The candy stuck to Judith's skin, leaving white and red splotches on her fingertips. "Ashamed, too, but he's also in denial. I don't think he can allow himself to go back to that night, the guilt of it. And so he's withdrawn from me and Lindsey."

"And how might all of this guilt and shame and denial be affecting Lindsey? This profound lack of communication within your family?"

Judith glanced at the door to the waiting area, imagining Lindsey sitting on the other side. "She takes it out on herself."

Judith closed her eyes and pictured Lucas's face as he had walked past her up the garage stairs going into the house. The expression of hopelessness. She had looked directly into his eyes and seen that he was no longer there.

"I did nothing," Judith said.

Unsaid

THE OFFICES OF EPSTEIN, BROWN, and Gilbert were plush with lustrous mahogany woods, buffed brass fixtures, tasteful art pieces. Judith and Peter followed Howard Pierce, three pairs of feet walking noiselessly on deep red-wine carpeting. They were all grim-faced, mentally preparing themselves for whatever would occur behind the doors of conference room number three.

As they entered, all chatter and private side conversations ceased. Karen and Dean Michaels looked up from a huddle with their lawyer, J.P. Epstein. Peter pulled one of the padded leather chairs out for Judith. Howard Pierce reached across the conference table to shake hands briskly with Mr. Epstein, and the men shared brief pleasantries, *Good morning . . . Chilly outside today . . . Weatherman said it might snow by next week*. A young paralegal buttoned his suit jacket and polished each lens of his glasses with a napkin, OHIO STATE emblazoned in gold across the front of his coffee mug.

Once Judith was settled into her seat between Peter and Howard, she surveyed the room with a growing sickness in the pit of her stomach. The Michaelses resumed their hushed conversation with Epstein as a court reporter took her seat and removed her cardigan, draping it across the back of her chair. Judith was freezing and wished she hadn't handed her coat over to the receptionist when they'd arrived. Both she and Peter had chosen understated clothing in dark colors, no jewelry or accessories other than their wedding bands. Judith glanced at

Peter, his posture straight, hands clasped and resting on the table in front of him. The fine hairs along the line of his forehead glistened with tiny beads of perspiration, and his cheeks were flushed. She wished he would remove his heavy suit jacket, loosen the knot in the tie at his throat.

A rumpled man banged through the double doors and slipped into a chair at the far end of the table. His shirt was wrinkled, and the handle of his briefcase broken so that he had to carry it tucked under one arm like a newspaper.

"Who's that?" Judith leaned over and whispered to Howard.

"Bill VanDeBerg. Attorney for the school district. He's just sitting in for this portion." Howard motioned for Peter's attention. "Once Judith is finished, they'll break for lunch, and then it'll be your turn."

"How long will all this take?" Peter asked, glancing at his watch as he removed it to reset the time, Judith knew, exactly seven minutes ahead of the clock on the adjacent wall.

"They like to get these things wrapped up before four," Howard said, mixing a splash of cream into his cup of coffee as Epstein stopped the receptionist and requested a glass of orange juice. Peter buckled the clasp of his watch, and Judith reached out her hand to place it over his, but when Mr. Epstein cleared his throat to signal the start, Peter pulled his hand away, tucking it under the table.

"Good morning, everyone," Epstein said after coughing into a handkerchief taken from his trouser pocket. The tip of his nose was bright red, and he sounded congested. "I trust everyone is

settled and comfortable. That said, I think we'll just get started."
He smiled across the table at Judith, opening his notebook. The
court reporter poised her hands, ready to type. Judith scooted to
the edge of her chair and leaned forward, straightening the hem
of her skirt.

"Mrs. Elliott, my name is J.P. Epstein, and I'll be taking your
deposition. Have you ever been deposed before?"

Judith shook her head. "No." Her gut tightened and she felt a
sudden hard urge to urinate, as if she might wet her pants if she
tried to stand.

"During the deposition, I'll ask you questions, and my
questions and your answers will be recorded by our court
reporter, Ms. Curzio over there. Do you understand that you
need to speak up, to answer orally in giving your answers so that
Ms. Curzio can hear you clearly? She won't be able to record a
nod or shake of your head."

Despite herself, Judith nodded mutely and then blushed. "Oh,
yes, I understand."

"Every now and then I may ask a question that isn't very clear
or for some reason you don't understand. If this happens, don't
answer. It's my job to ask understandable questions, so I'll clarify
myself if you don't understand. Okay?" Epstein smiled and blew
his nose into the handkerchief, a loud, honking sound.

"Okay," Judith answered. She glanced at the Michaelses from
the corner of her eye, but they were watching Epstein.

"I also want you to understand," Epstein continued, "that if
you need a break at any time, for any reason, just let me or Mr.

Pierce know. We'll finish your answer if you're in the middle of one and then see about the break. We're all aware of the difficult and painful subject we're about to discuss, so we'll take this slowly and gently. Okay?"

"Okay, thank you," Judith said.

Dean Michaels reached an arm out then and put it around Karen, sliding her chair closer to his.

"We've got water and coffee set out." Epstein gestured to a buffet table along the wall. "So feel free to get up and get whatever you want during the deposition. Okay?"

"Thank you."

"I'm sure Mr. Pierce has already informed you, but let me reiterate. If you want or need to speak with him at any time, please finish your answer if you're in the middle of one, and then you can speak with him. Okay?"

Judith nodded again. "Sorry. Yes. Okay."

Epstein continued with his explanation, and Judith was sworn in. The first questions were general ones about her background. Age, address, occupation, education, and so on. In her nervousness, Judith rushed through her replies, stumbling over the words. By the time Mr. Epstein finished with the preliminary questions, she was amazed to see that barely forty-five minutes had passed. She already felt exhausted.

"Now, Mrs. Elliott, how long have you and your husband lived in Fairlawn?"

"About a year and half."

"And you had two children, correct?"

"Yes."

"A son, Lucas, age sixteen at the time of his death, and a daughter, Lindsey, now age fourteen?"

"Yes." Judith felt her voice weaken, her speech growing slower at the mention of Lucas's name.

"Now, Mrs. Elliott, it was your son, Lucas, who was the gunman during the shooting at Roosevelt High, February fourteenth of last year, and who then took his own life. Correct?" Epstein softened his voice and took his time getting through the question, watching Judith's face as he laid out each word.

"Yes." She stared up at the ceiling, into the bright fluorescent lights, to blink back fresh tears.

"I'd like to backtrack a bit here. Now, when your family moved to Fairlawn twenty-one months ago, did your son react negatively or positively to the move and subsequent change in schools?"

"Um, positive, I guess. He didn't seem to mind too much."

"Did he have many friends at his previous school?"

"A few from his grade."

"Did he make many new friends at Roosevelt?"

"Uh, one good friend. Travis McDonnell."

"Would you have described your son as a loner?"

Judith knitted her brows together. "Loner?"

"Yes, isolated, antisocial, withdrawn?"

"No," she said quickly. "More like rejected or not included by his peers."

"Okay, but still not highly social or outgoing?"

"No. I suppose not."

"Was he involved in any extracurricular activities?"

"No."

"Sports, clubs, part-time job?"

"No. He liked to spend time on his own, painting or drawing."

"How did he get along with his teachers? Good, fair, or poor?"

"Fair, I guess. They never raised any concerns to us."

"Any discipline problems at his former schools?"

"No."

"Problems with peers at former schools?"

"There was a boy in our old neighborhood. We had some problems with bullying."

"And how did you manage those problems?"

"We talked with the bus driver, the principal, the boy's mother, but it never seemed to help."

"Did you try anything like counseling or therapy, mediation?"

"No."

"And how about when he enrolled at Roosevelt. Any problems there prior to February fourteenth?"

Judith glanced at Howard, but he only nodded at her to answer the question and went back to taking notes on his legal pad.

"There were some problems," she said.

Epstein flipped through a stapled stack of papers. "School records indicate there was a physical confrontation on January thirtieth between Lucas and Matt Michaels, for which Lucas received morning detention for initiating the fight. Correct?"

"Yes." Judith recalled the red drops of blood across the kitchen floor.

"And then there was a February second incident in which Lucas smashed the windshield of Matt Michaels's car in the high school parking lot, correct?"

"Yes."

Howard set his pen down and stared at Epstein, listening closely.

"Were the local authorities involved?"

"Yes."

"And your son was taken to the police station?"

"Yes."

"But no charges were filed?"

"No."

"Karen and Dean Michaels agreed to drop the criminal charges and just accept payment for the broken windshield, correct?"

"Yes."

"And your husband had stated that if the charges were dropped, you and he would deal accordingly with your son, take care of it yourselves, correct?"

Howard raised his pen. "Objection. Mrs. Elliott was not present at the police station during this conversation."

Epstein dismissively waved his hand at Howard, and Judith looked back and forth between the two men, unsure whether she should answer. She felt Karen Michaels staring at her now, her eyes boring into Judith's face.

Epstein moved on. "Now, Lucas had previously dated a girl from his grade, named Kristin Danforth, correct?"

"Yes."

"To your knowledge, was this his first serious girlfriend?"

"To my knowledge, yes."

"And how long did they date?"

Judith sighed and did a quick mental calculation. "From about October to the beginning of January."

"And she was the one who broke the relationship off?"

"Yes."

"And then began dating Matt Michaels?"

"That's the way I understood it, yes."

"Did your son seem to take the break-up hard?"

Judith hesitated and shifted her eyes to Mr. VanDeBerg at the end of the table, hunched over and scribbling on his notebook. "Yes, I would say he did."

"Did he seem depressed?"

I don't want anyone but her. Ever. Judith nodded and pressed her fingertips to her upper lip.

"Please answer orally, Mrs. Elliott," Epstein gently reminded her.

"Yes," she said. "He seemed depressed."

Epstein sneezed three times and wiped his nose. "Excuse me, I apologize. Did you try to speak with Lucas about this depression or his feelings over the break-up?"

"Well, you see, I, I thought that—"

"Mrs. Elliott," he said, sounding reluctant to interrupt her. "Please. Yes or no answers will be sufficient."

Judith pushed her finger harder into the chapped skin of her lip. "No," she whispered. "I didn't try to talk to him."

"How about after the windshield incident?"

More tears stung the corners of Judith's eyes. They blurred her vision as her chin trembled, the exact display of emotions Howard had tried to preempt with hours of coaching and practice sessions. She thought of the recent appointment with Dr. Haji, finally confessing everything that had happened after the broken windshield. She prayed that J.P. Epstein didn't somehow know about that night in the garage and ask her about it, press her to discuss it with Peter sitting just inches away.

"No," she whispered again, aware that the court reporter was straining to hear her answers.

"Did you seek out any psychiatric counseling for him, talk with the school guidance counselor, or take him to your family doctor?"

"No," she shook her head, and a line of tears broke free, spilling down her face.

Epstein took a deep breath and rubbed his head, appearing almost as if he dreaded what he was doing. "Were you aware that he had been drawing and painting violent images in the weeks before the shootings?"

"No."

"Did you ever look at the artwork he brought home from school or kept in his bedroom?"

"No."

"Were you well acquainted with his friend, Travis McDonnell, the boy he obtained the gun from?"

"No."

"How about Travis's parents?"

"No," Judith reached for a tissue from the box resting in the center of the table. She saw that Karen Michaels had also begun to cry, silently, with her head bent down as Dean rubbed the back of her neck.

"Is it true that when you were first interviewed by the Summit County Sheriff's Department following the shooting, you told them that you didn't even know Travis's last name or where he lived?"

"Well, we, I didn't say I never knew his last name, but I couldn't remember it."

"But you didn't know his address? Correct?"

"Objection," Howard said. "It would not be reasonable to expect her to recall someone else's street address after she had just been given devastating news about her son."

"But it is reasonable to expect that she or her husband would have had a last name and address written down somewhere in their home, or at least a telephone number. Isn't it true, Mrs. Elliott, that even though your son had spent an entire weekend at the McDonnell home unsupervised by adults, just two weeks prior to the shooting, you did not have an address or phone number for the McDonnell family?"

Judith looked helplessly at Howard as he gestured for her to answer. She then looked to Peter on her opposite side, but he only stared down at his hands, his jaw set in a clenched line as if he might crack his own teeth.

"No, we did not have an address or phone number," she finally answered.

"And didn't your son gain access to the gun he used on February fourteenth during the weekend he was unsupervised at the McDonnell home?"

"Yes," Judith said, teardrops falling from her chin onto the lapel of her jacket.

"And you were unaware he had been target practicing behind the McDonnell house during the course of that unsupervised weekend? Practicing with the very gun he stole from the McDonnell residence and used on February fourteenth?"

"Yes."

"Do you need a break?" Howard whispered to her. "We can take a break."

Judith shook her head. "No, no. I'm fine."

Epstein paused to offer a tissue to Karen and then another to Judith before continuing. "Mrs. Elliott, did you see and speak to your son the morning of the shootings?"

"Yes."

"Did you notice any changes in his behavior or demeanor? Anything out of the ordinary?"

The blue backpack flashed through her mind, the smell of the blueberry pancake batter as she'd poured it into the skillet. "Yes," she said.

"What did you note as different about him?" Epstein made small quotation marks in the air with his fingers as he said "different."

Judith paused, knowing the weight of her answer. "He was calm," she said.

"Calm?"

"Yes. Looking back, he seemed calm." She paused, choking up again. "Like he was at peace."

"What did the two of you talk about?"

"Nothing, really. Just, you know, breakfast food and dishes and he asked me about nicknames and then he wished me a happy Valentine's Day and was out the door. And then that was it." Her mouth trembled again and she wiped her nose with the tissue.

"Mrs. Elliott—"

"They made him miserable!" Judith cried out. "Matt and all his friends. They never gave him a moment's peace! Lucas never had a chance!"

"How dare you!" Dean Michaels slapped the table with his hands and jumped to his feet.

"Judith, don't do this!" Howard hissed under his breath, and put a firm hand on her arm, but she jerked it out of his grasp.

"The name calling and taunting and getting pushed around," she continued, pent-up words that she had vowed never to speak out loud tumbling forth. "The humiliation he had to face every single day he walked through those doors—"

"You've got some nerve, lady!" Dean pointed a shaking finger across the table. Karen Michaels covered her face with her hands and burst into sobs that rocked her entire body.

"I insist we take a break," Howard said, pushing his chair back. Peter shrank away from Judith and the table and everything around him. He lowered his head into his hands, cupping his temples as if he wanted to plug his ears with his fingers.

"I'm sorry. Please, I'm sorry!" Judith put her hands to her chest and tried to take a calming breath. "I didn't mean to say that. I, I didn't mean to imply . . ."

Karen reached up and tugged at Dean's sleeve, quietly begging him to sit down. He finally unclenched his fists and returned to his seat but gripped the armrests until his knuckles turned white. J.P. Epstein's posture was tense, his watery eyes darting from Judith to his clients as if he were prepared to bolt from the room the second the situation turned physical.

Judith looked directly at Dean. "I'm sorry," she repeated. "I didn't mean to imply any blame. No matter what went on between Lucas and Matt, I will never justify what my son did." She scooted to the edge of her chair and sat up straighter. "I know my last words to him were nothing of importance. Please, believe me when I tell you that I have replayed that morning over and over in my head a thousand times. That second when he hesitated in the doorway before leaving, like he wanted to tell me something but then changed his mind, and if I had stopped him and asked, even once, if there was something he wanted to talk to me about, then maybe four people would still be alive today and none of us would be sitting here right now."

"Mrs. Elliott," Epstein said. "I completely understand the profound difficulty of this but we—"

"No, you don't understand, Mr. Epstein, you don't understand at all."

She turned to face Karen as she spoke, her voice thick and painful in her throat. "Yes, there were moments. I, I know that's what you want me to say, that there were moments Peter or I sensed something was wrong, knew something was wrong and didn't act on it. Yes, we squandered . . . we squandered opportunities to do more, to help him. And I think about those moments all the time, replaying them in my head over and over until I could go crazy." Her voice broke as she stared across the table at Karen, pleading with her eyes, her hand stretched desperately out in front of her. "I don't know how I'll ever find a way to live with it," she whispered. "It will haunt me until the day I die."

Howard shifted in his seat as Mr. Epstein shook his head, trying to compose himself and regain control of the situation. "Mrs. Elliott, I really—"

"Stop," Karen said loudly, startling everyone in the room. She lowered her hands from her face and wiped her eyes.

Mr. Epstein turned to look at her. "Excuse me?" he said, confusion clouding his face.

"Stop," Karen repeated, finally looking Judith in the eye. "Enough. Just leave her alone."

"Mrs. Michaels, I highly advise against this," Epstein sputtered as Dean tried to pull Karen close to him, instructing her under his breath to stay quiet.

Karen brushed both men off and stood, gathering her purse and jacket. "I said let her go."

✍✓✎

WITHIN TWO DAYS, JUDITH AND Peter each received a single-page letter informing them that the suit against them had been dropped at the request of Karen and Dean Michaels, signed, J.P. Epstein and Associates. That same morning, while Peter was at work, with the letter folded and tucked in her back pocket, Judith telephoned a dozen different contractors until she found one willing to come to their house and tear down what was left of the sun porch. She wanted it done by the end of the day and offered to pay triple their normal asking price. A crew of eight men was at her front door within the hour.

They went at the skeletal remains with sledgehammers and saws, tossing the rotten boards into the back of a pickup truck. Judith and Lindsey watched, standing in the middle of the kitchen, as the planks of wood were shattered with hammers and torn away by crowbars—nails and wood chips flying as fine dust and grime drifted over counter tops and cabinets, until every last bit of the framing was demolished, then hauled away. The plastic sheeting was pulled down and the original sliding glass doors replaced, then finished off with sheetrock mud and trim. Judith wrote a check and sent the crew on their way before dinnertime.

When Peter came home, he clattered into the garage and through the kitchen with his usual oblivious distraction, hanging up his coat and keys and dropping a pile of mail on the counter. He was sorting through his briefcase at the kitchen table when Judith quietly entered the room, sizing him up, the refurbished wall and deck doors just a few feet away from him, still unnoticed.

"Hi," she said, and he looked up from the paper in his hand, startled by her voice.

"Oh, hi. I didn't see you."

"How was work?"

"Fine." He went back to his reading.

"Did you eat?"

"I had a late meeting, so I just grabbed a sandwich on the way home."

"This came today." She handed him his copy of the letter from J.P. Epstein. He unfolded it and read quickly, his eyes sliding back and forth over the page, his expression blank.

"Okay, then," he sighed, slipping the letter into the breast pocket of his jacket. He loosened his tie and slid it over his head. "Now that's behind us."

Judith nodded. She watched him move to the liquor cabinet, open a bottle of merlot, pour it into the last remaining glass from their Riedel stemware collection. He sipped the wine as he opened the mail, tearing up advertisements and solicitations.

"Did you notice?" Judith finally said, moving towards the wall.

"What?" he said and looked up at her. "Oh. When did—"

"Today." She ran her hand over the damp spackling. "It needs painting, but I think it looks good."

Peter stared at the doors, at his reflection in the glass Judith had wiped and polished just minutes before. He blinked, stepping closer to the glass as if expecting the reflection to speak. Judith waited for words, something, anything about the porch— why didn't she discuss it with him first, how much did it cost, who did she hire—but he only took a long drink of wine, then turned away. His attention went back to the mail, his briefcase, organizing piles of paper across the table. Picking up the remote, he switched on the small countertop television and flipped through the channels until finding the local news.

Judith went to the TV and shut it off. "Peter."

He dropped the remote onto the table. "What?" he said, and shrugged his shoulders.

"What do you think about the suit being dropped?"

"I already said. It's good. We can get on with our lives."

Judith sat down in a chair at the table and toyed with the gold fountain pen Peter had removed from his coat pocket. "I'm glad you think so. We need to talk about that."

"Okay," he said.

"We need to make some concrete decisions about Lindsey and school. She's been working with a tutor now for a year. I think she needs to get back into regular classes with other kids."

"I agree."

Judith took a deep breath. "But not at Roosevelt. Not in Fairlawn."

Peter crossed his arms over his chest. "What are you saying? You want to move?"

"Yes."

"Where?"

"There's a music school in Philadelphia she's really interested in. It's a good school, a respected school for some of the most talented kids in the country. Her music teacher is convinced she's good enough to get in. A fresh start in a new city might be what she needs."

"Philadelphia?"

"Look, you and I both know deep down there is no way we can ever send her back to the school where, where . . ." Judith couldn't bring herself to finish the sentence.

"So, Philadelphia? That's your solution?"

"She wants to go."

He reached out and gripped the back of a chair. "If not Roosevelt, then we'll find a school somewhere else in Akron. We don't have to move to another state."

Judith sighed and rubbed her forehead. "Peter, moving is not just for her. We all need a new start. Someplace where everyone doesn't know who we are. We could get into some family counseling with a good therapist. Dr. Haji said she could recommend—"

"Dr. Haji," Peter interrupted. "This was her idea?"

"No," Judith shook her head, frustrated. "No. This is what Lindsey wants. This is what I want."

"But who gives a shit about what I want, right?"

"I never said that. Of course I care about what you think. This is why we're talking."

He pushed off the chair and picked up his wine glass, turning his back to her as he paced the floor. "You're just giving up and running away. Well, I refuse to be driven out of town like some fugitive from the law. *I'm* not the one who did it."

"It's not running away," Judith grimaced. "Jesus, Peter, I'm trying to find a way to save our family!"

"Great," he spat. "This is your best idea. Uproot us. Move. New city, new house, new school. And for me, new job. Just fuck it, right? He can find a new career at this stage of his life, no problem."

"Peter, Lindsey needs help. She needs something drastic. For Christ's sake, we all need help."

"Look!" he shouted, so loud she jumped. "Look," he repeated in a softer tone. "I'm not moving. I'm not dumping a career I've worked for my whole life as some kind of self-inflicted punishment. I need some things to stay the same."

Judith closed her eyes and held a deep breath, desperately running lines of dialogue through her head, some magic phrasing to make him understand. "Please," she pleaded with him. "Lindsey can't stay here. I can't stay here. The constant reminders will kill us both." Judith lowered her head. "We have to go, whether or not you come with us."

Peter slumped into a chair, his body collapsing, muscles gone slack and useless. Judith moved next to him and knelt on the floor, laying her hands on his knees. "We need to help each other," she whispered. "Please, come with us."

He reached out to set the wineglass on the table. As he did so, the delicate stem snapped in half, red merlot spilling over his papers, seeping under his briefcase. Shoving Judith aside, he grabbed a handful of napkins, frantically sopping up the wine. But his papers had already turned crimson, the ink smearing. He held up his hands and stared at his palms, fingers spread wide and covered with a red stickiness.

"I didn't do this to my son," he wept. "I didn't do this. I didn't do this. I loved him. I didn't do this." He rubbed the wine off his hands onto his shirt, slacks, anything he could reach.

"Oh, Peter." Judith tried to pull him to her, to caress his face with her hands.

He pushed her away. "You see? You see? It wasn't all my fault. You did things, too. You kept secrets. It wasn't just me."

"Please, don't do this," Judith begged. "Come with us. Don't stay here alone. We'll get some help."

"Just go," he said, rising to look again through the glass doors, leaving Judith still on her knees, embracing an empty chair. "Please go," he whispered to his reflection.

Judith left the room, backing away from her husband as he leaned his head against the cold windowpane and sobbed.

LINDSEY'S BEDROOM WAS DARK, QUIET. She was lying on her side in a tight ball, the comforter pulled up to her ears when Judith entered.

"Lindsey?" Judith lowered herself onto the side of the mattress. "You awake?"

"Yes."

"Can I sit here for a minute?"

"I heard you two downstairs," she said, her voice muffled under the covers.

Judith ran her hand over Lindsey's tangled hair, easing her fingers through it until each snag was worked out and the silky strands fanned themselves across the pillow.

"Are we going to move now?" Lindsey finally asked.

"I think we can do anything we want," Judith answered, sliding under the covers with her daughter to sleep for the night.

Save Me

CAROLINE SAT BEHIND THE WHEEL of a shiny black convertible with the top down. She tapped her fingers on the dashboard to the beat of the music playing on the radio. "You like?" she asked, stroking the polished gearshift with her gloved hand. Her nose and cheeks were bright pink from the cool spring air. A colorful knit hat was tugged down over her ears.

"Nice," Judith said with a smile, easing into the leather seats. "What's the occasion?"

"Decided it was time to trade up. Do something nice for myself for a change." She offered a cigarette from her crumpled pack, but Judith shook her head.

"I know, I know. I need to quit," Caroline said from the side of her mouth as she lit one dangling between her pursed lips. "Next week. I'm getting hypnotized. That's how my mother kicked it ten years ago."

She poured Judith a steaming cup of coffee from her thermos. "I heard the lawsuit was withdrawn," Caroline said, tossing the last of her coffee into the street. "Must be a relief."

"I suppose," Judith said.

"So, what's with the sign?" she gestured to the metal For Sale sign stuck in the grass of the front yard with paper flyers rolled into a plastic canister attached at the base.

"We're moving. Me and Lindsey." Judith carefully sipped the hot liquid in her cup but still managed to burn the tip of her tongue.

"You and Lindsey," Caroline repeated.

Judith nodded, looking up at the dark windows of the house. She thought of the brown boxes stacked in the corner of the bedroom and in the hallway. Boxes she had unpacked less than two years ago. "Just me and Lindsey. Peter's staying in Akron. We're separating."

"Jesus," Caroline breathed. "I'm sorry."

Judith could hardly believe the words coming from her own mouth. Peter had already moved into an apartment across town and was looking at buying a condo as soon as the house sold. His closet had been bare for almost a week, dresser drawers hollow, and the bathroom stripped of all his shaving creams and cologne.

"Where are you going?"

"Pennsylvania," Judith said. "We'll establish residency so Lindsey can enroll in the Philadelphia High School for Creative and Performing Arts in the fall."

"Wow," Caroline sighed. "Alone in a new city."

"Yeah," Judith said, considering the weight of Caroline's observation. "She's ready for a new start. I'm ready."

"What will you do there?"

Judith thought about this for a long time. "Take care of my daughter," she finally answered.

"And Peter?"

Judith shrugged. "He's chosen to find his way alone."

"Well, I think we should do something to mark the moment," Caroline said, starting the engine. "Grab a hat and blanket from the back seat, sweetheart. We're going for a ride."

THE STREETS WERE EMPTY, THE houses in hibernation the same as their occupants. Judith burrowed under a wool blanket and wiped her running nose on a bright purple scarf Caroline had provided from that bottomless bag she always carried. Judith's stocking hat threatened to blow off once they hit open highway, and she pulled it down to her eyebrows. Caroline appeared unaffected by the chilly wind. She continued to smile, cranking the radio up over the howling noise.

They traveled east outside of town until they reached the Highway 14 bridge across Lake Rockwell. Caroline stopped at the center of the bridge, parking close to the rails. They were unable to see the water through the darkness but could hear the gentle lapping of waves against the wind. Their puffs of breath mingled with a light, wet snow that had begun to fall.

"I can breathe out here," Caroline whispered. "The cold in my lungs reminds me I'm alive."

Judith sucked in a deep breath, enough to send a satisfying streak of mild pain through her chest. "I thought it was spring," she laughed, holding her gloved hand up to catch the lazy, drifting flakes. "My tulips are already blooming."

"I have something to show you." Caroline rummaged through her corduroy bag and extracted a packet of photos. "I finally developed the last roll of film in my camera."

She flipped through the glossy stack, choosing one particular picture from the middle and handing it over to Judith. "Look at this one," she said, holding it under the weak light from the dash. "It's from last year's winter concert."

Judith squinted, recognizing Hannah in the forefront, seated at a piano on a stage, her back straight and hands poised above the keys, her long hair in a neatly braided ponytail. As Judith leaned closer to study the picture, she saw Lindsey's face, just over Hannah's shoulder, in the string section to the right, chin pressed to her violin, the bow a blur of movement. Both girls mirrored the same expression of concentration.

"How about that," Judith breathed. "I remember that concert. Hannah played a solo."

"Yeah. She was great." Caroline stroked another picture from the stack—Hannah posed in a pleated dress in front of her piano at home. "I'm starting to lose the particular lines of her face," she whispered. "That's what I hate most now, losing my grip on memories, clear pictures of her in my mind."

"The sound of his voice," Judith added, brushing the fine layer of white crystals off the dash. "Or his laugh."

Caroline, in turn, wiped the steering wheel clean. "You know, I keep thinking that if I'm strong, if I stop grieving for her and move on, so will everyone else. She'll be forgotten."

"Maybe that would be good for us," Judith said. "If Lucas were forgotten." She held up the photo of Hannah and Lindsey. "Can I keep this?"

Caroline nodded. "I printed doubles." She tilted her seat back.

Judith tucked the picture inside her shirt and reclined her seat next to Caroline's.

"New cars, new cities, new houses," Caroline said, blinking away flakes of snow that stuck to her lashes.

"Yeah," Judith said.

"This," Caroline whispered.

"What?"

"This is life. Getting on with it, isn't it?"

৵৻৵

SHE PARKED IN FRONT OF the house to let Judith out, the same spot at the curb where she'd always parked, where they'd sat together so many times before.

"Well," Caroline said. "Take care of yourself."

"Yeah. You, too." Judith opened the door and hesitated next to the car. She reached into her coat pocket, her fingers closing around the block of wood, the splintery grain rough against her skin. While packing and cleaning out her side of the closet, she'd come across it, stuck between two sweaters on a shelf, forgotten. The sight of the words again and their possible meaning were so very changed, reading the passage on this side of Valentine's Day. Now she knew it had been Lucas who had carved the words and hidden it in the wall. Another plea he'd sent into the universe, gone unnoticed and misunderstood. Like so many others.

Judith had again looked up the passage in the Bible, Psalms 69—now translatable as thoughts and feelings directly from Lucas, a transmission from her son's grave, something he'd been unable to articulate during his life. Reading the thirty-six verses, she understood that the wood had never been intended as a cry for help. In the end, it was the most unexpected source, religious scripture of all things, to provide him the words to describe what had painfully carved out his insides, words that he bent and applied to mean exactly what he wanted.

Save me, O God!
For the waters have come up to my neck.
I sink in deep mire, where there is no foothold;
I have come into deep waters, and the flood sweeps over me.
I am weary with my crying; my throat is parched.
My eyes grow dim with waiting for my God.

More in number than the hairs of my head
are those who hate me without cause;
mighty are those who would destroy me,
those who attack me with lies.
What I did not steal must I now restore?
O God, thou knowest my folly;
the hidden wrongs I have done are not hidden from thee.

Let not those who hope in thee be
put to shame through me, O Lord God of hosts;
let not those who seek thee be
brought to dishonor through me, O God of Israel.
For it is for thy sake that I have borne reproach,
that shame has covered my face.

I have become a stranger to my brethren,
an alien to my mother's sons.

For zeal for thy house has consumed me,
and the insults of those who insult
thee have fallen on me.
When I humbled my soul with fasting,
it became my reproach.
When I made sackcloth my clothing,
I became a byword to them.
I am the talk of those who sit in the gate,
and the drunkards make songs about me.

But as for me, my prayer is to thee, O Lord.
At an acceptable time, O God,
in the abundance of thy steadfast love answer me.
With thy faithful help rescue me from sinking in the mire;
let me be delivered from my enemies
and from the deep waters.
Let not the flood sweep over me,
or the deep swallow me up,
or the pit close its mouth over me.

Answer me, O Lord, for thy steadfast love is good;
according to thy abundant mercy, turn to me.
Hide not thy face from thy servant;
for I am in distress, make haste to answer me.

Draw near to me, redeem me,

set me free because of mine enemies!

Thou knowest my reproach, and my shame and my dishonor;

my foes are all known to thee.

Insults have broken my heart, so that I am in despair.

I looked for pity, but there was none;

and for comforters, but I found none.

They gave me poison for food,

and for my thirst they gave me vinegar to drink.

Let their own table before them become a snare;

let their sacrificial feasts be a trap.

Let their eyes be darkened, so that they cannot see;

and make their loins tremble continually.

Pour out thy indignation upon them,

and let thy burning anger overtake them.

May their camp be a desolation,

let no one dwell in their tents.

For they persecute him whom thou hast smitten,

and him whom thou hast wounded, they afflict still more.

Add to them punishment upon punishment;

may they have no acquittal from thee.

Let them be blotted out of the book of the living;

let them not be enrolled among the righteous.

But I am afflicted and in pain;

let thy salvation, O God, set me on high!

I will praise the name of God with a song;
I will magnify him with thanks-giving.
This will please the Lord more than an ox
or a bull with horns and hoofs.
Let the oppressed see it and be glad;
you who seek God, let your hearts revive.
For the Lord hears the needy,
and does not despise his own that are in bonds.

Let heaven and earth praise him,
the seas and everything that moves therein.
For God will save Zion and rebuild the cities of Judah;
and his servants shall dwell there and possess it;
the children of his servants shall inherit it,
and those who love his name shall dwell in it.

Judith handed the block to Caroline. "Here," she said. "I want you to have this."

Caroline took the wood and held it up to the green lights of the dash, reading the crooked words. "What is it?"

"You told me once that you just wanted to understand," Judith said. "I think this might be the best explanation I can give you. That Lucas can give you." She glanced over at the dark, naked windows of the house, thinking of the echoes that now filled the rooms in place of furniture or photos or potted plants. "Go home, Caroline," she sighed. "Wake Dan up, share this new car with him. Make him talk to you. Don't let this tear your relationship apart. You've lost one person you love; don't lose another."

Caroline pressed the piece of wood to her breast. Judith turned away and started to walk towards the house.

"Judith," Caroline called. It was snowing harder, and her hair and the interior of her car were carpeted in white—the last memory of Caroline Myers Judith would keep forever.

"It's okay to miss him," she said. "No matter what he did, he was your son. Your little boy."

Judith lifted her face to heaven as a tight cry escaped her throat. She spread her arms out wide from her sides like an offering, shivering, smiling, tears flowing down her cheeks to mix with the wet snow which seeped into her skin, replenishing her thirsty body. "You are my friend," she said. "Maybe my only friend."

The wind whipped at the sash of her coat and swirled a dusting of snow around her feet. She watched Caroline drive away, red taillights fading into the distance as the sleek black car rounded the corner at the stop sign, then disappeared.

May 29 - Philadelphia

This has been such a busy, crazy week, I don't know where to begin. Lindsey's graduation ceremony from CAPA High on Sunday was beautiful. Elegant, with the music and flowers and all. The class elected her to give the opening speech. Her words were very moving. She played her last concert as first chair violin (two years running) with a solo and was given special recognition for her scholarship to Cambridge. As I sat in the audience watching all her friends and teachers applaud her, I exhaled a breath and thought, *Yes, she will be okay.*

Her flight leaves tomorrow at seven in the morning. Earlier this week, she spoke on the phone with her roommate—another music major (cello) from Ireland. They seemed to really hit it off. She has already packed and shipped most of her things to the dormitory for the summer term. Her courses are ambitious, tough for a freshman, which is why she wanted to get a head start before fall. Dr. Haji asked me the other day if I was worried that she might be taking on too much, too early. Alone in a foreign country at a new school. No, I said. She's handled worse.

Penny was also here last week for the graduation. She and Mark have officially set their wedding date for January 12, when Lindsey will be home on holiday break so she can provide the music. They're having it in Cleveland, his hometown. Virginia is driving them crazy, overplanning with her leather organizers and etiquette books *and registries. Penny still swears it's going to stay just a small and simple affair, but with Virginia at the helm I see swan ice sculptures, champagne fountains and matching pink organza bridesmaids dresses.*

Lindsey said good-bye to her dad last week at graduation. He didn't bring his new wife. Stephanie is her name. She's due in a few months and couldn't fly. I've never met her but Lindsey showed me one of their wedding photos. She's young, has a pretty smile. Lindsey says she's nice. I knew he had met someone else when he finally asked me for a divorce. After two years of separation, it was time to make it official. I was ready. No more alimony, no more child support. Just Judith.

Lindsey said they're having a boy. How strange for me to hear this. After being married to him for eighteen years, I know what he's doing and it makes me very sad for him. He's trying to show everyone, mostly himself, that he can get it right. That he knows what he's doing. He'll have another boy to prove that Lucas was my fault, not his. I wonder what he tells Stephanie.

We talked briefly at Lindsey's party and I congratulated him on the wedding and new baby. I even hugged him good-bye when it was time to leave. It struck me, then, how different were the paths of grief we chose to travel, how different our burdens have been.

I often find myself back at that breakfast table three years ago, Valentine's Day morning. The family portrait we once made. Peter, Lindsey, Lucas and me. For all our good and bad, we were a family.

And there was love. However imperfect, mistreated or crooked, I know in my heart there was love.

I think of that beautiful house at 817 Culver Lane, now occupied by strangers. I think about the hole in the wall where the sun porch was supposed to have been. That drafty, giant, gaping hole that is no longer there.

And sometimes, late at night when I can't sleep, I think about Caroline. Where she is, what she's doing. I tried looking her up last year when Lindsey and I were back in Akron for Christmas. I drove by her house, but someone else's name was on the mailbox, and she and Dan were no longer listed in the telephone book. I hope they are still together.

I miss her. I hope wherever she is, she's playing the piano again.

It's three o'clock in the morning right now. Lindsey is sound asleep, curled up with her favorite pillow and her violin case on the floor next to her bed. I am wide awake. I'm full of so much at this moment, brimming over with all these emotions and memories. Pride for my daughter, happiness for my sister, sadness for my ex-husband, and uncertainty for myself, alone and without a clear plan for my future. Uncertainty, but also hope. I breathe. I blink. My heart keeps beating, miraculously. I enjoy the sunlight and soft breezes and my new African violet, which bloomed for the first time yesterday.

I have learned to smile again and it astounds me.

It is still so hard to think about him. Overwhelming, if it sneaks up on me when I'm not prepared. I've devised a deliberate, planned system of coping. When I want to think about him, when I feel I'm ready and able, I fall away from the world and fold into myself. Only then can I remove the box containing Lucas out of the deep corner of my heart. Only then can I open it up and sort through. I pull the items out one at a time, like secret photographs. Lucas riding a tricycle down our driveway. Lucas tearing apart wrapping paper at Christmas and birthdays. Lucas helping his little sister climb the birch tree in the back yard. The smell of his hair after a bath. The smudges of paint on his shirts whenever I sorted the laundry.

The things I can actually touch, I keep stored in a plastic container under my bed—a ratty blankie, clippings from his first haircut, a baseball mitt, a package of charcoal sketching pencils, three stained paintbrushes that smell like turpentine, his class ring wrapped in a scrap of velvet.

This is how I remember my son, the only way I can without succumbing to the grief that would keep me from getting out of bed. When I am finished, I close the lids and put the boxes back in their place until the next time it is safe to bring them out again.

I have asked myself over and over again if he has left his footprints in heaven or in hell, even though I do not want to know the answer.

In my wallet, there are four pictures I clipped from the newspaper, yellowed and worn at the creases. Hannah, Matt, Ed and Lucas. I carry them with me always, for I am part of them and they are part of me. It has been in the space between my tears, my words, my silences and mistakes that I am finding a place to heal. That tiny space between birth and death where we squeeze in all the things we get wrong, and all the things we get right.

Acknowledgments

A heartfelt thanks to the dedicated staff at River City Publishing, especially my dream editor, Jim Gilbert.

To all the talented members of my writing group for the many nights of critique, ideas, and community.

An enormous thanks for generous early readings of this story in various stages by Chantal Corcoran and Jenni Hobbs. I am profoundly indebted to the brilliant, patient eyes of Jackie Jensen and Dame Murl Pace.

To Mike Manno and the Polk County Sheriff's Department for legal advice, the University of Iowa Book Doctors for two crucial suggestions, Lindy Shaw for taking my violet photos, and Jason Hobbs for all the man-hours on my website.

To my parents, Myron and Sue, and my family for their unending love and pride in me whether I write a book or a grocery list.

And to the Fred Bonnie Memorial, for giving a nobody like me the chance of a lifetime.

A Conversation with Kali VanBaale
and a Reader's Group Guide
for
The Space Between

Reader's Guide

1. What is your impression of the Elliott family in the opening scene? What do their interactions say, if anything, about their relationships?

2. How is Judith's hobby of raising African violets indicative of her personality?

3. Do you find irony between her treatment of the tender, difficult plants and her treatment of her son?

4. How would you describe Judith? How did your opinion of her change?

5. How would you describe Peter? Do you find him sympathetic or unsympathetic?

6. How does Judith handle her grief differently from Peter? Do you feel they display a common difference between men and women? How does this affect their marriage? How does it affect Lindsey?

7. At their first meeting, were you surprised when Judith decides to get into Caroline's car? How do you feel about Caroline's willingness to forgive?

8. How did you feel about Judith when Kristin comes to the Elliotts' house to return the class ring and Judith slams the door in her face? Why is making amends with Kristin such an important part of Judith's healing process?

9. How important does Dr. Haji end up in the lives of Judith and Lindsey?

10. Did you agree with Karen Michaels's actions during the deposition for the lawsuit?

11. What is the significance of the unfinished sun porch? In what ways does it end up playing a role?

12. Lucas's only communication with the reader in the story is through Judith's flashbacks with Dr. Haji and his hidden block of wood. Do you feel you understood him better by the end of the story? Does Judith?

13. *The Space Between* explores an approach to school shootings rarely examined in public or by the media. Did your views change as the story progressed?

A Conversation with Kali VanBaale Regarding
The Space Between

1. How long did it take you to write *The Space Between*?

I spent nearly three years writing this story—one year on the first draft and two more on editing and revising—but sat on the idea without putting down a single word for over fifteen months. It is such a sensitive, minefield-laden subject that I didn't want to mishandle it by jumping in too fast. I also didn't want to take it straight from any of the stories covered on the news. I wanted Judith to have her own voice, to tell her own story, and to find insight as to how something like this happened within *her* family.

2. How much of this story was taken from news headlines?

My first seed idea for this story came to me two years after the Columbine tragedy. I was six months pregnant when the shootings occurred, so it was a very scary, confusing time to be bringing a child into the world. On the second anniversary, I was watching the news and old footage of that April day and my thoughts kept coming back to the mothers of the shooters, how they would ever begin to put their lives back together. I kept wondering if they rushed to the school like all the other parents—worried, terrified, and trying to find their children, oblivious to what had really happened. The image of a woman then came to me, standing in front of a row of buses as they unloaded, searching for her son in the crowd like so many other mothers, only to discover in the same second that not only was he dead but he was the gunman. My driving force from that point on was uncovering what would happen to this woman and her family. In order for me to tell any story, I must start with a fresh, compelling character banging around in my head with such urgency that I can't go another day without getting the words out.

3. Are there any autobiographical elements to *The Space Between*?

Fortunately, I've never suffered the profound loss of a child, but I have known and been close to several families who have. I am convinced that I could have never written this story had I not been a mother myself. I know in my heart that I could not have *imagined* the loss of a child without first *knowing* the overwhelming love and responsibility of a child.

Looking at the words of the story now, I do see much of myself in Judith in terms of her lack of confidence as a mother, always second-guessing herself and plagued with doubts. Having two boys myself, I am familiar with reactionary parental behaviors, unconsciously withdrawing from situations in which you feel you have no answers or all the wrong answers.

4. Did you find Judith a likeable or unlikable character? How about Caroline?

Judith was like a living, breathing person to me, and I always felt sort of protective of her, worrying about her during the course of the story and wanting for her to somehow be okay by the end. But she was also a frustrating character to me, indecisive and passive when she should've been stepping up sooner to take control. I wanted to shake some sense into her at times. Regardless, I did like her because she was all too human and bravely faced her faults as a wife and mother.

As for Caroline, she was a strange, fun, and sad character to write, so yes, I definitely liked her from the first scene in the car. At times, though, I wondered if she was too forgiving, too understanding, but then I realized by the end of the story that forgiveness and understanding were the sole reasons she went to Judith's house the first night. Caroline had already made up her mind that she wanted peace in her heart for this boy and his family and was simply searching for the validation, which she finally got.

5. Who is the intended audience?

I understood that by choosing the point of view of the mother of a shooter, I ran the risk of appearing as if I were taking sides, though that couldn't be further from the truth. In no way was I trying to turn this into a who-suffers-more kind of contest. Grief cannot be measured or compared. Loss is loss. I wrote a voice that spoke loudest to me, one side of a multisided tragedy, which turned out to be Judith's. Whether a reader pities or blames her, the story still brings up many complex issues for which there are no easy answers. The very nature of our society breeds gray areas in parenting that the average parent is not always equipped to handle. We are often quick to place blame after a tragedy, demand answers, justice, and punishment, but at the end of the day, no one sets out to *raise* their child to commit a heinous crime like a school shooting. Then again, at the end of the day, logic such as that still isn't much comfort to the families who senselessly lost a loved one. See . . . no easy answers.

6. Who are your favorite authors, and how have they influenced your work?

The Book of Ruth by Jane Hamilton is one of my favorite books simply because I fell in love with Ruth Dahl's narrative voice. I also loved the tiny, heartbreaking nuances of *Ordinary People* by Judith Guest, the masterful layers of *The Hours* by Michael Cunningham, and anything by Anne-Marie MacDonald for her huge, gutsy plotlines and brave choices in subject matter that would make other writers squirm.

I do enjoy the works of Edith Wharton and Jane Austen (all hail the woman who created Mr. Darcy), but, admittedly, I'm attracted mostly to modern fiction and tend to read what is current and closest to my own style of writing. I've been most influenced by Elizabeth Strout, author of *Amy and Isabelle* and *Abide With Me*. I took a point of view workshop taught by her at the University of Iowa Summer Writing Festival several years ago. She spoke so passionately about giving fictional characters an *honest* voice, about how on the first page of a story, as writers, we ask a reader to trust us, to take our hand so we can lead them through the story, and that it is our job to not abandon them or lead them astray. The two days I spent with her changed my writing forever, and I have enormous respect for not just her talent but also her integrity.